*Dedicated
to Uli
who loves and lives
both
Truth and Story*

Dear Gwen + Don —
This comes with much, much
love. May we have days
of great joy "in retreat" and
playing together —
Scott

THE RETREAT

A Novel By
CAROL KORTSCH

The Retreat
Copyright © 2012
Carol P. Kortsch

Published by Prose Press
Pawleys Island,
South Carolina 29585

proseNcons@live.com
www.prosepress.biz

ISBN: 978-0-9851889-4-8

Comments: ckortsch@global-partners.com

Cover design: Jon-Marc Kortsch
Interior art: Allene Riley Kussin

Grateful acknowledgement is made to the following for permission to reprint previously published material:

Eighth Mountain Press: "*Kindness*" poem by Naomi Shihab Nye, from "*The Words Under the Words: Selected Poems.*" copyright 1995. By permission of the author, 2012.

Graywolf Press: "*The Way It Is*", poem by William Stafford, from "The Way It Is: New and Selected Poems," copyright 1998 by the Estate of William Stafford. Reprinted with permission of The Permissions Company, Inc. on behalf of Graywolf Press, Minneapolis, Minnesota,

New Directions Publishing Corporation: "The Thread" poem by Denise Levertov, from POEMS 1960-1967, copyright 1966 by Denise Levertov. Reprinted by permission of New Directions Publishing Corp.

Tom Jay: for the excerpt, "The Seeker's Path", from his interview with Heron Dance, as quoted in the 2006 Heron Dance Day Book and Planner. Permission granted by telephone conversation with the author, Aug 2012.

Truth and Story

Truth and Story were twins who lived together
in the same house
in the same village for fifty years.

They were much loved in their community and went
together every night to visit all their neighbors.

For their visits, Story dressed elaborately in costumes.

She wore elegant robes, strings of seashells, pearls
or glass beads, garlands of flowers,
fanciful wigs and crowns or hats.

Every night Story looked a bit different
but always intriguing.
Truth never wore clothes at all.

When they made their rounds each night, everyone they
visited embraced Story warmly and greeted Truth
more distantly with great respect.

One night Story was too ill to make the traditional visit,
so Truth went without her.

The visits lacked the joy and warmth they had when
Story went along.

After several nights of visiting alone and feeling
bereft without Story,
Truth decided to comfort herself by making the visit
dressed in some of Story's finery.

That night wherever Truth went she was warmly greeted
with great hospitality, and embraced, for you see,
Truth dressed as Story is easier to embrace.

As told by Dr. Lyn Mueller,
recorded in
The Story Way of Knowing in the Context of Community.
by Sara L. Sanders.

BEFORE THE RETREAT

We felt the rustle of change in early springtime. It was clear the shift had broken through. They would not arrive until September, but we knew they were on their way. They would make it here eventually—at least most of them. Over the centuries, we have learned that it takes a long time for human bodies to catch up with their souls, if in fact they ever do.

Winter's energy held on longer than usual; it had been centuries since that northern power had gripped us so powerfully in her bony clutch. One white storm after another blasted through, ripping off layers of cedar shakes from the little cottages and dumping such a load of ice-encrusted snow that even dear old oak could not stand it. Some of her most treasured limbs bent beyond their capacity, then splintered and remained hanging under the blanket of snow—a dismal specter of her approaching death. It did not help that we often heard the pine trees in the Conservation area next door snapping like fireworks while being slowly stripped of their branches. The landscape remained frozen, numbed in suspense, barely able to breathe under the dark weight of frost.

1

For weeks, from the outside, there appeared to be no movement in the old house, either. The mice reported that the kitchen stood empty—molding in the cold, if that was possible. It was as if the cook had gone to bed and he too had frozen in place. Maybe he was deciding to leave again, as he did decades ago. It gave us such hope last fall when he came back. We wondered at the time how to let him know how much we welcomed him home. Like the oak, he seemed sorely mistreated by life.

When the ice finally melted around the first snowdrops, no longer could we remain silent or be silenced. Our collective voice emerged, blasting apart the icy shards of winter and dripping the fresh oils of cyclical renewal into each creaky joint of this ancient land. We discerned it was time for reconnection. As kindred, each of us activated a deeper dimension of aliveness that spring, as if the frightening visitation of untimely death had scared the life back into us, propelling us to be unusually fertile and present. Even the rocks cried out for attention.

It appeared to be an omen when the stones on the top of the old cairn in the memorial garden lost their balance. The sun melted the ice that had been holding them upright, and after a century of standing tall they toppled over, spilling into Cook's favorite patch of daffodils. He had helped plant the bulbs years ago, so he noticed the calamity right away.

We knew he was going to be all right when, huffing and puffing, he lovingly set each rock back into place again. We wonder if he heard us cheering and clapping. He appeared to have finished his task and was about to go inside, but after our celebration, he turned around and wandered back down the garden path, picking a posy of freshly opening buds. We imagined he intended it to grace the kitchen table, where he often kept cut flowers, but it surprised even us when, with tears running down his face, he solemnly laid the bouquet on the rock cairn and bowed his head.

We hoped he would notice how, in response, the daffodils turned to him in gratitude. Even the ones crushed by the rocks thanked him, their bruised petals vibrating with color.

He probably did not see them, because his eyes continued to overflow with tears while he gripped the upright rocks as if absorbing their last ray of strength. He seemed most reluctant to let them go.

Yes, life shifted that spring. Each of us moved differently, flowing together with an upsurge of vitality. It was time. If you had been looking closely, like us, you would have watched the story of the retreat unfold.

FRIDAY

CHAPTER ONE

"Extend and receive welcome. People learn best in hospitable spaces. In this circle we support each other's learning by giving and receiving hospitality."

SAM

We listen intently from our timeless places as they sit in the circle. It is Friday afternoon, and he is the first to speak of why he came. We hear him telling his story: parsing thoughts, building credibility. We hear him heaping words together into a carefully edited professorial resume, spiced with a dash of humor and a lick of drama. Then, unexpectedly he finds himself uttering something he knows, but until this moment had never been able to verbalize.

"That was my moment of revolution, my personal Bastille Day."

Our hearts stir with anticipation. Was it really the moment when everything changed? Is there really one moment when the deadly tide of societal imprisonment reaches its apex and a person turns toward freedom? He obviously didn't run naked in the streets to celebrate his liberation, but somehow it does appear that his mind took flight, escaped the box of his brain, and cut loose his body.

As a studious, reserved college professor who specializes in behavioral psychology (who had just been privately enjoying the lurid details of a historical romance), it is clear that he certainly did *feel* for the moment like one of those French revelers. Of course, we know he couldn't say all of that, certainly not in the first hour of the retreat.

We hear him hiccup as a sob claws its way up the back of his windpipe. He doesn't describe how, on that day of revolution, he grabbed a Twix bar and buried his escaping sorrow in sweetness. What is evident today is that once more he is provoked, mesmerized by his own words and captured by the spirit of death that haunts at the most unexpected times. Sitting here with everyone quietly looking at him, he has to clear his throat at several points when memory washes through his system. He even searches under the chair looking for solace but finds only his water bottle and swallows slowly to regain his composure—one breath at a time.

We understand that his circular soliloquy is serving as a polishing rag, dusting off a rarely used source of light within him. His buried anger gleams with energy, his peripatetic thoughts reach for clarity, but after checking out the kindly faces in the circle, it is apparent that he consciously sets aside the desire to be completely authentic. "Better to stay safe and not run into the roads of life, not looking where you are going," we hear an inner authority say.

"My name is Sam. I'm a psychology professor. I live in suburbia, about ten minutes away. My answer to the question, 'What brings you here today?' is to tell you a story from my daily commute last spring.

"My two-hour sentence on the expressway mostly consists of whiling away the minutes with NPR and an array of CD books, selected to match my moods and interests. One day I was feeling particularly ornery and bored. Nothing was working for me: political biography, psychology, religion, historical fiction, even a goodie-bag of usually tempting snacks held no appeal. It was not a day for either carrot sticks or a Twix bar!

"I rolled down the window to breathe. A deep gulp of exhaust fumes from an idling semi-trailer changed my mind. I closed the window, quelling the desperate urge to unfasten my seat belt, bolt onto the green median strip, and lie down in the spring grass … maybe even strip off all my clothes!"

Sam laughs, but sobers quickly. "Then the deer caught my attention. A magnificent buck with a set of three-point antlers lay splayed out on the grass, exactly where I had envisioned lying. At first I thought it was a hallucination, but those lifeless eyes were staring at me from his twisted neck, as if he were still trying to break free, still engaged in the bolt across the highway that must have killed him.

"That was my moment of revolution, my personal Bastille Day. In the silence of the car, I became the wild creature, pondering the deer's insane dash for novelty, the longing for better feeding grounds. Maybe the deer spooked. Maybe desire became the executioner. Better to stay safe and not run into the roads of life, not looking where you are going.

"I had poured myself into a lecture that same day, feeling I had summoned up all the courage I could muster. I knew I had found some fresh depth—one I wanted to be able to repeat. I had been teaching with the Socratic question, 'How do we as humans find strength and energy to work and live well?' Remarkably inspired,

I felt I had reached a new dimension of teaching. Even the classroom interaction with the students was stellar … until … until … a student said a very unkind thing about me."

He hesitates, searching for appropriate words. *That picayune comment fractured my heart—just like that buck. A dead professor lying prostrate in the hall, felled by a freshman's idle joke … talk about losing my external and internal motivation.*

"Some of you must understand how teaching can be very difficult at times..." He is scanning the room now, searching for a human connection, hoping for some kind witness. His eyes land on a young black woman with a coiled snake tattoo on her arm. She sits bolt upright, directly opposite him. She appears locked in position, nodding her head, but smiles back at Sam sympathetically, her eyes glistening with tears, offering him enough encouragement to continue.

"I am still trying to figure out how to find the strength and courage to work and live well. … I guess, maybe, that is still my question. Why couldn't I see that before? That's why I was teaching so well that day. Yes!" … *Oh yes, now I remember. It was so strange how, as if in response to my question, the trucker behind me leaned aggressively on his air-horn. 'Up-yours,' I thought, stomping on the gas and shooting forward down the open road.*

Sam straightens and speaks firmly. "I will no longer tolerate that commute every day. Like the deer, my spirit is daily overwhelmed, killed by the seeming necessity to drive to my job. I was not made for that. The deer was not made for that. I came here today because there must be a better way—a more harmonious way to live for the rest of my life."

MICHAELA

Startled, Michaela jumps at the power of Sam's conclusion. For an instant she considers bursting out with a friendly obscenity, but instead keeps smiling at him. He has unlocked a part of her story—about the day she decided to walk home from work. It too had been a decisive day.

Usually she was so overloaded with papers to mark and books to read that the short bus ride became essential transport. That day, as the last dawdling child left the classroom, she had surveyed the disaster scene around her and on impulse picked up her handbag and a bottle of water that she had been planning to drink all afternoon and marched out the door. She felt like slamming it, but true to her nature she denied herself the satisfaction. Leaving the classroom in such disarray was already highly unusual for her. Just as she sensed the first warming ray of sunshine, she turned back with a sigh. She remembered that she needed to go to the restroom; she had wanted to do that all afternoon, too.

The day had started in crisis mode. At 6:30AM, Emma began screaming from the shower that the hot water was freezing cold, as if Michaela had purposely planned this indignity just for her daughter's personal torture. Then, after stepping off the stairs and slipping in a pool of icy water covering the laundry room floor, she'd found the imploded water heater. After several hasty phone calls, further back-talk from Emma, and the preparation of a quick-fix lunch—overly loaded with nitrites, sugar, and BPA—the two had separated in a sullen silence. They both hurried out into the rain, flying down the busy street in opposite directions to their respective schools.

Michaela's ears were still ringing with Emma's verbal rampage as she sat on the morning bus attempting

11

to comfort and calm herself, gallantly staving off the impending pity party that had been ramping up for a dismal celebration all month.

Emma is simply impossible! It's curious how teenage girls seem to know exactly when to escalate a fight with their mothers. It's as if she deliberately needles into the core of all my anxieties, determined to undermine sixteen years of responsible and loving parenting.

Then she'd had to face the terrors of the classroom all day. Prepubescent children on a wet spring Monday before a week of spring break—this was the stuff of educators' nightmares. Everybody was teetering on the brink of breakdown after an onerously lengthy and frightfully cold winter. And there was still a week to go before any respite. Somehow, Michaela had found her way through the day. She was often surprised at the depths of her capacity to teach, no matter what hurdles had to be overcome; she knew that she was a very caring and competent teacher, but days like that one tested every fiber of her being.

With ten years in the classroom, she had learned that she had to find the students exactly where they were—almost join them for a moment in their rebellion and angst—and then quickly move to engage them, to use that often-deadly energy in a constructive manner. Teaching in an urban setting felt like creatively taming myriad tempests brewing in a daily teapot. This was one of those shadow seasons when everything loomed out of proportion and could fly out of hand in an instant, if not carefully negotiated and managed with thoughtful attention.

Michaela knew her young charges, like her, were at the mercy of an inner city environment that reeled with intensity. It was her job to stoke and fuel the fire of deep learning that held at bay all the other intruders on a child's life. Thus her classroom looked like a cross between a nature preserve and the city dump. Michaela somehow managed to supervise it all; she attempted to find fun or a purposeful lesson in everything.

This was why Emma drove her crazy. As a mother, she could do nothing right, and home became the war zone. It had taken her years to understand how to form an alliance with each new class, how to inspire their best inner resources with a microscopic school budget and paltry administrative help. But being a mother to her teenager seemed an even harder job; she'd felt completely helpless that day.

Finally the rain had stopped and the sun was strikingly warm. *Spring really is here.* Michaela noticed how her body turned instinctively in the opposite direction—away from home. *Am I running away? Is it okay to give up for few hours? Where can I actually go, anyway?*

Her cell phone buzzed and she ignored it. Again. *I can't face Emma right now. If she calls one more time, then maybe I'll have to answer, but she is undoubtedly wondering where I am and demanding to know why there's nothing good to eat in the house. Let her figure it out for herself ... she's old enough to manage on her own.*

A raucous commotion diverted her attention. Down an alley, two enormous black crows were fighting over something repulsive. About to turn away in disgust, she looked again, this time with less human disdain. She noted how regal the birds looked, their stately posture as they stalked their turf: pecking and preening, taking turns to compulsively caw at each other while the other ate, flapping their wings in competitive ritual. Michaela felt her heart lift.

What amazing bright and clever eyes. This is royalty

in drag. I could have easily missed them. Hmmm, "Raven Speaks"—we just read that story in class. A Native American tale about black birds that bring messages from the Underworld. The children were asking if it was true. I told them every tale has truth, but each one of us has to stop and listen to find the truth from inside of us ... then we'll know what to believe.

A synchronicity? ... For me? God knows I feel dragged though an underworld. Michaela laughingly stretched out an arm to wave goodbye to the birds, who had been scared off by the shriek of a police siren. *Of course this is for me. I wonder what message the crows bring?*

She soon found herself walking in a part of the neighborhood she rarely visited, but knew there was a community garden tucked in between blocks of old row-houses. The most dilapidated crack houses had been torn down and turned into a well-maintained public space.

Ah, here it is. How beautiful everything looks emerging from winter's storms. Oh, look! Someone has set up a bench in the rose arbor—just what I need today. Michaela wiped away the tear that had latched onto her eyelash. *Let me just sit here for a while ... until I am ready to go home again.*

God, I am so thirsty. Finally now I can drink my water.

Smiling now, Michaela also reaches for her water bottle. Clutching it for support, she braces her back against the chair and joined the group where Sam had left off.

"My name is Michaela, I'm a teacher too…"

GEORGE

George feels the blood in his legs pulse. He longs to be at home, settled in his well-worn, plush recliner

14

with his legs up. *What am I doing here? Whatever made me decide to come? I have no idea how to answer this question.*

His legs had begun to ache just as the jet began its descent for the stopover in Denver. Flying often left him numb in his extremities: the pressure changing, the throbbing and pinching of his blood as it coursed through his body. Knowing just enough about biology to worry, he wondered if he was at risk for heart disease, blood clots, or heart-stopping systemic failure. His doctor had been encouraging him to pay closer attention to his lifestyle. He knew vaguely that something was out of sync in his system, but he wasn't clear what it was.

He moves his generous body uncomfortably on the hard seat, glancing at the rest of the participants. *Am I the only uneasy person in the room?* Unobtrusively, he moves his hand up to rub his shoulder. *Damn, that really does hurt. What a lousy start to the weekend. Maybe I shouldn't have come.*

The suitcase falling on him had certainly amplified his agitation. He realized then that he was angry. Fuming, in fact. The blow on his shoulder had awakened a surge of emotional energy that had been building inside for a long time.

That nutso woman, hurtling down the plane aisle with her flying luggage, reminded me of my wife and three daughters. They all seem out of control to me. Living at warp speed, never stopping to think about what they are doing or why they are doing it. They drive me crazy. I am forever on call as the handyman in the house. Mr. Fix-It. The nice guy available to drop everything to help the women. I am tired of taking forks out of the garbage disposal, unstopping tampon-plugged toilets, and re-caulking the shower stall to save the downstairs ceiling from falling in. I am tired of bailing out overdrawn bank accounts; my hard-earned money used like caulking, stopping up the leaks from unthinking, unnecessary expenditures.

George shakes his head. *It is not that I don't like women. I rather love them all. But from my perspective they simply don't engage their brains much of the time. I know I am frightfully prejudiced even thinking like this, but God knows I learned a long time ago that it's brain power that has served me well, saved me in fact.*

Getting away this weekend was supposed to be a relaxing thing, and now I am even more worked up than when I started. I come away looking for peace, trying to get away from work and family pressures, searching for some freedom ... and now I feel even worse.

George squirms again, his attention drifting to the past. As a kid, he was already on the lumpish side. He never could compete with the jocks and the lotharios of adolescence, so using his clever little head, he'd found his way into the science club, and from there into founding a manufacturing and sales company that designed and fabricated laboratory instruments. His work demanded he spend a great deal of time traveling to international trade fairs and exhibitions and attempting to balance his frustrations at work with the frustrations of home.

It had become unavoidably evident to George that his life revolved around managing and maintaining a circle of unreasonable people who simply demanded too much of him: his wife, his girls, his co-workers, and his clients, all wanting, it seemed, yet another piece of his ample flesh.

Restless and agitated, he feels it again—like on the plane—and a helpless growl almost escapes through his clenched teeth. *If only I really could get away from it all. I'd like to leave everything and everybody behind. I've always loved Colorado. If I hadn't got back on the plane*

16

in Denver, no one would ever have known what happened to me. I still could make another life for myself. He had visualized building himself an outback cabin: hauling river rocks from the creek for the foundation, crafting a massive stone chimney, and fly-fishing to his heart's content. We can sympathize; his getaway fantasies are set in the pristine forest of his youth.

He shakes his head like a wet dog. *I must be very angry to have considered such a shocking thing. Walk out on all the people I love the most? Leave a business that I've poured my life's energy into? Turn away from all I've ever known? How sad and awful... a hopeless move. A frightening attack on myself most of all...*

For a moment, we watch as he floats dissociated in the quiet room. Returning, he reluctantly reminds himself why he had, perhaps, made the choice to travel to a faraway, unfamiliar city, solely to go on a weekend retreat.

The brochure said this retreat was *"a time to foster personal and professional renewal through setting aside time and space to reflect on life and work."* George knows, or at least some part of him knows, that he needs this time to be alone. He urgently needs some kind of renewal before his life explodes. He knows he needs help, but doesn't want to be alone on retreat. That had seemed too depressing, so he deliberately chose to gather with a group of strangers with whom he had no connection. As a bonus, with potential business contacts in the region, he could write off the trip as a work expense.

He had congratulated himself on having the foresight to book a rental car for the next three days. As usual, the retreat center offered transport to and from the airport, but he used his lifelong policy of always having an escape option. *Just in case I need a car to get away from all these strangers.* George feels the tiny beads of sweat rolling off his forehead. He lifts his arm to wipe them away and winces with the increased pain in his shoulder. *Buck up—get it together, man. It's almost your turn to tell them why you came. Remember what the facilitator said. She offered us a hospitable space—a place to learn by giving and receiving. You're a salesman, you know how to do that—relax.*

GERRITT and LEONA

They sit on either side of the room, taking turns to glare at one another helplessly, and then each looks down at the floor. The mid-life shadows on his face hide the gangly immigrant Dutch boy in glasses who was curious about everything, the boy she had gratefully been paired with in chemistry class. At first glance, she continues to portray the vivacious, African-American city girl, the athlete who has recently moved to the suburbs; but from inside, it is also clear that she has ripened and has barely snacked on that lush bounty.

This had been her idea—she had seen a brochure advertising the retreat at a yoga seminar, and unbeknownst to him, he came to offer penance. She would never have accepted this as a token gesture, but after twenty-eight years of good enough partnering, it seemed they owed it to each other to exit into the world as friends; and in a way that women often are, she still prayed for the possibility to rebuild the trust he had so devastatingly broken in their marriage. She almost requested separate rooms, but thought that might strike people as weird, inviting too many shame-filled questions.

Like always, they had little left to say to each other that afternoon. It was normally a forty-five-minute trip, but there had been an accident and the afternoon rush was horrendous. As they sat in the stop-and-go traffic, the silence between them felt particularly ominous.

So here they sit, plunged in communal silence, embarking on this retreat together, spending a weekend reflecting on their messed-up lives with a group of strangers. Maybe they should have chosen the marriage seminar offered here next month, but most of us sensed it was probably too late for that. Maybe they might find a way to regroup personally, as individuals, and somehow find a compass bearing for separate futures. Humans often seem plagued by the instinctual force to chart the course of their lives together, glued to endure the indignities of a life-long, three-legged race.

Maybe it seems perfectly reasonable to arrive here late this Friday afternoon, after the rush hour, at the end of a strenuous work week. Maybe it is a thousand times better than wallowing in the morass of weekend misery when each moment together is reduced to a forced march of relationship, a plodding progression toward the unknown. They have nowhere else to go just yet. Being with each other "until death do us part" is all they know. They are surely at the end of the road.

When Gerritt and Leona drove into the driveway, when our ancient home beckoned them to enter, both felt consumed by a deep silence, sucked into a weight more ponderous than experienced before. It may surprise you that no guardian at the gate protected them from what was waiting; no caretaker shielded the group from their unwieldy presence. At Terra Center, everyone is always welcome.

MEI

Esther-Mei, or Mei as she prefers to be called, had exited smoothly from the limo and, after a few quiet words to Wan, her chauffeur, walked attentively along the curving path to the old stone center, absorbing the ambiance of this spiritual haven. She stopped at the mammoth wooden doors and took a long extended breath, inhaling and then exhaling, before grasping the brass knob.

Moments later, relieved and smiling to herself, she wandered down a path toward one of the small cottages. She was most gratified to have her own room. Mei cringed at the thought of sharing her space with a complete stranger. So far everything felt wonderfully right. *For an institution, this place has remarkably harmonious Feng Shui,* she thought. Of course we agree.

Thank goodness it's working so far. Signing up for this weekend was such a last-minute gamble ... so unlike me to not make all my usual diligent background checks. What a relief my intuition has not betrayed me. These past months it has been hard to trust any part of me. Coming here is such a giant leap of faith ... but I am so elated to finally, finally get away all by myself. No one knows where I am except for Wan.

Mei is in mourning. Her husband of thirty years died in late winter, just like our beloved oak, shaking her world and forcing her to rebuild her life as a widow, as a Chinese woman, and as a Christian. Their successful family business had weathered the founder's loss, rolling along efficiently and smoothly. But Mei has been feeling stifled, strangled by all the expectations on her. It has been nine long months, and she is intensely aware that she needs fresh air, physically, emotionally, spiritually, and intellectually. Her psyche has begun to revolt against the assumption she will continue in her assigned role as the gracious feminine version of her husband. She has been praying daily for some guidance,

<u>for some light to follow</u>. We watched her envision how every morning this past month, she had intentionally knelt down in front of her family altar and asked for help.

She prayed to everyone: to the God of her father, to the ancestors of her mother, and to Jesus, who had seemed to her to be the most likely to understand her dilemma. She then did something that she had never, ever done before. She spoke to herself. She quietly declared with all the faith she could muster, *"Pay attention today. You will find your answers hidden in everything around you."*

When she saw the brochure, she knew it was an answer to her intentional prayers. She was destined to be at the retreat. There on the front cover were the words from Thomas Merton: *"There is in all visible things ... a hidden wholeness."* What better summation of her longings and desires? She had been exploring some of Merton's books recently and had concluded that if he were still alive he would be the one she would go to, searching for new meaning in her life.

Now, two weeks later, plunging into the sea of the great unknown, she feels full of hope, yet cautious. Mei knows how vulnerable she is. Not only does her wealth attract people like flies, but also her graceful demeanor, polished through years of careful attention to detail, seems a magnet for needy people. Strange folks are always trying to hang onto her in some way, looking to her for their answers. Equally exhausting since the death of her husband has been people's insistence on saying how good she looks, how brave she is, even how much God shines through her.

It makes me feel crazy, she thought. *No room for me to be Mei. I am sick and tired of being everybody else's*

21

"wholeness." I just hope this retreat isn't full of helpless souls looking for some instant spiritual deepening fix.

I did like the woman leader, though. She had a funny name ... I can't remember what it was. She seemed so genuine and honest. I think that telephone conversation with her helped me risk, set aside my fears. I really am looking for a new inner wholeness.

The cottage door was stuck. Mei had to shove several times on the old white batten-board slats while pressing the black farm latch before finally bursting unceremoniously into the room.

Oh, my God ... what is this? She picked up a pumpkin-colored folder. *My maiden name—Lee. Esther-Mei Lee. How did she get here?*

She laughed aloud, remembering that in completing the registration form, this was her little trick for disguising herself. What a shock, after all these years, to meet her nineteen-year-old self again. *I really am craving anonymity this weekend.*

The no-frills room was simple and clean. a simplicity she is unfamiliar with, but that perfect for today. Less is more. She had an hour before the initial reception, so she picked up her folder, found her wide-brimmed sunhat, and strolled toward a secluded place in the sunny garden, where we sent her our fragrant greetings. As she curled up on a bench to peruse the contents of the folder, she had a surprising mental flashback to a precious family heirloom—an ornately decorated manuscript that stayed locked in the china cabinet. On very special occasions, she loved to hear the click when her father unlocked the cabinet with a well-hidden key, and then proudly told a story while displaying the opulent wonders of an ancient world, illustrated in the pages of the book.

Now, sitting in the circle this Friday afternoon, Mei

hears herself click open as she begins to speak. Like words and drawings on the pages of a tightly bound book, she has been squeezed into her life: bent, folded, and glued into place between restrictive, although elegantly decorated covers. Now it is time to break out of the bindings of her life.

CHAPTER TWO

"Be present as fully as possible. Be here
with your doubts, fears, and failings, as well as your
convictions, joys, and successes, your listening as
well as your speaking."

THENA

In a cozy alcove off the main meeting room, Thena sits, quietly waiting for Dylan to arrive. Her short, curly, gray-flecked hair coordinates with her gold dangly tree-frog earrings (a precious gift from her zany daughter), reflecting her self-image as an easy-going individual with a splash of humor without losing class. It appears that Thena would never wear painted wooden parrots or spotted geckos.

This morning, after rush hour, she had driven rather distractedly to our idyllic place hidden on the edge of the city beside a state nature reserve. We had seen her scrambling around with her head down, busily organizing reams of papers and preparing materials for the weekend ahead. Now in the silence of waiting, she becomes conscious that a multitude of meetings and conferences with haranguing advocacy groups and anxiously zealous parent committees have left her worn out. She becomes aware of the tinny residue left from working non-stop for a month, even on weekends, since late August.

Typically, she would arrive a day before to give herself time to relax into a more reflective rhythm for the weekend, but given yesterday's emergency board meeting she'd forfeited the luxury of a more spacious beginning. She wistfully recalls her cabin, her private hideaway in the Canadian Gulf Islands, centered in the place where mountains, evergreens, and the ocean all meet. *Since my vacation on Anvil—that seems ages ago. The days spent kayaking around the islands ... the horns of the ferries echoing across the channel ... gulls streaking by me. How I miss the wildness and smell of the ocean, the unforgettable scent of western cedar permeating the air, the seclusion of the forest embracing me in green ferns and damp moss. How I long to be back in that deep rest with nature. I wish I could fly away there now.*

Thena exhales audibly, briefly noting a fly buzzing incessantly at the window screen. *And here I am again, getting ready to work another weekend, leading this introductory retreat with all new people—and, to top it off, my latest responsibility is to mentor Dylan.* She sighs again. She likes Dylan, her latest facilitator-in-training, but today this suddenly feels like one more responsibility, one more duty she has to perform.

What am I missing? What do I need for myself from this retreat?

We can't help but smile as the part of her that knows the answer to this question lifts the window screen and

26

releases the fly from its prison.

... I wish I could let go more naturally of the need to lead. I am tired of this old familiar role of Athena, my namesake: the ruler, the liberator, and all-knowing wise woman. Please let me find a way, one more time, to let go of my force, my driving energy, and trust this gentle retreat process of letting everybody do his or her own inner work.

Remember, I do not have to "be in charge." My work is to slow down and pay careful attention to myself, so I can more compassionately honor each person who comes today, Dylan included.

She hasn't talked with him today but had caught a glimpse of him an hour ago through the dining room window. He was jogging down the path toward the Conservation area while she was tucking away the last crumbs of a superb, homemade key-lime pie. She envied his youthful vigor, a liveliness that bubbled spontaneously out of him.

He is full of an elixir from the gods. Oh, how I would love to tap into that kind of energy today. It feels so natural and flowing ... like a vigorous sea breeze on Anvil.

It was their first time working together as a team, but during their conversations over the past months, she had become curious, sometimes sensing that energy in him as a kind of restlessness; like an untamed animal's, as if part of him was diverted, "out for a jog" somewhere in an inner wilderness.

It should be interesting working with him this weekend—for many reasons. Ha! I may not be a jogger on the outside, but I sure can keep a remarkable pace. But Dylan feels like a different breed of person.

Thena was not only older by more than a decade than Dylan, but rich in years of experience facilitating groups of every kind. She had risen out of the field of social work, a care-giver of people, to now being an organizational caregiver to a statewide network of groups that served special-needs children and adults. In fact, this week several board members had encouraged her to stand as a candidate for chairperson,; a job that would certainly demand her full-time energy. She was not at all sure she wanted to be pushed to the top in the bubbling froth of regional school board politics. Besides, she had other more concrete personal goals she was considering pursuing—like how to develop more group circles. This really was what she relished doing, what drew her to spend her weekends away from home.

Thena loved this model of large group formation. About ten years before, in an unusual twist of fate, she had signed up for a seasonal series of retreats: a group of fifteen educators who met for eight weekends over the space of two years. It had been a life-changing process—a slow and gentle inner revolution that continued to challenge.

Now this national community of facilitators branched across many disciplines—not just teachers but medical professionals looking for alternative forms of education, and religious leaders from many faiths who cared profoundly about communal group process. She had witnessed repeatedly how these groups provided a unique relational matrix for personal growth for any thoughtful person looking for change.

As she gazes across the expansive lawn, the movement of swallows catches her eye. Darting in and out under the eaves of the old rafters, their freedom momentarily assuages her hidden ache, releasing old memories. The birds remind her of her hippie parents—free-floating, wheeling in currents of radical social change, yet still grounded in intentional community. Her birth and early years had formed Thena from the inside out, and here too she was offering humans the potential for radical change in a healing communal process. Momentarily revived, her mind reels with inspiration bursting with ideas of how much more she could do in this retreat work.

This is why I'm here to lead this group. Tired, yes, but not without hope. Maybe Dylan is a gift today for my flagging soul. I need some youthful inspiration.

She picks at her cuticles, noting that the nail polish hastily applied earlier in the week no longer covers up the telltale signs of last weekend's gardening marathon. Over the past decade she had become an avid gardener. Initially, she'd found it a welcome relief to be alone— getting her hands dirty in soil instead of people's lives— until like her work, it had become an obsession. Last weekend had been just that, an all-out, two-day work blitz. *I hope my lotus presentation tomorrow will be well received by the group. ... I wonder if I've gone overboard. Maybe I shouldn't have taken the risk.*

Seesawing emotionally, the muscles in her jaw fluttering with ambivalence, Thena wishes now that she had taken the opportunity earlier to go for a calming walk out-of-doors, but it is clear that she has neither the time nor the capacity to appreciate our home or the wilderness sanctuary next door. For relief, she then turns her attention back to the printed weekend outline.

She had worked diligently: preparing handouts, organizing sessions, looking after all the registration questions. Thena was grateful to the Terra Center for hosting much of her weekend work. She felt at home here, knowing that the logistics were organized by the small but capable staff of the environmental group that had refurbished the former Benedictine mission house to use as a training center.

They too are so young and zealous—ha! Except for my buddy Charles. Thena chuckles to herself, realizing they must pay attention to the cook and his schedule this weekend. Even though she had reflected a great deal on the program for the next three days, she knew every retreat experience is markedly different. They had not been tempted to pull out stock sessions that had worked in the past, so she and Dylan had each taken many hours to consider how to serve those from diverse occupations who had registered. Each person—a seeker—searching for renewed authenticity in his or her professional work and personal life.

Just like me. I feel like I need deeper renewal too, in both my private and professional life. I just wish I had a whole day to myself before everyone else shows up.

She glances at her watch, surprised, noting her hardened and tightened breathing waiting for Dylan to arrive. He is only ten minutes late. Not a big deal, but being on time was one of those things that had always been important to her. "Staying on time is a gift to everybody," she often remarked to anyone who might be listening.

We see her close her eyes, trying to center herself, and watch as her impatience lurks like a vulture on the periphery of her consciousness.

Eventually, Dylan slips into the room smelling of a rain shower. His tall, muscular body glows with recent physical exertion. As he hugs Thena, she relaxes instinctively. *Maybe I am not alone in this leadership thing after all. Here is somebody who feels fully alive and present in himself—someone quite different from me. Maybe someone I can learn to trust.*

After a few minutes of catching up on their recent days, Thena searches for the file on her laptop for a Jan Garbarek piece that she wants to use later.

"Listen to this, Dylan—what do you think about using this after dinner, before the evening session? Let me play it now. It might be a good way for us to arrive here now, to let our souls catch up with our bodies."

The alto sax soars above them as they naturally fall into the quiet, sinking more deeply into the soft sofas of the sun-filled alcove. Thena feels the evocative music hollowing out a light and welcoming space inside and around her, and wishes the same for the sixteen others soon to arrive; strangers to each other embarking on a living breathing voyage of souls.

CHAPTER THREE

"What is offered in the circle is by invitation, not demand. This is not a "share or die" event! During this retreat, do whatever your soul calls for, and know that you do it with our support. Your soul knows your needs better than we do."

DYLAN

Finally, it is time to start. Thena just scurried off to use the restroom while Dylan nervously scans the room once more, counting the chairs in the circle.

Eighteen. Better count them again just to be sure ... how inauspicious it would be to not to have a place for someone. A shame that someone just cancelled out yesterday. Don't people realize how disruptive it is to opt out at the last minute? He hears Thena's voice of experience in his head saying: "It is what it is."

Oh, well. Thena told me it's always like that, to learn to accept—you simply never know who will be there until you start, so don't be so uptight. Besides, you can rely on her, she is crazy thorough in her planning. Can't believe how much effort it takes to prepare for one of

*these weekends—never would have imagined it during
my first retreat. Everything felt so peaceful and artfully
simple. Well, here goes, I guess it's my turn now....*

As Dylan self-consciously tucks in his shirt, and
runs his fingers through his jet-black hair, we see the
flashbacks as they streak across his consciousness:

*Arriving and relishing the warm welcome, yet aware
of so much conflict inside. Those haunting wolf dreams
that threatened to devour me from the inside out. So
terrified of going to sleep, even keeping the night-
light on, which made me feel like such a dope. What a
ghastly cycle ... crazy-making. I couldn't figure out how
I seemed so chronically out of control when my outside
world remained quite normal.*

*It's hard to realize that it's been five years: scoping
out my first group like this one, tentatively exploring the
rough edges of my crappy inner world. God, I still can
remember that feeling of being swept along in a flooding
river, held in by steep banks, but guided by some much
deeper reality. All that emotional turbulence unearthing
forces that led me downstream even deeper into my
fears. What a weekend, to somehow mysteriously face
those lurking shadows, and then that unforgettable
surge of hope—the instant I knew that the wolf was my
friend, not an enemy.*

Dylan's broad shoulders relax as he folds his tall
frame and sits down in the empty circle. Re-inspired,
he gazes around at each chair, and we feel his thoughts
like prayers energizing the space. No longer caught
by the angst of counting, he envisions life-changing
opportunities for each who would sit there in a few
minutes. He longs to pass the baton of change to each
person, longs that they would leave as he had left from
his first event—surprisingly at rest, recharged with
courage, and staggering with fresh realization of all he

didn't know.

As a community ourselves, we sense how much Dylan loves being a part of groups. Evidently they had been his thing for years, freeing him to try this model out—intuitively he knew that nothing unleashed his creative energy like a group. After a wildly social time at college, he had wandered for a decade as an ardent seeker, from seminar to seminar, training group to training group, searching for the latest way of being in ✗ community. Balancing music, art, environmental, and social concerns—eventually he had settled into a career as a music teacher in an alternative city school. For fun, in his spare time, he initiated a threesome of drummers who played back up for community events and music gigs.

Gradually, I've changed ... especially learning to slow down and pay attention to life. My insides don't churn as often, the way they used to ... although, interesting, last night I did have another wolf dream.

His body visibly stiffens and in visceral reaction, Dylan holds his breath.

Without warning—as rarely happens in our private space—the outside neighborhood intruded with ferocious intensity. We were momentarily stunned by the unwelcome sounds of two dogs snapping and snarling and a man yelling to subdue them. Shocked from his reverie, Dylan also becomes aware of other voices and footsteps tapping down the hall. He bounces to his feet and taking several deep breaths, intentionally pushes beyond his panic.

Today, I must lead. Probably my recurring dream of last night is connected to that. God knows I'm such a blundering neophyte, but I've tried to be honest about that with Thena. I can only lead from my authentic self—warts, wolves, and all.

It is five o'clock on a warm afternoon in late September when the first knot of people walk expectantly into the meeting room. Dylan comes alive before our eyes; his genuine, boyish smile makes everyone feel at home. We watch the color return to his cheeks as he shakes hands and personally welcomes each participant.

Dylan's mind flows with first impressions, but beyond that immediate experience he mostly senses their intense curiosity, how they check each other out, quite aware that they are also sizing up their two leaders. He also sees how each one glances around the room, taking in the large empty circle of chairs, and how most hover cautiously on the outside, sipping a cold drink and nibbling a few of the delectable hors d'oeuvres. Like us, his heart goes out to each trembling hesitation, to each querulous misgiving about ever stepping foot in this door. He senses the rising decibel level of anxiety as people run out of wise and insignificant things to say.

Just when Dylan was about to catch her eye and plead: "please—for heaven's sake—let's begin," Thena reaches for her Tibetan bell.

VANESSA and GEORGE

In the midst of the human hubbub, we were the only ones that noticed how Vanessa froze when he entered the meeting room.

The bell had just rung, and in the far reaches of her mind she is listening to the woman facilitator saying something about finding a seat and starting the circle in five minutes, but with shaking hands she is forced to stabilize her glass on the table, and instead turns her back on him and the circle now forming.

He's here—I can't believe my eyes. It's the man from seat 27C. How on earth did he get here? He didn't come on the shuttle. Why him, of all people? Crap, look at me, in a tizzy, all over again.

Some of us previously had been relishing her company in the garden that afternoon; she is one of those dear souls we simply can't help but cherish. Since getting off the plane from Denver, Vanessa had obviously felt like she was in heaven; her thoughts cascading in rivulets of joy at everything she encountered. *What luxury to be pampered by the staff in this idyllic world of spiritual life and numinous energy—this place is loaded with good vibes. Oh my, look at those flowers ... oh, and the waterfall. This is too good to be true...*

Thus, she had dreamily wandered the grounds for the past few hours, feeling like she'd left behind her old life with its basket of worries, and was being lavishly replenished with bouquets of happiness. She loved her private room with her own bath and even indulged in a leisurely soak in the tub. Then, feeling bold, she decided to put on her most dramatic dress, the flowered one that Arthur never let her wear, but the one she adored. She reveled in the bold lilacs that flowed across her ample bosom and danced in clusters around her knees. Arthur always wanted her to keep her knees covered in public— apparently it was something about his mother—at least that is what she said as she inspected her knees in the mirror and declared them beautiful, although a tad on the pudgy side. She had sallied into the reception with such confidence that it quite took our breaths away. There was no doubt that Vanessa wanted to portray in effervescent color that she was a garden in bloom—and quite proud of it.

When she turns around again to locate a seat to hide in, the transformation of her body is positively ghoulish: slumped over, face hidden, the lilacs now scrunched into indecipherable purple wads of color that clash with the spring-bud green of the background fabric. She bends so far over that like an old tea-pot she accidentally tips forward into her chair when she slips on a stray folder on the floor.

How embarrassing for her. Somehow his arrival brought with him all her forgotten angst, her critical, self-hating ways, and her childlike fear of being her true messy self. Mr. 27C is no doubt an ugly uninvited reminder that she can never be good enough.

*　　*　　*

George sidled in late to the reception after waking up from a long overdue sleep, the first restful nap he could remember for years. At home, there was always too much going on to fully relax.

He makes a beeline to the food table, quite thrilled to find a fine spread of canapés. *Too bad there's no wine. A light Pinot Noir or a fruity Riesling would be perfect for this hot afternoon. Oh, well, the place sure looks like a charming old monastery. Now if only I didn't have to talk to anybody. I am so tired of meeting strangers.*

Just as he sighs with resignation, the young facilitator Dylan comes up and extends his hand, pleasantly attempting to make him feel at home. George eyes him with a certain suspicion, noting his youth and rather zealous demeanor, and hopes fervently that he is not expected to match his enthusiasm. He tries to maneuver to the other side of the room and sit down, by himself, in that cozy circle of chairs. It is now when Thena invites them all to do that very thing.

George smiles. *How very convenient.*

SAM and RAQUEL

Raquel holds up her hand as a signal, to no avail. Deep in the corner of the room, Sam has his back to Thena so he hears neither the bell nor Thena's invitation. He keeps on talking to Raquel in a sonorous voice. During the last few minutes, amid the whirl of the reception, they had discovered they were both doctors: she, a doctor of family medicine, he, a doctor of psychology. Work had seemed like a safe topic to explore among a sea of strangers.

If Raquel were honest at this moment she would tell us that she has come determined to be a fly on the wall, to be anonymous and silent. She hopes to avoid all extra attention. This retreat is all about finding time to be alone and get away from the noise of the recent months. Clueless, Sam keeps on talking at full volume.

Here it is all over again, déjà-vu—the story of my life—trapped and rendered immobile, caught by accident in the cross-fire of someone else's life.

She eventually manages to extract herself from the corner while gently nudging Sam to turn around and find his seat. Apparently chagrined, he hustles red-faced to one of the two remaining empty chairs.

Thena smiles warmly as if she had not noticed anything amiss, instead drawing the group's attention with a few well-chosen words of greeting. After briefly introducing herself and Dylan, she looks around the circle, engaging each one of them in her warmth.

"I invite you to be quiet for a few minutes, to settle into this space, to let your minds, bodies, and souls arrive in this circle—to be as fully present as possible. It has taken a lot of energy for us all to get here. Let's honor ourselves and all that brings us together today."

She gently rings the bell in her hand, and as the last vibration of the bowl fades away, the room becomes very, very quiet.

Despite the silence, Thena's mind whirls on. It is

clear that she is wondering why one chair is empty. As she scans the room her jaw hardens with a twinge of frustration, then she closes her eyes.

Alycia and Evan—that's who it is. First it was Alycia who said she was coming, accepting my invitation to come pro-bono because she is the board chair of the Terra Center. Then she asked if instead, Evan, her husband could come in her place; now neither of them are here. They only live a stone's throw away, so I wonder what's going on. I really wanted them to experience this weekend program; she especially could be such a financial support and recruiter for us ....

Thena shifts in her chair, plants her feet more firmly on the ground and opens her eyes to reorient herself back inside the room. She sees George sitting opposite her and with gentle eyes observes the spasms in his jiggling legs. She recalls his telephone call a couple of months ago. He had been brusque, almost rude, asking if this was "some hidden religion or some pyramid sales thing that you're trying to sign me up for? I am a salesperson so I know you must have some product. It seems like an expensive weekend to not be perfectly clear about what I am going to get."

She had laughed then, not at him, but in the delight of being able to say simply, "George, our product is to give you space and time to rediscover your own deep self, to reconnect who you are with what you do. And to do this in a group of others who are doing the same thing."

Who would have thought it? George did come. Now, here he is, sitting in the circle. Amazing—you just never know who ends up showing up.

Eventually her mind drifts into stillness. As a facilitator, she always finds this part complex. How challenging it is to be present, to remain in a mindful

40

state and not become overly absorbed with everyone else. Even though it is critical to stay deeply connected with the group, she must be in this retreat, too—that is always the other half of her job.

Aha—if only we could help her understand more clearly, but today is not the time. If only we could settle her heart—for once and for all—to trust the present moment. But alas, Thena's mental gymnastics reflect only a glimmer of understanding about the complicated world of human choice.

How often we watch humans as in a pinball machine, popping out of place and caroming down unprepared and dismal tracks in the wilderness, when only a step away lie other solitary paths rich in communal adventures. The monks, particularly ones like Charles, have shown us much about this powerful cycle of intimacy: of joining, and staying, of questioning and leaving, and of coming back full circle to find what you never lost. Humans constantly mistake the source of perfect action.

This afternoon once again we nudge each other to spin, to keep alive the movement in this blessed silence. We refresh this space with the comfort that comes from the bond of centuries; that glue that still guides us on separate paths while we move in harmony. In the silence this afternoon, we attend to each human soul as each hovers expectantly around that still-point within; some move faster and some slower, many are bouncing wildly in and out of their persons.

We always circle slowly—in the other direction— this gyroscope of time has many threads, many paths to peace.

CHAPTER FOUR

"Speak your truth in ways that respect other people's truth. Our views of reality may differ, but speaking one's truth in a circle of trust does not mean interpreting, correcting, or debating what others say. Speak from your center to the center of the circle, using 'I' statements, trusting people to do their own sifting and winnowing."

RAQUEL

Disturbed by the silence, Raquel finds herself staring at her toes, momentarily wishing she had made the time to get a pedicure. The woman's feet beside her gleam with the shine of wine-berry red.

Why do I feel so edgy and hyper-conscious of myself? I used to love being quiet. What is happening to me? God, listen to that tachycardia. I'm way too intense. Pull it together, girl! This is not a psych eval. Nobody is pressuring you.

Opening her eyes, she wills herself to focus on anything else other than her own beating heart.

As Raquel looks around the room, she becomes

aware of how calming this feels. Except for the empty chair, the room pulses with life: men and women, most of them middle-aged, but a few younger "thirty-somethings." *Looks like I am on the younger side of this crowd.* She catches the eye of the woman therapist all the way from Canada who had been on her shuttle ride and they exchange a quick smile. *Glad we have some diversity and color in the room: African-Americans, a Chinese woman, and some curiously dressed folks who evidently wear their colors.*

This gentleman beside me has an armload of actinic keratoses—looks like it's time to see his dermatologist. Oh my—check out that tattoo! Striking, physically fit black female, magnetic coils around right arm—is it a snake?

God. Look at that dress. Peri-menopausal white female, high BMI. That flowery shroud looks like a garden tent—something my mother would wear.

Now he definitely looks like the youngest here—late twenties, Causasian male, throw back from the '60s, spots of rosacea on his face, odd clothes—rough leather necklace around his neck, unusual leather sandals, and jagged patches of old cow-hide on his rough hemp shirt...

Raquel drinks it all in: brightly colored scarves and pieces of fascinating jewelry that glitter with dozens of buried stories. Absorbed in this reverie, Raquel witnesses waves of external movement that match her inner condition: fingers fluttering and scratching, hands rubbing together, knees shaking, and feet twitching. Most of the group has their eyes closed, yet their faces burn with hope and concentration. Raquel senses the longing beneath their skin.

Or, is that my longing? she wonders. She watches as stillness creeps over these warm bodies, feeling anticipation rise within her as she reaches out connecting in some mysterious way with each one of these diverse creations. Surprisingly, she finds herself less pressured by the silence, more softly open now to being present in this circle of quiet.

In time, Thena rings the bowl again and after offering a quiet thank you to everyone, she begins by talking generally about their next days together, and then hands the details over to the other facilitator. *Thank God, she has a soothing way of speaking,* thought Raquel. *I couldn't abide some heavy-handed leader right now. Yikes, this guy seems rather high energy. Enthusiastic— cute dimple on his face, makes him look even more youthful—wonder how old he is? Left-handed, no ring—like me it seems—he keeps waving his hand in the air and pointing to the flip chart.*

"Boundary Markers." Raquel looks with interest at the list of group norms that Dylan is speaking about. There are eleven of them—short, to-the-point statements. She hears him reading carefully, weighting each word with meaning. Underlining the importance of "providing a safe, supportive space for each one of us," he says.

Eventually, he offers a short time of quiet reflection to consider the personal significance of these statements. She hears him asking the group, "What ones seem highlighted for you today?" But mesmerized, Raquel has lost track of much of what Dylan said.

"Extend and receive welcome. People learn best in hospitable spaces. In this circle we support each other's learning by giving and receiving hospitality. Be here with your doubts, fears, and failings as well as your convictions, joys, and successes, your listening as well as your speaking."

This is exactly how I was feeling during the silence. I followed my own need and discovered the part of myself that responds in warmth and tenderness, even to Sam and his loud awkwardness. I sure hope I can live out of this hospitable place instead of the coldly clinical, diagnostic world of my mind. Maybe this weekend I can try to welcome the more raw spaces of my psyche, I'm aware how beaten-up I feel. I sure need this gift for myself, to learn to give and receive welcome—even to all my anxiety. I know it's a symptom of something...

SAM

Across the room, Sam exhales. This was exactly what he wants and needs—time to be quiet and listen within—time to take in the presence of this group of modern-day pilgrims. He had quickly settled into his normal Quaker experience of reflective silence. It was like coming home. He could stay this way for hours and shed the burden of having to say anything at all. We watched as his earlier experience of shame melted into nothingness in the silence.

He was grateful for the print-out on the boundary markers because sitting on the angle beside the flip chart made it difficult to follow. *And even though Dylan has a loud, clear voice, he tends to talk too fast, resulting in his energy knotting up words into an amorphous bundle of noise. Rather bewildering, actually. He is a nice, earnest guy though.*

Sam thought about many things that he rarely said. His mind overflowed with ideas, concepts, images, and perceptions. For much of his life he had trundled along, making meaning mostly by himself, but recently had been drawn to attend Quaker meetings, especially because of the silence. It brought him an unusual peace to be still within a circle of others. After his encounter with the deer, he had set aside a lot more time to be still. *These group norms sure look similar to being in meeting. Lovely wording, though. Never seen it quite so succinctly described. I love this notion that I can be present by **"invitation rather than demand."** A great reminder that I can be myself, all my idiosyncratic channels of thought. I like this statement about **"speaking your truth in ways that respect other people's truth."** I've always believed that. But I have so many strong and unconventional ideas and badly need to try them out— to go public. Glad Sheera isn't here to shut me up. She hates it when I am outspoken ... although I really am a private sort of person. Now there's a duality...*

He notes Dylan's face flushing as he speaks again. *What's he saying now? He sounds rather contemplative but also suddenly more cautious.*

"As I have been talking with you, I became aware that the point about speaking my own truth and not interpreting or correcting or debating is what calls for my attention today. When I heard this for the first time, in a group like this, I became more personally cognizant of a lifetime of being corrected by all manner of goodhearted and authoritarian people." He laughs. "Starting with my grandmother."

A few of the group snicker knowingly, but Sam notices a middle-aged woman in a flowered dress sit up straighter in her seat, frowning anxiously, as if worried that maybe she is one of those authoritarian grandmas.

Dylan continues. "It was in my first group that I realized how much I longed for open space to bumble and fumble around: a place to risk, to make mistakes, and a place to gloriously succeed. A place to be entirely normal, fully human. I realize as I start to lead these groups, I don't want to fall into the trap of having to

47

be the perfect leader. Like Thena here. Ha!" He laughs nervously at his own joke. "I hope as a new facilitator, I learn to be fully me. In living this out more publicly, I am counting on you to not try to fix me, nor advise me by setting me straight. Still, I do invite you to speak your own truth. Please tell me what helps. Tell me what I do that isn't useful for you. I really do want to know.

nor judge me

"I am a classroom music teacher, so I know how important it is to learn and grow in a mood of nonjudgmental acceptance. I also know that each one of us is at the core that kind of being. So, like you, I enter this circle a learner: scared, raw, and kind of rough around the edges, but also excited about being fully present with you this weekend."

From the other side of the room, Thena picks up the thread of leadership and thanks Dylan for opening his heart. It's time for more introductions around the circle.

"When you are ready," she says, "tell us your name and a few words about yourself. If you like, speak about any question you bring to this weekend or anything that you hope for from these days together. Like Dylan just did, speak into the center of the circle, rather than to each other. Maybe one of the guidelines has been highlighted for you—it might have given you words to focus a little more clearly on something important in this season of your life. Please, let's always remember to leave room for silence as we speak. I like to think of silence as another member of our group which, like each one of us, needs lots of welcoming space."

Thena's simple natural invitation needed no further explanation. For a while again, silence found a comfortable place in the room.

Sam surprises himself by hearing his own voice. "M-my name is S-Sam." It was completely atypical for him to speak first in a group but after stuttering through the initial shock, he plows on:

"I- I'm a research psychology professor. I live in suburbia, not far from here. My answer to the question, i-is to tell you a story from my daily commute last spring."

He feels himself trembling as he tells the story of the deer. It is only when he gets to the end and says "…I came here today because there must be a better way—a more harmonious way to live for the rest of my life" that his confidence rises enough to risk even more personal disclosure.

"Wh -when you sp-spoke, Dylan, about bumbling and stumbling as you grow and learn in life—this is exactly what I was thinking earlier, when I bumbled into this group, talking when everyone else was quiet. I usually don't tell people this, but I want you to know that I have lived all my life with significant hearing loss and need your patience and help. Can you please speak clearly, so I can hear and keep up. Thank you all for your understanding."

MICHAELA
"All alone I heal this heart of sorrow …
All alone I raise this child
Solid stone is just sand and water, baby …
Sand and water and a million years gone by."

Michaela could not get these words from Beth Nielsen Chapman out of her mind. On the train that afternoon she had stumbled across it in her iPod and the lyrics immediately found the same distressing emotional groove as if it were 2001.

Over ten years later, and I still get lost in this melancholy. I thought I had left it behind. Why did I listen to that song? I don't even like it anymore.

49

Now the song, playing repeatedly, is all she hears. The only other distraction was the cloying fragrance of the woman sitting next to her. *That smell is going to kill me. Her perfume matches the outrageous flowers on her dress. I can hardly breathe, this circle is so quiet.*

"... all alone ... all alone ... all alone." I have not come to dig up my past sorrow. This was not what I came to this retreat to do. I must look forward—not backward.

The music now seems to come from the outside and gains in intensity. As she fights back tears, a black stone catches her attention. The shiny river rock supports the candle in the circle's centerpiece. It breathes simplicity: an ivory candle, a black rock, a dried lotus seedpod, and several branches of maple and spruce radiating their leaves in colorful arcs. This is the focus for eighteen pairs of eyes.

She tries to find something else to focus on, some way of escaping the emotion threatening to overwhelm her. Unexpectedly, the words on the flip chart stand out: ***"Be present as fully as possible. Be here with your doubts, fears, failings, convictions, joys, successes ..."*** *Maybe this was what the male facilitator meant. He has just encouraged us to consider new ways of being with difficult parts of our lives.*

What am I supposed to do with this gush of grief and frustration? All the exasperation, the inner eye rolling that is my stock response in public settings. I rarely speak my feelings aloud, but I sure am a judgmental bitch a lot of the time ... especially to myself.

Michaela turns over ideas in the dark stream bed of her mind, peeking under the black rocks of sorrow, glistening in their uncertainty. During the silence she sits expectant, sifting her thoughts. *"Solid stone is just sand and water and a million years gone by." It feels like a million years ago ... left alone—a puddle of water,* *my life blown apart in a terrifying storm. Jake, my only* *love, never coming home, leaving me with little Emma.* *So much time gone by. So many long days forcing myself* *to move on—work, going to school, moving on, always* *moving on. Alone—except for Emma.*

It dawns on her that she identifies with the stone: the amalgam of gritty sand, water, time. *One tough woman ... it has been the only way for me to be. So what if I feel like a bitch sometimes? I am real and solid—and* *beautiful like that river rock.*

Michaela comes back consciously into the circle upon hearing Thena's invitation to speak. Sam inspires her with his forthrightness and gives her a fresh start, helping her recover more of her usual confident self. It still takes a great deal of courage, but she does open her mouth to say simply:

"My name is Michaela. I'm a teacher, too. I'm in the middle of some big changes in my life. I'm a single mom and teach at a primary school in the city. My only daughter is getting ready to go off to college next year." She pauses for a bit, checking if it is still safe. "I've been sitting here in the silence wondering why a certain very painful song keeps coming to my mind. I hope to find some answers to that during these days together. I'm also trying to figure out if and when I should go back to school for more graduate work. I think maybe from all my life experience, I'd make a great principal one day."

The silence seems to deepen after she speaks.

They hear each other's names now, one by one, as each drops tempting tidbits of information into the room.

"I'm Maria," says a big-boned woman in a resonant

voice. Drawing our attention, we regard her auburn hair swept up in a loose bun framing her face with a simple elegance, her sturdy body draped in a silk shawl the same color as her hair. "I am a professional singer. I came here because my partner is struggling with a long-term chronic illness and I have chosen to be her primary caregiver. I am looking for strength, how to keep on going when my partner is suffering so much." She seemed about to continue, but then grows quiet.

It is clear that Thena's emotional batteries are re-charging; clear that she treasures this time in the circle when finally all the words and images from applications and telephone calls become en-fleshed in vibrant story. She waits expectantly, her soft grey eyes shining with encouragement, honoring each charged utterance.

Zach, the young man with the leather necklace, looks around at everyone then says, "I figure I'm probably the youngest person here. I hope I can find my place with people who look and feel a lot like my parents."

Everyone laughs, albeit a bit nervously, acknowledging the truth he just spoke. He rambles on for a while about his two recent jobs as a youth minister: one in a rural church and the other in an urban situation. The circle listens openly to him, silently already aware of their need to give him more than his share of time to dump his frustrations into their midst.

Vanessa chokes up listening to him, she's thinking of her youngest—her own Arthur Jr., so unlike his shy and stable father, wandering off by himself, somewhere in Asia right now. She speaks tentatively, introduces herself by name, and then burbles on for a few minutes rather disjointedly.

"I live in Arizona, it was a long way to come but a very dear girlfriend told me about this, she said that her retreat was the best thing that had happened to her for a very long time. I agree—she has definitely changed. I think I'm looking for change, too. Not sure what that might look like but my problem is that my husband Arthur is ready to retire, but I'm not. My work in the hospital is really rewarding but quite stressful. Oh and I should probably say, I'm not medical—I run the volunteer organization. It's a very large group. I manage 472 volunteers. I'm the director."

It is not clear to anyone exactly what is most important for Vanessa right now but we are captivated by what she is not saying, by all that is sitting in the corners of her mind waiting to be explored. Like her garden of wonders dress, she resonates with a profound energy that has no words but draws our inquisitive concentration.

One thing she is aware of and doesn't say is that her private embarrassment with George still steams on the front burner of her mind, and in order to balance herself, she is aware of pathetically (that's her word for it) trying overly hard to be clever and coherent. Finally, she reigns in her thoughts and concludes simply. "This weekend, I need time to hear myself think."

When she reaches this point with such astonishing clarity, George has a flash of recollection. We see him jerk his neck around with the question on his face: *Do I know this woman?* Then, just as quickly, he falls back inside his troubled flesh. Instead he is reveling in the wish to hear his wife say that exact thing. Privately, he has long thought she should take the time to hear herself think. *What a brilliant way to describe what I would like to hear from her. I must file that idea away to bring to her attention when I get home.*

He remains silent, but is clearly wavering. His legs continue to bounce with explosive power. This open group space, although initially inviting to his easy-going public self, is unsettling to him. Clearly, he is rapidly being displaced by an inner porcupine attempting to sit on his quills.

George had been relieved when Dylan clearly said that no one was forced to speak here, *"**Only speak by invitation, not demand**." Maybe I'll take the leaders up on this and remain silent for the weekend. I wonder what that might feel like.* His insides prickle in excitement with this freeing thought.

Michaela, sitting beside him, could not help but notice his uneasiness. From the moment they sat down, he had been fidgeting with the handout sheet, folding and refolding it into little squares. *Hey mister, relax. You feel like you wandered into the wrong group. You don't seem to fit here today. Do you really want to be here? Strange—so opposite to this guy who is talking now.*

Gerritt now takes his turn. He speaks quietly yet forthrightly while looking at his wife across the room. "Leona and I are both in a major transition. Our two children have left home and we have had some difficult challenges. I realize I've been a workaholic for much of my career. I love the scientific research I do but I need time to sort through future decisions."

He takes in a gulp of air. His voice cracks, slowing him down. "I was surprised to feel some sadness about all this in the quiet of the circle … a few minutes ago …"

"Yes," says Leona, jumping in and rescuing him. "Being an empty-nester *is* sad. I have been happy to discover yoga, though. It has been *really* helpful to discover how my body teaches me so much. Ummm ... I admit, though, that my excitement in my new work as a yoga instructor has taken me way off-balance. I hope to get more balanced this weekend."

Thena listens thoughtfully to the two of them, wondering what their real story is. *Something important brought them here; they look incredibly stressed. Couples don't often come together to my retreats. It's going to be interesting to watch how this evolves.*

Mei realizes she can no longer hide. She wants to speak ... *now, before it's too late. I must say something, but how do I speak with integrity and yet honor my privacy? I like this idea of the "inner teacher." This point stands out for me. What a radical way of thinking about God—my teacher inside. Inside me.* She decides in an instant that the one thing she wants to practice this weekend is to speak from her heart.

"I am in conflict," she says. "A part of me wants to tell you everything about myself and another part wants to be private. I don't know how to resolve that, so the best I can say for now is that I am pleased to be here. I know I was sent here for some reason, so this weekend I want to practice being authentic, speaking directly and only from my heart."

It is curious how word sparks fly from conversations like this, igniting a ready torch in other souls, mirroring some deep and waiting part of the listener and quickly fanning a response that bulldozes away the often insurmountable fears of authentic group process among strangers. How curious, too, that we had no time to savor the power of Mei's words, to offer her space to bask and be nourished by the rich wisdom of her soul, because in response, Raquel almost leaps across the room to hug her. The room reels, compelled by the unspoken magnetism.

We witness Mei's shudder of alarm. (Simultaneously, we tune in to how much she fears untoward lunatic attractions, and also aware that as Raquel leans forward out of her chair, she herself teeters precariously on repeating what was so recently done to her—"caught by accident in the cross-fire of someone else's life." Yes, humans reacting from their emotional wounds *are* entirely predictable—if one can slow down the process long enough to notice.)

We noticed then that Raquel sashayed into the complicated dance of humor that so often precedes the real deal. Craning her neck, she attempts to read Mei's shiny plastic name card. "I didn't hear your name? My? Is it? No? May? Well, OK Mei—I think I've got it." They both laugh a touch hysterically at the rhyming game, and then finally she soberly speaks directly to Mei. "My name is Raquel and I am so grateful for what you just said. I also want to learn to be authentic and trust that I can speak out of all my conflicted insides." She pauses.

After clearing her throat several times as if a crust of words had formed in her chest, she squeezes out the following almost in one long extended breath. "I am a physician, I just came back from Africa, where I was working in the aftermath of a war zone for ten years. I know that somehow the war got inside of me. I am struggling, fighting to get my old life back, and yet missing Africa in every pore of my body. I am in complete culture shock. I really pray that this weekend might be helpful somehow, as I feel quite at the end of my rope."

Again, no one speaks for a long time. Eventually it becomes clear that all those who want to share have done so; even George finds his own way to delicately say his few carefully chosen words that allow his spirit entry into the group rather than leaving him on the fringe like the distant observer of his youth.

After honoring the spirit of this earnest beginning, Thena announces it is time for dinner. The tantalizing smells from the kitchen are overpoweringly inviting.

CHAPTER FIVE
DINNER

Charles had been waiting. Dinner has been ready for twenty minutes. It is not that he is an overly punctual person; in fact, he fully values the need for flexibility when it comes to serving food for retreats such as this. But Charles' inordinate fondness for the finest of food, prepared and served in its prime, inspires him to serve vegetables steamed delicately, not mushy and sodden like so much institutional fodder. He adores fresh rolls, crusted in their buttery richness, divinely tender when swept out of the oven into the mouth. He could not bear to see a salad wilting or water beading all over the ice-filled jugs, leaving damp puddles around the carefully assembled floral centerpieces on the stark, round wooden tables.

Unfortunately, the refreshing cold soup now slightly warm, had lost its prime, and his fragrant decorations of wispy herbs had begun to sink under their own weight into soupy oblivion—not a good thing for his choice gazpacho, probably the last batch of this season, made from fresh vegetables meticulously picked early this morning before the hot sun came up.

He hears voices approaching the kitchen. Finally. He breathes a sigh of relief.

Becoming the cook last year was the best of all worlds for Charles. He has his own private space to work, with an ever-changing world of vulnerable and hungry humanity to serve. And even better, he could daily offer the most priceless gift, the divine blessing of lavish generosity, pressed down and pouring over. His Italian grandmother oozed like oil through his pores as he stirs his way through the gastronomical seasons. Every time Charles pours virgin olive oil into a sizzling pan, he grins, bowing his bald head in gratitude, remembering his grandmother.

The story was told that the last thing she did before leaving her ancestral home was to cut stubby, budding sprigs from several of her precious olive and fig trees, then wrap them in damp cloth in an old cigar tin from her dead husband, killed in the Great War. Upon arrival on mainland, she hastily planted the little cuttings in pots of earth, even before the suitcases were unpacked. It was said that Nonna had actually wanted to take a dozen fertilized eggs from her favorite White Leghorn hens, but her sons convinced her she could not keep them safe and warm on her lap all the way to America—and besides, where would she find a broody hen in the city? Nonna objected that her mother had carried chicken eggs with her, tucked into her warm bosom when they were forced out of Sicily decades before. But she had to agree that it would be a longer trip to America.

We note that it never takes long for a newcomer to the retreat center to become aware that Charles, the cook, is the human and spiritual pulse of this property. What they do not realize, as we do, is that Charles has a long and complicated history with this place and with the Church.

Pasquale Sertano, as he had been named at birth, arrived unexpectedly between worlds; he was born prematurely on Ellis Island. He had the complex fortune to arrive, not in the middle of the Atlantic Ocean, but in the immigration detention center on Easter Sunday, 1938. He was one of the 355 babies born to immigrants on the island, in transit to their new homeland. His rotund young mother had hidden her pregnancy from the officials. When Charles arrived, hatched out of the skirts of this shy and scared young bride, his grandmother had welcomed him as if baby Jesus himself had shown up—a potent blessing to be born an American citizen, a symbol of all the hope and promise in the world that had brought the Sertano family to these shores.

Charles arrived as if he, too, could not wait for freedom. His grandmother and her two sons, with their fresh brides, had finally found their way to leave before war erupted again. After the devastation of the first war and the death of her husband, his grandmother's grief turned into a steely determination to lose no more of her family to war. As the matriarch of the family, she made it happen. They packed up and left their home in southern Italy, and with some help from some of the more questionable government authorities, Nonna thought she had left the conflict zone behind—only to be put into the Ellis Island detention center upon arrival in port.

In 1938, Ellis Island no longer bustled with immigrants as at the turn of the century, but had been demoted to an eerie place of detention for anyone who looked suspicious. The Sertano family's illegally doctored papers did not pass the vigilant inspector, who was intent on keeping any enemy Italians from infiltrating the East Coast. The immigration board would not meet until Tuesday, so it was a long and difficult weekend, dismally sequestered from their Easter celebratory dinner with relatives in New Jersey who had sponsored them.

Thus when Charles arrived unheralded, his grandmother knew without doubt that he was an Easter symbol, and as one who came from God, thus belonged to God, not to the family. Just like her fiery insistence in crossing to this new land, nothing was going to stop Nonna from seeing Charles entering the priesthood. From that Easter Sunday on, he was given in an arranged marriage to the Church.

Tonight at this Friday dinner, here he is: clearly the body and the blood, the life energy, of the ghost of the former mission house. No longer priest, but cook, he consciously relishes the moments when he parades out of the kitchen carrying one of his supreme culinary creations, as he held high the host before spiritual pilgrims. Charles, once the novice priest, now is back at this abundant communion table providing a new kind of food and drink for the hungry supplicants.

But tonight, hidden beneath his tender ministrations, right at the spot where his splotchy apron fastens around his middle, we know Charles feels off-center, somewhat disoriented. All summer he has been emotionally on edge, balanced precariously in the often-confusing haze of transitional space. Curious to him, although completely understandable to us, he often physically feels the vital energy of the past surge through him. At times he lives outside of himself, inside the ancient walls of the physical building. He attempts to comprehend mysterious urges that seep into his pores, wraithlike, that stir him, seeking to bring the former back to life.

We heard him pottering around the herb garden,

talking to himself the other day, "I feel as if I am already becoming one of the "balcony people," those invisible souls watching from heaven's sidelines. I can't figure it out, but seem to have spent most of this summer cooking, escaping my emotional reality. Whatever. What's an old man meant to do? I've always harbored a gloriously plump chef inside me, so I guess now I am one."

*   *   *

Thena sticks her head rather sheepishly into the kitchen and still standing at the kitchen door, apologizes profusely for their lateness. She knows Charles well enough by now and realizes he is the benevolent authority to be reckoned with around here.

"Well, you better get it together for tomorrow because I have a really fine feast planned for Saturday night."

As Charles gently chides Thena, a sudden memory washes over her. She sees herself sitting with her grandmother during a Shabbat service and hearing the rabbi give a sermon from Isaiah. *"Let your soul delight itself in fatness."* At the time, as a young teenager, she had laughed at such a cracked-up idea, thereby implanting this ludicrous memory. Fatness was surely an evil, avoided at all costs.

Now, she senses her grandmother mirrored in Charles's face. Momentarily suspended in time, she stares at the portly cook, but aware only of the presence of her favorite Bubbie, her inspiring life force during all the difficult years of adolescence. How many times had she soaked in the rich, wealth of her divine kitchen ... such fat goodness.

Charles remains riveted to the spot, a basket of hot rolls floating at the end of his arm. *"Here it is again, that energy, moving through me as if I am not even here at all.*"

"God, Charles, I just saw Bubbie, my grandmother…" Thena trails off in confusion. "It … it smells so good in here," she mumbles, then shrugging her shoulders, she turns to the dining room.

Charles gently lays his hand on her arm, stopping her. "I don't have time right now, but come back sometime and tell me what you just saw. I'd like to know more about your Bubbie. She sounds important."

As the two of them move into the dining room, the group hushes expectantly.

"Folks, I'd like you to meet Charles, our cook here," Thena announces. As you can smell and see, his food is delicious. Charles is a special friend of mine, and I hope you can get to know him, too. He can tell you all about this property and its history because he used to live here when it was a mission house for the Benedictines. I am so glad he came back to serve us in this way. Enjoy your dinner!"

Charles beams with pleasure and then hustles back to work, a little more settled now. He is clearly still caught up in the moments with Thena, realizing with awe that once again the invisible had whispered.

As he moves around the room, in and among this diverse group, he feels one of them for the next hour. He relishes their heartfelt appreciation of the fine quality of his food, but also revels in their conversation, in the remarkably personal ways that strangers make themselves known to each other when they sit down together at a table to eat good food. All their hungers and longings show up out of hiding.

He watches as a heavy-set man dressed in a well-worn business suit, with tie askew, inhales two large platefuls of food quickly, and then with his face flushed in pleasant exhilaration proceeds to regale his tablemates with inconsequential stories, clearly enjoying an audience, but with little awareness that he now holds the table hostage. A delicate-looking Chinese woman catches Charles's eye and they smile at each other in quiet recognition of the situation.

This man's name card is tucked into his jacket pocket but he reminds Charles of Brother Phillip, a red-haired Irish priest who always managed to get the whole table laughing but somehow left Charles feeling hollow and dry, as if the excessive humor masked some bottomless emptiness. He also poignantly notes that this lady has a finely tuned resonance like his dear old friend Antonio Piccione, the gardener. Antonio, the man who had rescued him when Charles lost the capacity to fight for himself.

Those awful days, when I was struggling with whether to leave the priesthood. My horrible depression that spring. But Antonio came every day, wheedling me out of bed into the garden. Dear man. I can't believe he lived for 105 years—the oldest Benedictine in the U.S. He used to tell me about the $8.67 he had in his pocket when he came in the big rush at Ellis Island three decades before me. No wonder I adopted him as the father I never knew...

A younger woman laughs loudly, bringing him out of his reverie. She has a touch of annoyance in her voice.

"No, it isn't always snow- and ice-covered in Alberta. We do have long winters but our summers are beautifully hot. You crazy Americans have been known to bring your skis to Canada in July. Think Montana—I live right across the border from there."

As Charles hears these conversational snippets, they tumble through him like jigsaw pieces cut from his memory. They existed long ago, all these life chronicles.

65

Nothing is really new; each story had been heard around these very tables, decades before. The past continues to whisper in his ear.

It was a bare, stark room then, with none of the gaily printed curtains, nor the hanging ivy and spider-plants in the windows that I love so much. The sienna-hued paint gives a sun-like quality to the room now.

But food has always been important in this place ... the sensuality of eating with my brothers—especially the silent meals. The quiet ecstasy of slow-eating, one meditative mouthful at a time. I loved how the silence hung like a friendly cloak from these walls. I know she is still waiting to envelop any one of us who stops long enough to pay attention to her presence.

Maybe Thena might like to try a silent meal with this group. I am sure the Chinese lady would like that.

CHAPTER SIX

"No fixing, no saving, no advising, and no setting each other straight. This is one of the hardest guidelines, but it is vital to welcoming the soul, to making space for the inner teacher."

Slowly, the well-nourished group members trickle back into the circle. The alto sax of Jan Garbarek floats evocatively up the hallway to the dining room, drawing in Maria, the singer, the last of the stragglers. Each person finds a small printed card placed on their seat. We watch as the spirit in the room visibly relaxes as the group responds to the invitation:

"You have nothing to do and nowhere to go."
~ a Taoist saying

Vanessa sighed when she read the message, and now gives Maria a generous, welcoming smile as she slides in beside her. She smiles again when she hears Maria respond to her card in the same manner.

Dylan rings the chime.

Raquel feels the silence melt into her bones and imperceptibly leech tension from her taut body. A tear runs down her face, surprising her, as if given silent permission for release. *How good to do nothing, just to sit here. What a hectic summer since coming home—a nonstop whirlwind of family and friends, and media interviews. But now in September—back to the same old exhaustion that engulfed me out in the African bush. I sure don't want that to happen again—I'm so afraid of being trapped alone inside my life.*

The disquieting mood of silence has triggered her again, so she is relieved when Dylan begins the evening session by handing out two poems printed on the same page, and garners even more comfort when he commences reading in his deep lyrical voice:

The Way It Is
There's a thread you follow. It goes among
things that change. But it doesn't change.
People wonder about what you are pursuing.
You have to explain about the thread.
But it is hard for others to see.
While you hold it you can't get lost.
Tragedies happen; people get hurt
or die; and you suffer and get old.
Nothing you do can stop time's unfolding.
You don't let go of the thread.
~ William Stafford

After a pause for reflection, Dylan asks if someone else might like to read it once more. Michaela is quick to jump in, her voice evidently well used to reading aloud in the classroom.

68

"There's a thread you follow …"

Raquel senses her vivacious femininity as such a contrast and for an instant looks at Michaela with a glance of jealousy, wishing for some of her ebullience, but then moves on, inspired. *Yes! I really like this poem— it speaks to me about the thread I have been following. I wonder what it is? What made me go to Angola, to such a burned-out country—to a place where I couldn't speak the language, a land decimated by decades of civil war? Why is it so hard to explain it? People want to give me a heroine's medal for what I've done, when mostly all I feel is hurt and tragedy, and how terribly tired I am.* **"Don't let go of the thread…"** *What does that mean for me?*

Before Raquel has time to try to answer her own questions, Thena begins to read the next poem in her calm, gentle voice.

The Thread
Something is very gently,
invisibly, silently,
pulling at me - a thread
or net of threads
finer than cobweb and as
elastic. I haven't tried
the strength of it. No barbed hook
pierced and tore me. Was it
not long ago this thread
began to draw me? Or
way back? Was I
born with its knot about my
neck, a bridle? Not fear
but a stirring
of wonder makes me

catch my breath when I feel
the tug of it when I thought
it has loosened itself and gone.
~ Denise Levertov

George shifts in his chair, thoroughly uncomfortable in every way. He had seriously stuffed himself at dinner, and his digestive tract is telling him not to do that again—although he had relished every mouthful. He had even gone back to his room after dinner and changed his suit for something more comfortable. Even more discomfiting was how ill at ease he felt right now, deeper down, below the indigestion. A barrage of buried memories about poetry assailed him.

Miss Simms—my gorgeous tenth-grade English teacher—was mad about the stuff. Reams of old words filling pages, making no sense to me at all. But how I loved just basking in the sound of her voice, awed by her beauty ... aroused with sentimental feelings that had nowhere to go ... and then being asked to come up with my own lines of poetry. Impossible! Surely, I won't be asked to do that again.

But maybe there is something here in these words. Why do I keep reading "barbed hook pierced and tore me?" Not a very pleasant nor encouraging idea. Even as a child I hated going fishing though Dad loved it. I always felt sorry for the worms and for the fish.

But ... maybe I'm the fish now. Like those feelings I had yesterday on the plane, the idea of being caught in my life and wanting to run away. I feel like a fish out of water—a horrible sense of being trapped at the end of my own lifeline.

Just then, Dylan invites them to repeat out any phrase from either poem that had caught their attention. George chuckles darkly to himself, but remains silent.

Raquel begins in a hopeful voice: "Not fear but a stirring of wonder makes me catch my breath."

"It is hard for others to see," Vanessa bursts out.

"Was I born with its knot about my neck, a bridle?" asks Leona.

Zach, the youngest person in the room, speaks forcefully, deep from his gut. "People wonder what you are pursuing."

Inside of herself, Mei marvels, "*Something is very gently, invisibly, silently pulling at me.*"

"Long ago this thread began to draw me," calls Sam

Maria gasps in a stage whisper, "Tragedies happen, people get hurt and die."

Raquel spoke again, this time, her words escaping with a clear finality: "Nothing you do can stop time's unfolding."

The hush in the room deepens. A gentle underbelly of quiet holds the disparate voices together, wrapping the group as a whole in the filaments of story that emerged, each a loose strand of the variegated threads of their lives. The past and the future twirled into the present moment. The poets still communicate through them all.

They even speak for George, who is choking on the barb of truth that he is desperately attempting not to swallow. His words remain stuck in his throat, silencing him.

Michaela considers it very natural to be given twenty minutes to go off alone, either to stay seated in the circle or to find a private place to reflect with these poems and a few well-chosen questions. She senses the significance of this time of silent meditation and eagerly finds a secluded corner of the room where she props herself on a pile of yoga mats and resolutely turns to the first question.

What threads have you been following in your life?
"I have been a teacher all my life," she writes in her journal. *"I started early by teaching my brother and my sisters how to behave, how to keep Mom happy, and how to keep Dad away from us. I learned what worked and then passed it on to them so they wouldn't get hurt like I did. I felt like I was the crash-test dummy of the family, the one forced through the most damaging situations so the others could follow more safely. I was the big brave girl who on the outside could face any problem and still show up as the teacher's pet. I was the one who faced up to the bullies in school. I had to learn quickly because Dad was a bully when he drank, and when he didn't drink he was even more scary and cruel ... "*

Michaela begins to cry softly. She had often wondered what kept her in such unpleasant schools, choosing the most difficult classes, while facing head-on the most unsupportive and challenging of all administrative staff. But in her heart of hearts she knew she was born to be a teacher. This is not a fragile thread. Clearly, it is a massive knotted steel cable that runs through her entire life. Never before has she experienced such a palpable sense of calling to her work.

Gerritt feels like he is the author of the first poem, but has just now read the words. *This is my story. This is "the way it is." This is how I have lived my life, holding this one thread I could never let go of. My research, my day to day work is the constant search for answers. Always plodding on. I know I am anything but a quitter; my work consistently shows my commitment. But what about Leona? What happened to me? "Tragedies happen; people get hurt."*
I knew I was wounding her when I fell for Carmen. I knew it was going to happen. I knew that somehow, this

was the way it was going to be. It all felt a little like a high school science lab experiment, when you already know the results of your actions before you even begin. So why bother trying to make good decisions? What the hell—life is just this way, all pre-determined.

His anger shifts the normally precise balance of his mind. He grows confused, lost in the paradoxical world of his own uncertainty.

How could it be? How can something so right, be so wrong? My experience with Carmen taught me more about myself than years of being safe in a placid marriage.

I know I was following some unmistakable inner direction—but consequently I lost my moorings in another part of myself. I've gone over this, millions of times. I give up. I quit trying to understand what I could have done differently.

Chris

He turns to the next question: ***"What stirring of wonder catches your breath when you feel its pull?"***

Gerritt stops in his mental tracks; he feels a stirring, a tugging from a messy, untended corner of his inner world. As a brain scientist he knows he is experiencing a cascade of chemicals, the brain transmitting information from one neuron to another, attempting to regain its normal functioning of speaking, thinking, and moving in response to all of these powerful emotional stimuli. He could hear a waterfall of hormones tumbling over themselves as they attempted to reconnect with his tried and true, well-trodden inner paths. Eventually, Gerritt's over-functioning brain becomes hopelessly overwhelmed.

He leaps off his chair, startling not only himself, but also those sitting quietly in the circle. *It's like being administered an electroshock treatment in public. How embarrassing.* For a time, he paced back and forth behind the circle, and then headed for the men's room.

Re-entering the room, Gerritt remembers Dylan had pointed out various resources that were available for this weekend if anyone was interested. At the back of the room, an inviting stack of art materials captures his attention. Mechanically, as if being moved by an unrecognized force, Gerritt selects a box of colored pencils and a large sheet of paper, pulls up a chair to the table, and begins to color "the invisible tugging and stirring of wonder in his soul."

He has just started when Dylan announces that it might be a good time now to form groups of three and share some of what they had been discovering. "This will be a short fifteen minutes, enough time for each person to talk for five minutes. Listen quietly, be attentive to your partners, and don't say anything in response as you would normally do. This is not a time to chat, but a time to speak from your heart as you wish—or to be silent. Be careful to listen openly."

Gerritt, unmoved by his typical commitment to conformity, keeps on drawing alone. As the triads huddle in small circles, he remains blind and deaf to all else happening around him.

The room buzzes with conversation, forcing everyone to pay close attention to their small group members, but we watch as Leona cranes her lovely neck over Dylan's tall shoulder. Evidently she could barely contain her wifely curiosity. By the distasteful look on her face we imagine her inner monologue: *What the hell is he doing? Hunched up like an idiot over the table like that ... is he really drawing? Didn't he hear the announcement to join a group? I can't believe that he is completely immersed in some arty thing. God, I'd love to peek over his shoulder. No, I will not be distracted by this man tonight.*

Leona abruptly turns her chair out of his line of vision, and tunes in to Dylan and Vanessa. We watch her trying to listen carefully to Vanessa but we note her ambivalence. Maybe she is wondering about how much she wants to share. Is it possible that Gerritt, for better and for worse, is *the* major thread in her life? We wait and wonder if she'll have the courage to talk about this when it comes her turn to speak. Does she really want to understand this personal dilemma that spans so much love and hate?

*　　*　　*

In the meantime, George had left the room. He felt compelled to remain silent, to get outdoors and clear his brain. He had found it an enormously difficult day, and it had been way too long since he'd sat outside by himself on a warm evening. It was past twilight, but he senses the sun's heat captured in the concrete and stones around him, warming him as he finds his way down the dimly lit path. Most of the lights had burned out (*...budget problems?* he wonders), but as his eyes adjust to the darkness, to his delight the path ends in a tranquil water garden. He gropes his way, sitting down cautiously in an old ribbed lounge chair. A towering potted bush gives off the most exotic fragrance he has ever encountered. The waterfall is still, and the hush of evening reflects back the silence of the quiet pond. Shadows of majestic dark foliage surround him on all sides. *I'll have to come back here during the day to see everything more clearly. I have stumbled into a genuine secret garden. How surreal...*

But what am I doing here? I almost feel caught at this retreat. What a relief that we can do what we need to do. I couldn't bear even trying to talk with anybody just now. I feel like a thrashing fish, snagged on the barbed hook of my life ... and it is clear I am acting like the fish out of water in this group. How aggravating. But I don't know what else to do, how else to act. I am so tired of pretending.

It feels so dark everywhere right now. The lights in my life seem to be going out one by one. All my contracts expiring, those promising deals this week, evaporating before my eyes. Just like this garden here—so dark, so much unknown.

Like the mysterious dark-leaved plants, he has few words to name the lurking shadows inside or outside. He remains motionless and after a long time, George stumbles back to his room and falls into another very deep sleep.

*   *   *

When the triads began to form, it had taken courage for Mei not to retreat to the prayer room alone. *That's what I do, so easily, go it alone. I've always done that.* She coached herself, remembering she had not come here to be by herself. She waited, still seated in the circle, trusting the right two people would eventually come and find her. She knew that if she moved a muscle, she would automatically slip outside to manage by herself. *That's what I've been doing for way too long*

After Thena and Michaela materialize in front of her looking for a third person, and the three of them pulled their chairs together, Mei found she was more than ready to be the first to speak. But five minutes barely scratched the surface. Like a dry pump on an old well, Mei only needed a little priming to reopen the silence of the past months. Her husband's death raised so many questions; dozens of them gushed out of her broken heart. Thena and Michaela listened compassionately, but tonight

76

there would be no answers for Mei, other than finding a simple harmony in the new connection with the outside world.

Later that evening, when she made her way to the greenhouse sanctuary space set aside for silent prayer and meditation, all she could do was fall on her face on the mat. She listened longingly to the sound of water flowing among the rocks in the indoor fountain. Eventually, she began to pray for wisdom to know if she should respond to Thena's last announcement.

Before she closed the circle for that night, Thena had spoken briefly about the Clearness Circles which would be held Saturday afternoon. Previously, Mei had carefully read the details of the plan for this unusual opportunity. She learned that the old term "Clearness Committee" came from the Quakers, back in the 1600's, when individuals needed a way to draw on both inner and communal resources to deal with personal problems because they had no clerical leaders to "solve" their problems for them.

Thena had concluded the evening with a stirring invitation to consider being a focus person tomorrow, to bring a troubling question or a pressing personal issue to a small group during this special discernment meeting. Mei was intrigued.

Can I trust this process? She wondered. *Do I actually believe that I have an inner teacher, a personal authority that will give me guidance and help me hear my own voice? Right now I am really looking for new direction.*

Will I be able to be real with the small group they choose for me? How on earth will they understand me or my heritage, the culture that is so much a part of me? Where I come from we don't do therapy or self-help groups; we have ourselves, our community of advisors

77

and guides. But they haven't helped me much, either. What would my church think if they knew I was coming for help here? Is God here in this process? God, are you here? Did you bring me here? Should I do this tomorrow? Please, give me peace. Eventually, Mei knew. *I want to do this. I want to trust others to help me, just by their listening—like tonight.*

She's humming a little tune now. We watch over her as she walks down the darkened path to her cottage room. Just as she gets to her door, we see her stop and tilt her head up to the night sky, as a plaintive child might, when asking for one more night-sustaining drink of water.

"Oh, dear God, please don't let them give me more advice, I've had enough of that. Too many prayers, too many other people's ideas, too much unasked-for concern. Thank you. Tomorrow I'll need to find out more to be absolutely sure, but for now I'm going to bed. Good night."

CHAPTER SEVEN
NIGHT

Night here at the Terra Center often brings surprises, even to us who are more accustomed to living in the shadow-lands; it is mostly in darkness that humanity inclines towards transparency. No longer are there so many tempting shadows to hide in.

As the lights switch off in meeting room, and one by one blink on and then off in the bedrooms, we sense the restless revolutions of psyche and mind; waves of excitement and despair, those toxins of insomnia that park themselves at the doorways of sleep. Even deeper yet, we intuit the roaming of spirits that must escape the confines of old categories of truth and falsehood, and must fly unimpeded into creative higher realms. It is now especially that the air teems with soulful prayers whispered on pillows, ones that blaze arrows through the night sky. And occasionally—how much we celebrate this—when bodies and souls unite, then the energy of love-making emerges, and disrobed in her full glory, dances high in the air like a fire-fly.

Yes, the whirling day activity of a weekend retreat

center pales in comparison to the nomadic tent—orchestra of night. Tonight is no exception.

*   *   *

Leona lies silent under the covers, not moving when Gerritt enters their room. She has been mentally turning over the events of the past few hours. She could not identify any specific outward change, but she feels that the logjam inside her head has subtly shifted. It seemed a hopeful day, reminding her of the winter ice break-up she had read about in northern communities, when townspeople placed bets on the hour the giant river of ice would start to groan and buckle, heralding the soon-to-be flowing water. She had heard that, at a certain time each spring, the ice jam literally explodes with energy, cracking like a cannon, releasing everything below the surface that had become unstable and under pressure.

That describes exactly how I am feeling, anticipating some kind of inner break-up, afraid and yet determined to wait until the dam breaks. How I long to be able to flow again, from the inside outward. Today I sensed some brand new movement. For a yoga instructor, that's exciting news.

She stirs, and then turns toward her husband expectantly, letting him know she is awake. He switches on the antiquated metal bedside lamp. *Speaking of explosions of energy, I can't believe how energized he looks. He seems to have lost years in the past hour.*

Gerritt's face flushes as he sits gingerly beside her, as if waiting to be invited to speak, waiting for a summons to the queen's throne. She smiles warmly, aware that recently she had been thwarting any attempt he had made to communicate. Chagrined, she realizes she had demanded this annoying sign of obeisance.

"Where have you been, Gerritt? What were you

drawing? You seemed so captivated!"

Gerritt cautiously produced his artwork, then quickly tucked it away again, safely behind his back.

"I don't know quite what came over me, Leona," he said. I became so distressed in the midst of my journaling. I would have exploded if I had forced myself to write one more word. It reminded me of the increasing frustration I have at work, creating research documents with tedious descriptions of the most intricate workings of the brain. I know what I'm doing. I do it well, in fact, I am an expert in the field, but it's virtually impossible to describe what goes on—and yet I keep trying.

"On top of that, every time I try, I know I come closer and closer to reality, to the real truth. But will I ever be able to prove that? I go forward, but never quite make it, only able to move just half the distance of the last time. In this work you get close, but you never truly arrive. Sometimes my work feels like a burden from hell. You can smell it, you can almost taste it, but you can never hold it in your hands and say: 'Here is the answer I was seeking.'"

He stops, breathless, as if bowled over by his rush of verbal clarity.

Leona sits up on her pillows. "So, show me what you drew. Tell me about it!"

Gerritt talks for a few minutes about his drawing, describing in colorful detail his journey into his inner world. He had drawn stark strokes of reds and blacks interlaced with contrasting pastel circles and earthy hues, an abstract panoply of color and shape, yet rich with vivid dimension. Leona instinctively knows that this is him. *This is Gerritt, the Dutch boy who always needs answers for everything. My golden-boy of science and rationality has been turned inside out. All his hidden messy divergence and contradictions are here, exposed on paper, and so beautifully and colorfully revealed.*

She feels the shock of being graced by this very private disclosure, and also confused as if somehow he truly intends this revelation for her. It was like seeing his inner naked self, stripped of all its order and rightness, and given honor, like a gallery showcase presentation, fit for only the most valuable pieces of art. She wants to touch the paper, to touch him, to feel with her hands this glorious springing rawness liberated from a lifetime of confinement.

"Thank you, Gerritt," is the best she can muster. "Th ..thank you for showing me, sharing with me. I am very happy for you."

The moment passes. They manage a few more perfunctory words that night, but a certain awe embraces them as they lie transfixed, side by side, both awake for a very long time.

MARIA

"Grace, it's me, I am so sorry to wake you up, to call you so late, but we only just now ended our evening session."

"Maria, is that you, I can barely hear you?"

"Sorry, I'll speak a little louder, but the cell phone signal isn't so good here and these old rooms aren't that soundproof. I hear a guy already snoring next door. It's been an incredibly exhausting but strangely helpful day. But how are you doing? I haven't been able to get you out of my mind. It was so hard to leave this morning when I knew you were going to be in such pain. How did your treatment go?"

"Terrible, same old battle axe of a technician who has to ram stuff into every orifice of my body. I want to do the same to her."

"Oh dear, not again. How awful. I'd do anything to

be able to take one of those horrible experiences in my body instead of yours. I think you know that. ... Could you swallow anything today? I'm so sorry I'm not there to help you be more comfortable."

"No, no need for you to suffer with me my dear, my one thought of gratitude today has been that you are on retreat—finally you are taking time to sort out your life instead of caring only for me."

"Aw, thank you Grace. You are such as sweetheart for being so persistent, pushing me to come. You know how guilty I feel doing what I want and leaving you on your own. But as always, you seem to figure things out for yourself. You've always been like that."

"Actually, I have always thought the same about you. I could never have traveled the European opera circuit like you did. I'm just the homebody."

Maria laughs quietly. "Yeah, you've said that hundreds of times. Maybe this weekend might help. You're the truly independent and free one in our relationship. I know everybody thinks that's me, that I am the strong one. All they ever hear is my voice. You've always been the one who could figure out real life. I've lived my life on the stage. I can't imagine how you find your way through every day right now, By now, I'd be groveling in some corner of an institution if I were you."

"I love you Maria."

"I really love you too."

"So what's happening in the retreat? Any cool people or just those who've been hiding under a rock all their life?"

"No there are some really good people, but what it's about is hard to put to words. Simple, uncomplicated, yet quite powerful. All we did tonight was read two poems about threads and it led me to write about singing, about you and our relationship, and then a bit about your sickness. It feels like I found a way of seeing some significant threads in my life that I've never looked at all together.

"I realize that up until now, you've been the only one in my life who I could really be honest with. Tonight it seemed so natural talking freely with a couple of complete strangers. Like can you believe it? I hope you don't mind, I had to tell them about you."

"Hope you didn't tell them everything."

"No silly, of course not, just that I was able to be real without having to act. You know, the big operatic thing. I almost didn't tell them that I sing, somehow it doesn't seem important right now. … oh, dear, are you all right? That cough sounds worse. I'm sorry, Grace. I don't want to tire you out. You really do sound awfully weak. Are you sure you are going to be okay by yourself?"

"I'm just fine. Now let's hang up and I can get back to sleep and you do the same."

"Okay. Goodnight my love. I'll keep my cell phone on so if you need anything you can call me. I love you. I'll call you in the morning."

ZACH

Shuffling his sandals along the threadbare carpet, Zach drifts restlessly down the hall. *I can't possibly go to sleep yet. These old folks sure go to bed early ... and I'm starved. I wish I had taken another of those heavenly cheesecakes that the cook offered us back to my room. Why couldn't I just be honest and grab another big one for myself?* In the snack area, he opens and closes cupboard doors, finding only a packet of airplane pretzels amid the plastic plates and utensils. *Somehow these seem entirely out of place here, and must be awfully stale, they don't even hand them out on planes anymore.*

Eventually, a different kind of hunger draws him back into the eerily still meeting room. He steps into the circle of chairs, now randomly scattered around the floor, left askew and out of alignment like so many group members that night. The center table draws his attention and he moves closer, attentively peering into the night shadows. Hidden under the fall foliage, he spies a box of matches, and on impulse lights the candle, dropping cross-legged in front of the decorated altar.

I haven't noticed this before. He reaches for a chocolate-brown seedpod about the size of his palm. *What a cool thing. How intricate and earthy, yet feather-light and buoyant—it's floating in my hand. I wonder what it is. Maybe it's a lotus? Yes, that's right. It's the same design on Steve's new CD, "Lotus Songs."*

It seems important for him to hold it for a while, cupping both hands around the candlelit bowl of the dried flower. He stares into the black holes where seeds once were, and experiences a mysterious depth and heaviness despite the lack of physical weight.

Where have all the seeds gone? Are they growing in some foreign, tropical land? I've never seen a lotus plant in this country, but I remember that Buddhists revere the lotus as sacred. It doesn't make much sense, but just holding this feels kind of unearthly, like a tiny glimpse of mystery.

What a sentimental nerd I am sometimes ... but I feel like this dried-out husk—as if I have scattered all my seeds for everybody else and have nothing left. Like, I feel empty these days. Nothing left to give out. How can I be so entirely empty and lifeless when I'm still so young? I feel like an old lotus pod. Did I ever really have a chance to flower?

Crap ... how morose I can get at times. Like some big old moose farting around the forest. I hate this part of me. Maybe that's not true, either, but nothing feels very sure right now. What's happening to me?

Ideas and word fragments explode in his brain, holding him rooted to the carpet. Afraid to move abruptly, afraid that he might lose this moment—that it would be swept away and he along with it. Rapt in his inner world, he grips the seedpod as if it were a lifebuoy of reality. He seems to need this symbol of faith right now, even though it emerged as light from the dark side of the planet and represents so much of what he had been told was not from God.

Zach had been raised in a Christian evangelical home in rural Ohio. His dad was a gentle man, a well-loved traveling preacher of the Good News mostly bringing encouragement and promise to those wounded by fundamentalism. Zach's more austere mother had never been able to let go of that tenacious grip. She'd efficiently raised Zach and his younger brother mostly on her own, immersed in a tightly woven, extraordinarily supportive church community.

When he moved to the local high school, Zach began to break free of his early formation in the rigid home-school system. Like a well-oiled machine, he had learned how to perform, to maintain an appropriate social equilibrium, but was still afraid to think for himself. He could never risk cutting loose, going feral like his more daring friends. He'd drifted through a Christian college, reveling in art classes and dabbling in drama; anything that brought him freedom and individual empowerment attracted him. When it came time to graduate, Zach realized he was not yet ready to stand on his own in the outside world, so it seemed most natural to go off to seminary—maybe a little more liberal one than his parents cared for, but nevertheless it was his decision to become a youth minister. Like his father and his mother, he continued to remain tied to the institutional church.

Eight years later, he had struggled through two jobs in two churches, the first in a small town where the parishioners persistently tried to hitch him to proper Christian girls, and the second in an urban setting amid the poorest of the poor. Now, overwhelmed by his proliferating confusion and lack of answers concerning the oppression of poverty, Zach was at the end of his rope. It seemed that not only had God abandoned him, but he privately worried that some of his church-work was compounding the complicated issues of social injustice. Divorce from the church loomed.

Earlier this month, just when he had decided to give notice of his resignation, a visiting speaker had glimpsed his dejected spirit and kindly invited him to talk. During the conversation the retreat was mentioned, and much to Zach's amazement, his new friend offered to help him find finances to get there. Thus he had landed at the door today.

As the candle burns on, Zach grabs a yellow-lined pad and a pencil off the back table and begins to write.

I was born in church.
I was bred in church.
Now I feel dead in church.

God - the ultimate paradox
Who are you, God?
All, everything or No-thing

One more time through the treadmill of pious activity and platitudes
I try to ignore the cloying odor of ancient religion grown moldy creeping into my bones like formaldehyde surrounded by the precious relics of the past.

We sit on the shelves of culture, totems and monuments of history
*   piled back to back, like an unused, overstuffed library*
*   propped up on spindly legs called church.*

Slowly spilling over and falling
*   ... one by one to the floor of despair.*
There is nowhere to go but down
*   letting go, being sucked into open space.*

Mystery
*   Depth*
*   Darkness*
*   Emptiness*
*   Void*

I find myself falling into fear
.... and mysteriously ... I feel new life stirring ... a wispy tendril of smoke rising uncertainly out of the ash heap of my inner wasteland.
the promise of light, warmth ... heat ... urges me on to explore.
Mystical stars of hope rise on the horizon of my consciousness.
Old sages of history emerge from the dusty tomes to guide my way ahead.

I feel lost, voyaging in the gaping wound of open space but I am not alone.
Who are you?
Who am I?

When Zach blows out the candle, he feels relieved. In the darkness, those uneven holes in the lotus pod do not look so ominously empty anymore. *Maybe I can sleep now. Not that I have any fresh answers, but at least I have words for my struggle.*

His whispers follow him out of the room:

> *"Goodnight God, whoever you are.*
> *Goodnight Zach, whoever you are.*
> *I hope I meet you tomorrow."*

SATURDAY

CHAPTER EIGHT
EARLY MORNING

For much of the night, the air hung thick and so charged we could barely move. The atmosphere in the meeting room burned on with the raw power of eons of unspoken energy. As the last young man trailed off down the hall to his room, he might have noticed that even though he turned the light switch off, the room perceptibly glowed until the dust settled. The mice reported that it looked like lightning bugs had come indoors, but we decided they were intoxicated from the abundant feast from the kitchen and dining room floors. Cook had gone to bed early. After all his exertions that day, he had been too tired to sweep the floor, leaving it for the breakfast crew to do in the morning.

From the outside we trace the aura of longing that rises in smoke wraiths from different windows, seeping out through the cracks in the old doorjambs. We watch eagerly to see where it emerges: some rooms crystal-clear, while others, especially two of the cottages, are shrouded in a fine cloud of prescience.

For those of us who do not sleep anymore, it has been a particularly long and suspenseful night. While we are relieved that the connection had brought most of them here to be together, the challenge is undeniably ours. Change always brings apprehension. One can never be sure of anything. Humans are notoriously fickle when it comes to shifting into the open and honest position; it seems their capacity to reach down into their depths is directly proportional to the amount of pain they are able to tolerate, plus their capacity to be thoughtfully present. That is our strength here in the underworld—or the above-world, depending on how you see it. We've been listing hopefully toward deep change for many earthly years.

It is not that we are disinterested voyeurs; it is more that we are so overly observant that we can hardly restrain ourselves from engaging. A night like this one has us on the tiptoes of expectancy. No wonder we hear human folks talking about how the night comes alive.

Take dreams, for instance. Do we mastermind those life-changing dreams that erupt into consciousness every now and then? Is this the work of spirit—those night visions, like heart trails that set a fresh course for a more abundant life? Or is this the inner work of the dreamer, who completes the most complex work when asleep? We would like to think we are a part of those momentous shifts.

Dawn cannot come fast enough for us to see what will happen next. Poor old Cook, once again, despite his bodily fatigue, has not been able to sleep. This year has been hard on him. It is clear that he exists halfway in our world now, so he inherits the best of both worlds, and unfortunately the worst of both. It is clearly most confusing for him.

We try to comfort him in his four o'clock sleeplessness, but he spends a couple of hours sitting outside, holding his head in his hands and trying to pray. We lament that he cannot just turn off his mind at night, the way he takes off his clothes.

For the others? There certainly was a lot of dreaming going on all night; we can't wait to find out how many will pay attention.

RAQUEL

Raquel wakes with a start, wide-eyed and wondering where on earth she is. She lies perfectly still, overcome by the sound of her beating heart. Gradually, she adjusts to the early morning silence of the retreat center.

How unnerving to have such quiet. Over the past decade, she had grown accustomed to the morning sounds of an Angolan village. The roosters scratching in the dust and crowing outside her window became her alarm clock, together with the murmuring of the women and the shrieks of little children passing by her house on their way down the dirt path to the river. So much daily activity unfolded before the scorching sun moved high in the sky. She also remembered lying in bed and agonizing, recalling that same path as a conduit of horror. A missionary had shown her his 16 mm movies of slave traders on the march less than a century ago, passing that very place as they forced their shackled prey down to the coast. Sleeping and waking, Africa has indelibly tattooed her signature on Raquel's heart.

This morning, as her eyes become accustomed to the darkness of her room, a vivid dream scrolls back across her consciousness. *This is what disturbed my sleep.*

She had dreamed of an unborn baby that talked. Sophie, her young stepsister, was the swollen mother-to-be, a picture-perfect cutaway sculpture of a pregnant woman from the anatomy lab. She can still see that naked little form, curled up and looking at her, speaking to her in a muffled voice. In the dream, Raquel leaned in closer to Sophie's belly, trying to decipher its plaintive crying. *"But, I have no name,"* and again, louder, with even more anxiety ... *"I have no name."*

Raquel flings off the bed covers and shoots to her feet. *How spooky is this? What is all this about? I guess I did hear yesterday that Sophie was finally pregnant after years of trying. But what does it mean ... "I have no name?"*

She throws cold water on her face, frantic to erase the imprinted images of the night. As she reaches for the towel, her wild eyes startle her, the mirror reflecting the terror in her heart. Peering over the towel, she glimpses the shadow of Africa, a familiar memory manifested in hundreds of similar overcast eyes. She recognizes traumatized patients reaching toward help, yet rigid with the fear that they would surely be hurt again. Raquel watches as her eyes glisten with tears, springing from inner pools of compassion. Instantaneously she feels the tide of fear recede, leaving her shivering in the bathroom. *Something profound is hidden in this dream—speaking to me. I don't know what it is about pregnancy, but pregnant women are starting to haunt me. I've got to get outside and go for a run, clear my head before I drive myself crazy.*

She throws on a pair of sweat pants, a light jacket, and running shoes, and then quietly creeps down the hall to the back entrance.

As she begins to jog, her mind wanders back to her beloved country. Sunrise has always been electric for her. In Angola, dawn was the only time of the day to escape to recharge her soul; the only moments when she would not be disturbed by the overwhelming needs of the sick. Most of them walked for days to see her. Hordes of very ill patients, coughing and spitting sputum, smelling of pus and unimaginable body odors, would begin lining up outside the outpatient clinic shortly after dawn. They would sit patiently all day waiting to be seen, and if they couldn't get help that day, they would be back in line the next morning. The little grass huts of the outpatient camp constantly overflowed, new ones needing to be built to provide shelter for the patients and their families.

The African patients often used to bring her their dreams, excited to tell them as part of their medical history. *It took me too long to value their dreams, let alone what they might be saying. I was such a skeptic, denigrating them as superstitious mumbo-jumbo. Medical school certainly never helped me decipher anything useful in a dream. It was only in those final months when I started to remember my own vivid dreams that I began to realize their potential value. I wish I had paid more attention. It might help me today...*

Raquel tires quickly, slowing to a walk before she even broke a sweat. *I feel more like the patient than the doctor this morning.*

VANESSA

Vanessa had awoken at five and leaped out of bed, anticipating meeting sunrise by the pond. She often woke early, doing some of her best thinking at that time of day. She had recognized recently that if she didn't find the opportunity to sit still first thing in the morning, then the rest of the day would rush past her, leaving her off-balance and out-of-sorts. This morning she picked up her journal, hoping to write about yesterday, to unravel some of the jumbled threads of her life.

She found her way along the old stone path in the

murky morning mist. *It's going to be another warm Indian summer day. Perfect for hanging outside in this beautiful space. I do hope we get more time to be outdoors. I love everything about this property.*

Yesterday she had looked longingly at a curved bench, like the one Monet painted, that nestled into a rock face beside the lily pond, but the quiet Chinese woman had already claimed it. Today she smiles with delight to be the first to enjoy the sanctuary as it slowly comes alive before her eyes.

Robins and wrens begin to sing. As their chorus swells, an entranced Vanessa witnesses the visible and invisible energy bursting out of the darkness in a crescendo of song that swells to an almost deafening climax, and then slowly ebbs into more quiet bird-working noises as the sun begins to glint off the pond water.

I wish I could sing like that! I'd love to sing passionately about my life right now. I'm feeling music that longs to find voice from inside me. Imagine waking every morning and being excited about the day, like the birds. I have been so stuck in this mid-life transition ... this upheaval of uncertainty with Tray leaving home, and my body going crazy with hormones. Have I lost touch with my personal everyday reawakening?

She reaches for her journal and began to articulate her feelings around this unsettling, yet oddly promising concept of change. The words form easily on the page in front of her.

> *I struggle with dreams.*
> *Who am I, what can I do with my life now?*
> *It is simpler to not dream at all than to feel the despair of letting my cherished aspirations fall into the clutter of life's wastebasket.*

98

I wish there were a way to go forward creatively,
to go slowly and steadily and not rush into the
chaos that my mind churns out.
How do I live in this fragile moment?

She stops and waits for a while realizing that even writing takes her away from the presence of this moment.

How my mind flits around inside my head—just
like a little fat Carolina wren that is chirping
loudly from tree to bush, and then circling back
and doing the same thing all over again.

Vanessa chuckles. *What a perfect image of my mind ... a very loud, busy Carolina wren!*

Like yesterday.
That anxious drive in the wild traffic.
The five-ounce tube of expensive face cream in
my handbag that security casually tossed
into the trash can.
Then the race for the gate ...

Her face flushes with chagrin just thinking about the scene she had made: *careening around the curve of the jet-way—suitcase lurching precariously, my red jacket straggling from my unzipped shoulder bag and wedging in my suitcase wheels, the ejected baggie of toiletries that skidded to a stop at the feet of an obviously annoyed flight attendant. Then, as the last one to board, frantically gathering my private belongings and with all those eyes on me struggling to heave my carry-on into the overhead bin. And finally, the man in 27C yelping with irritated surprise when my suitcase nearly brains him.*

Then to see him here—the man from 27C at the same retreat! How lucky that the bag just glanced off his shoulder. I tried to apologize, but all he did was cower in his seat with his head tucked under his arms. Hopefully, he doesn't recognize me, but just knowing he is here reminds me of all the secret things I loathe about myself.

> *Yesterday it all erupted to the surface: all the messiness, all the fumbling—classic traits of the inept, hysterical woman seems to be bubbling out of my pores, just like my over-packed suitcase with its bulging contents. This is the part of myself I am usually able to hide. I remember how Mom used to mock me about these times of acute ineptitude...*

Grieving lips

Grieving as therapy

Clearly, Vanessa's recent months in therapy had begun to teach her to be more tender, more compassionate with herself, but this was the part of her imperfection that most got to her. In fact, to the public eye Vanessa knows she appears as a stellar model of mid-life social responsibility. As the director of the volunteer program at a hospital, she maintains a high profile of benevolent authority and competence, while inside she still harbors the anxiety of a little girl. This was what had finally driven her to her therapist's door; she is exhausted from living in two different worlds.

> *God have mercy on me—no wonder I need a retreat. I sure hope Elizabeth knew what she was doing when she insisted I attend this event. She even gave me her airline miles. Such a dear friend ... something of a seer for me. She always*

*seems to sense the way and nudge me into new
directions. After all, it was Elizabeth who
introduced Arthur to me, and that gift is one of
the treasures of my life.*

*Maybe this retreat will be kind of like another
Arthur. Maybe some whole new love will emerge
into my life—if only I can keep all my anxiety and
bumbling awkwardness under control. I must
keep reminding myself of all the good work I do.
I have accomplished a great deal in my life and
I know we also all have weaknesses. I mustn't let
yesterday's beginning discourage me today. I
wonder what this retreat really is all about? It
feels like a pilgrimage into uncertainty.*

*Yes, that's it—uncertainty. I hadn't realized how
unsettled I've become: my frantic rushing to the
airport, my jumbled possessions scattered on the
floor, my stuffed baggage mirroring my
overwrought emotional self. Nothing feels tidy
and controlled anymore...* my emotional self bound to draw unwanted attention

The bright azure butterflies on her scarf match the
butterflies fluttering in her stomach. Vanessa's mind
reels off her fears: *What if Arthur dies and leaves me by
myself? What if Tray has a terrible accident and never
comes home again? What if the next hospital board
meeting passes all those budget cuts? What if...*

To give her credit, it had been quite an act of courage
to sign up for an event that she knew so little about.
Truthfully, she is a homebody. She prefers to live her
private life secure in her home and family, and the work
that she loves, grounded more like a caterpillar than a
butterfly.

*...in the airplane, catapulted into thin air, flying
by the seat of my pants. Flying into the future
with nothing sure about this adventure but a deep
awareness that somehow the unknown was
beckoning me. I remember pressing my nose to
the window and seeing the desert patterns of
water that for millennia had etched channels on
sand and rock. Delicate filigree of sandstone
embankments. Caverns and walls of river-
carvings. Everything changing. Eroding, drying
and getting flooded all over again.
Such immense vastness.*

*At jet-speed, time passed below and through me.
Somehow, this is also like me .... I felt the beauty
in the aging rock and bore witness to the part of*   e.g.
me that was wrinkling like the rivers, furrowing   skin
?   *out new ground for fresh life. One stream of
action leading into another. Networks of motion.
Giant granite boulders, strewn randomly about
the landscape, forcing rivers to flow sideways,
building fresh pathways. Seeing from that height
gave me momentary comfort. It dawned on me
how unusual it felt to be living inside and outside
the plane simultaneously.*

*Yes! I am on course—to somewhere. I am the
snaking river, the fluid brown caterpillar gorging
out a canyon face. I feel my own unfolding, a
freedom as I fork and bend like the water below.
Big boulders do not have to stop me from
change...*

A picture of the mountain homestead she had seen

102

from the airplane arises in her mind. It appears barely a speck from the air, but clearly a human habitation on a tiny scrap of cleared land, a thimble-sized glassy pond, and several outbuildings. She had wondered what it must be like to live there, how it might be to subsist in that lonely place.

I never realized how afraid I've been of leaving the security of home and work, yet how I long to move ahead toward some kind of change. As much as I like my work, I think I would get horribly depressed if I worked at this same job for the rest of my life. Am I finally able to risk something new? What do I want in this next phase of my life?

She feels it rising in her—a further torrent of words, a letter to her son, a letter to herself.

What do I want to be when I grow up?
Thirty years between us, and still I ask myself the same question ...

For over an hour, Vanessa sits huddled over her journal, and then she gets up to look for coffee. S*urely somebody has made a pot by now.*

GEORGE

George is hanging around the coffeemaker, waiting for it to stop dripping. He had been tempted initially to drive out and look for a Starbucks, but he discovered the coffeepot ready to go, with a note attached: *"First person up—all you need to do is push the start button."*

The coffee smells intoxicating. He wishes wryly that his start button would come on as easily as the coffee machine.

Overall he had slept remarkably well, but the same disquieting feelings he'd had last night begin to bubble up. He is tapping his foot impatiently when the amply built woman called Vanessa comes bounding through the door from the garden in efflorescent bloom. Upon seeing George she appears to wilt momentarily, then she squares her shoulders and finds herself greeting George graciously, asking how he is doing. As they fill their coffee mugs, after struggling through a self-conscious conversation about the weather and the day ahead, Vanessa quietly laughs and says simply, "You don't remember me, do you?"

George winces. He has absolutely no idea what this woman is talking about, but she continues to speak, thus saving him from any awkward attempts at guessing.

"I met you yesterday. Well, 'sort of' met you. I am the wild woman on the plane who almost dropped her suitcase on your head. How could you forget me? I'm so relieved I didn't break your neck—my suitcase was ridiculously heavy. I felt like such a dolt, but I could have died when you showed up here at the same retreat yesterday afternoon. Isn't it strange how life happens sometimes?"

George sucks in his breath sharply while trying to drink his hot coffee. Yes, he certainly does remember, but feigns a spell of coughing to give him time to respond. At last he smiles, hunches dramatically, and makes a joke about his shoulder injury and Quasimodo.

"I'm getting out of here," he tells Vanessa. "The sunshine calls, and it's too early to be around crazy women with hot coffee! See you later." He heads off for the pond, relieved to hear her giggle.

LEONA

Leona emerges from the meditation room glowing, energized by her early morning yoga routine. She had left Gerritt in the room almost an hour ago, passed out in bed, his colorful drawing from the night before still open on the bedside table. She realized her body was crying out for attention. Yoga was her way of getting to the core of herself. Once her body focused, breathing rhythmically, she consistently found strength and calm from the inside out. This morning, though, it had been harder to re-connect with this daily rhythm.

As she'd rolled out her mat and bent her body into her first sun salutation, she felt a wave of release but she found it uncanny how as she stood solid and supple on the balls of her feet in tadasana, mountain pose, a strange feeling of being liquid and leaky washed through her. *Incredibly soft. Weirdly unripe. Like a soft-boiled egg still protected by the comfort of a hard shell but very apprehensive of being cracked open.*

Leona swayed and lost her balance, almost falling off her solidly planted feet. *of Don's death*
This whole thing with Gerritt's affair has knocked me so far off balance that I have no idea where to go from here. It's getting clearer every day that he has been the biggest shell of protection in my life. What a challenge to think about going it alone, much less doing it, like diving off into the deep, a plunge of true separation. Is this what must happen? Do I really want to become whole and separate, even more immensely vulnerable? I have No choice

She kept moving in the sequence of asanas that she knew so well.

Leona had always thought of herself as independent and separate—fully confident in her capacities to survive and walk through life's vicissitudes. Her parents had both courageously grown out of poverty during her childhood, becoming a family of influence. She rather liked all this about herself. It gave her power.

How disturbing now to come to grips with this emerging part of herself—one that remained afraid, silently panicking as the open door loomed ahead of her. She hates her paralysis of the past months.

But everything constantly changes. Being separate is to mourn the loss of the other. I have spent a lot of my life joined to others. My parents, Gerritt, the children ...

Breathe. Relax. Trust the changes to come. Her first yoga instructor used these words like mantras, and now she heard herself repeat them. *"When you are ready ... go gently ... soft belly ... relax ... just like your breath, let peace come."*

Yes, I am more than my fears. It has been impossible until now to let go, afraid of breaking apart completely. I've imagined that all my life-force, my energy, would drain out of me, leaving me dry. A fragile egg-shell, useless and empty. A bag of dusty bones.

As she moved through her final floor poses, rivulets of tears rolled backward into her ears. She lay still, letting the gentle washing continue as her tough shell of independence cracked and made room for a softer being to flow, inside and out.

Finally, in savasana, lying still like a corpse, she gave in and surrendered every part of her body. For the first time, she had the experience of allowing the earth to carry her. *I am being protected. The Universe is able to hold me in arms that are bigger and more gentle than I had ever imagined ...*

It took a long time to come to her feet and face the day, but as Leona opens the door of the prayer room and walks out, she knows she will never be the same again. She is ready now, prepared to sit in silent meditation with the group.

1pm Friday, Sept 6 On the Leroy.
I'm not ready yet

106

THENA

Thena rings the bell at exactly 7:30 AM. She knows that others will dribble in, but it seems important to honor those few who are already sitting in silence. She recognizes her own need for order and that many of the sojourners need their private space in the morning. Others welcome the unusual opportunity to sit in a quiet meditation within community. Thena finds that the quiet communal presence evoked in this half hour graces the rest of the day in a mystical sense, one she does not easily describe. This is why no matter how tired she is, she always comes expectantly to this early morning circle. It is unusual for her to be so observant of ritual, as she has never been easily drawn to religious form.

Thena loves it that these retreats leave space for individuals to be themselves, with no attached label of religion, politics, or class. This spelled freedom for her, and she fervently wishes to pass this gift to anyone interested. As she glances around to see who is here this morning, she can't help but observe a new glow about Leona. Riveted, she wonders what she is sensing. *I did not notice Leona this way last night. How extraordinary to be introduced to her now at such an energetic level.*

Thena's instant response passes, but she is left holding the afterglow of something fresh—*like a delightful whiff of a newly bathed baby. What a strange association. It leaves me yearning for that same freshness inside me. What about Leona touches my own subconscious needs?*

With profound longing, Thena sits open and waiting in the silence of the next half hour.

CHAPTER NINE
BREAKFAST

The dining room buzzes with conversation as people slowly wander in to breakfast. Michaela hesitantly looks around the room, wondering who to sit with. She feels tentative and suddenly out of place, as if the shadow of her teenage daughter had arrived unannounced.

Damn, I knew this tight t-shirt of Emma's would stand out too much. Why did I have to try to look cute and sexy? How did I possibly imagine that I might meet a man here? Maybe I'll sit with the singer, she seems interesting.

Maria smiles a welcome but keeps eating her toast and scrambled eggs.

"Nice day isn't it? I'm so glad to get out of the city. Are you from around here?"

"About an hour and half away, in the country," replies Maria rather distantly.

"Last night you said you're a musician, a singer. I'm curious. What kind of music do you perform?"

"Opera—most of the time, but for now I'm off the circuit," said Maria with an air of finality.

Well this conversation is going nowhere. Did I miss

something at the meditation time? I really shouldn't have given in to the snooze button. I'm probably the only one who didn't make it—maybe she's unimpressed with me, doubting my sincerity.

As Michaela looks around the room for help, she notices that the other conversations also fall into tried and true social patterns. She hears smatterings of uncomplicated topics: groups of three and four chatting about work or recent vacation activities, lots of polite and interested listening. The extroverts drawing in the less talkative ones.

It sure seems like we're dancing around the more complex issues that have brought us here. Oh well, let's keep it simple—after all it is only breakfast time.

Anyway, what on earth can I say to her that has any importance? Is it possible that she's a real opera star who has traveled the world? No wonder I feel like a shrimp emotionally beside her. Look at that fabulous bling around her neck. I wonder where she got that? Definitely not from Macy's.

A woman was talking behind them in a voice louder than necessary. She seemed concerned about her cat, worried that her husband might not feed it. A male voice replied, chuckling about what happened when he by accident locked his cat in the hall closet overnight.

Yikes. Wherever I go, inevitably the cat-lovers emerge. Makes me itch to listen to them.

For a moment, Michaela considers joking with Maria about this, but then quashes the idea and remains circling in her unspoken social anxiety until Dylan arrives, sitting down beside them in a whirlwind of energy, his tray clattering on the table, his hair so wet it almost drips. He obviously had emerged straight out of the shower.

"How are you two wonderful women doing this

Wade :A

morning? Both of you are looking quite radiant and serene sitting over here in the sunshine, I just had to come and bask in your company," he announces cheerily.

"Well my friend, you just made my day," gushes Michaela. "Did you just get out of bed, like me? I thought I was the only one who slept through meditation this morning."

"Well actually I just came in from a run ... uh-oh! There goes the boss. She just gave me her knowing look that it's time to get to work," Dylan says good-naturedly.

Thena was striding out the door holding an apple and a bagel.

"She looks like she's taking her food back into the meeting room to finalize the morning sessions. I'm sorry—I better do the same. I really had wanted to get to know you both. I have a sense that music runs deep in our blood and wanted to find more of that connection. Maybe next time."

And with a flourish, he abandons us again to our silent misery. Michaela swallows her disappointment with the last dregs of her coffee, then asks kindly, "Maria, may I get you some more coffee?

*   *   *

From our perspective, Thena appears to be operating in ultra-high gear. Of course, we understand there is a lot to think about and accomplish as a group facilitator; there are always glitches in the plans and bumps along the course of each hour. This time it doesn't take long before we understand the real reason for her urgent pace this morning.

"Our gentleman who didn't make it last night has now arrived; I just met up with him in the hall. Dylan, can you remember to introduce him before I get going? His name is Evan. Did I tell you that his wife is the board chair of this Center? I gave her a special invitation but in the end it appears she sent her husband. Interesting…

"… also because I am taking the lead for much of the morning, please remember that it's your job to talk about the Clearness Circle plans, to make sure that by lunch we have the names of those who want to be focus persons. Have you heard from anyone else?"

"So far Mei is the only person who has spoken to me," says Dylan. "I guess we still hope that three people will volunteer, each group is so different. Do you know what happened in the last group of my seasonal series? Six of us volunteered. After all those retreats together, we didn't want to miss out on the opportunity. But it was way too many people, so the leaders had to move the process along by picking straws. Seemed to me like a simple solution that worked mysteriously well in the end. I wanted to be a focus person but my name wasn't picked; later on I realized how good that decision was. I wonder what will happen today? "

He had rambled on for a while in his affable way, then something makes him pause and turn directly to face the older facilitator. Looking her straight in the eyes he softly asks:

"Thena, how are you feeling about your presentation?"

We can see that Thena hears his question deep in her gut. She has to stop for a breath or two before she can reply. Then she speaks haltingly.

"I don't know, Dylan. I'm in a complicated place right now. A part of me is happy and available to do my work with this group, but another part of me is … is calling for attention. I'm not clear yet what that is all about. I think …"

She hesitates, and to our relief she finally stops her forward momentum. The words no longer need to be forced out of her mouth. Gradually the taut worry lines between her eyebrows soften and as her body relaxes, she smiles at Dylan.

"Thanks for being sensitive and asking, it helps me to slow down and go gently into this morning. My pace can be so frenetic at times."

She pauses again. "Especially since later in the second half of the morning, I am offering a very personal object lesson, my lotus presentation. Remember when we talked about this? I was a little nervous about how abstract it might feel for some people. Our famous writer friends, like Mary Oliver, Rilke, or Wendell Berry, can always draw the group's soul to the fore with their poetry. But experimenting with this personal slideshow is new territory for me. I can only hope that the group will find what they need from it. I guess we'll see what transpires."

"Well, I can't wait to see it, completed, with all your pictures," says Dylan. "Remember—trust yourself, my friend. That's always what you tell me!"

It is good to see Thena and Dylan laughing together as the first of the group members make their way into the meeting room.

*   *   *

Gerritt listens carefully as Dylan starts the morning welcoming the newcomer. He is curious that Evan has just arrived, even though he lives only a few minutes away. He sees a handsome, balding, black man wearing a beat-up Eagles football jacket. He reminds him of an aging line-backer emerging from the locker room.

"I'm sorry to be late, hope I didn't miss too much from last night. I just couldn't make it any earlier." Evan introduces himself as a businessman who runs a nonprofit sports center for underserved kids. He doesn't say much more, but something resonates for Gerritt when he hears Evan speak.

I'm not sure why, but I am quite drawn to him. It's not the content of what he just said, but more about how he says it. The way he communicates has a brittle, rather resolute air, as if he is stating the obvious, leaving no room for personal emotion or public response.

that's what it won't to be like

Is Evan trying to give us the sense of his being at ease, as if his late arrival is entirely appropriate behavior? Ha! He sounds a bit like I do when I think I'm about to get swept into an emotionally loaded situation with Leona, or the Dean. I get tense, like a starched shirt inside, but act as if I am not affected at all. How amusing to see this in another man!

Gerritt smiles to himself again, when after what seemed like a tense silence, Vanessa is compelled to express a warm fuzzy welcome to Evan on behalf of the entire group. It is evidently her way of making him feel comfortable, but she clearly is clueless that her sympathy might draw even more attention to an already uncomfortable man in an uncomfortable situation. *She sounds so much like Leona—that is exactly what she might do to attempt keep everybody happy.*

Good grief, listen to me—I'm the one with the monkey mind today.

As he struggles to settle into a reflective silence, he makes the mistake of gazing for too long at his wife who sits calmly meditating with her eyes closed. A lump rises in his throat, and then expands to fill the whole room when he hears the first notes of the haunting Celtic musical opening that Thena has chosen. *Am I going crazy? Why is this circle so loaded for me? Everything anybody says affects me.* This may be me, I fear

He is grateful for the diversion when Thena begins to speak.

114

"This morning I'd like to draw our attention to our personal identity and integrity. I invite you to look at some of the connections between who you are and what you do. Frederich Buechner in his book, *Telling Secrets* said that:

> *We try to make ourselves into something that we hope the world will like better than it apparently did the selves we originally were. That is the story of all of our lives ... and in the process of living out that story, the original, shimmering self gets buried so deep that most of us end up hardly living out of it at all. Instead, we live out all the other selves which we are constantly putting on and taking off like coats and hats against the world's weather.*

W
O
W
!

"This morning I hope that each of us will see in some new way our original shimmering self." Thena's eyes gleam in harmony with her words.

Once again, like last night, Gerritt trembles with agitation. Viscerally he feels the division: One part of him keeps piling on all the hats and coats of disguise he can find, and the other part of him clearly is tearing them off and about to tell the world each one of his secrets.

Now if only I can stay calm and seated in this chair, and not bolt like last night.

I think of the 2½ year old being brave when Mama has to go to Edmonton w/ baby for 6 weeks. The 3-yr-old doing dishes. The toddler who begins walking @ 8 months & speaks clearly @ 12. The precocious child reading @ 5 & the Bible @ 6! 115 The youngster who loves speed, bikes, stilts — anything that moves FAST.

CHAPTER TEN
THE MÖBIUS STRIP

After reading the Buechner quote again, Thena passes around a stack of long narrow strips of paper. They are blue on one side and green on the other.

"Imagine this as a very simple representation of your life. Think of one side as your outer life, that which we all can see: your external life of work, your persona that you show to the world. Consider the other your inner world: that part of you rich in values and beliefs, full of your personal thoughts and experience, all that which is mostly hidden from view.

"Think about how this inner and outer definition works for you. If it's helpful, take a few minutes and list words that best describe your ways of being both 'private' and 'public' on the two faces of your strip."

*   *   *

Michaela likes this distinction; it makes immediate sense for her. *This feels like the key to what I am looking for this weekend.* On the green side, she writes quickly:

Strong, Confident, Capable, Loving, Teacher, Mother.
On the blue side she hesitates, but then notes in minute
script: *Fearful, Angry, Child, Empty, Sad.*

*How strange! Look how I automatically list what
seem like opposites.* She stares glumly at the paper,
aware how quickly she has lost her positive emotional
bearings. *Categorizing my life in such black and white
terms is hopeless—surely there are other important
inner values in my life. How about Honesty, Justice ...?
Yes, this seems more accurate and fair.* Michaela fluidly
pens a few more lines and then gazes around the room,
curious to see how everybody else is dealing with this
act of self-disclosure.

Across from her sits Evan, earlier her heart had
skipped a beat when she saw his handsome frame arrive
in the circle. *Now he's slumped over his papers, his eyes
glued to his feet—evidently he's like me—so quickly
disheartened, a world away, lost in his thoughts. It's a
shame he's married, he might have made a great catch.
Look at Sam—he's really into this exercise. Now if only I
could find a man that looks like Evan and acts like Sam.
Look at his energy! It's spilling out of his entire body:
from his ruffled hair to his wrinkled shirt and his uneven
socks, he's truly a man squeezed by the juice of life. I
wonder what he's writing? What I would give to land a
man with that kind of vitality.*

Michaela hears Thena's voice again. This time she
thinks she hears a change, a slight tremor rising, as she
moves on with her presentation.

"Think of yourself as a child. Was your inner and
outer world the same? Small children are remarkably
undivided. Yet, as we all know, how complicated life
becomes. Allow me to share a little of my story to
explain. I grew up as a sixties child from an African-
American father and a Jewish mother. My parents

both ran from their cultures and families into a hippie commune in California. I was raised in a remarkably free and easy world as a genuine little flower child."

She smiles broadly, remembering with pleasure her earliest years at Sunflower Ranch. "Thank God I was named Athena, not Sunflower or Solstice, like two of my friends. Being named after the goddess of both love and war was very appropriate. When I was twelve, my Dad was killed in Vietnam, so on the outside my name fits; although, as a young child, it was hard to be authentic. I was too aware of all the incongruities I observed in the adult world. It was especially difficult after my dad's death, when my mother escaped the real world and turned to marijuana as her best friend."

She turns in the circle, making eye contact with those who are available. "Okay, so here's my question again:

"How about you? Think of yourself as a child, when do you remember being free and entirely your own delightful self? Was your inner and outer world the same?"

Silently, the group ponders. Many are journaling thoughtfully, but it is clear that Dylan is having trouble focusing today. He knows that Thena's remarks have been genuinely unguarded and it affects him, hooking him out of his own journey of self-exploration and sending him into her world, escaping unconsciously into the world of figuring out others.

From his earliest days, he has intently watched the world go round. When his dad moved the family to Uganda on contract for USAID, he had morphed into a child of the global village: curious and alert, learning from and imitating almost anybody he met. Now he is sitting in the circle being thoroughly entertained by watching everybody around him.

George is looking positively happy. I wonder what he's thinking. He has been so prickly since he arrived. Looking slyly to his left, Dylan becomes unbearably curious, wondering what Mei is writing. He notes that she hasn't looked up for the past ten minutes. *She is such a silent but strong presence in this group. Who is this reclusive woman anyway?* Then, rolling his eyes upwards, he grins to himself, almost chuckling aloud. Mei has written all over her paper strip in beautiful, flowing Chinese characters.

You nosy bastard—serves you right for looking. Mind your own effing business. You know she'll speak when she's ready.

Off-balance, he closes his eyes attempting to center himself, but opens them quickly. He senses Michaela, realizing she has been staring at him. Quickly he looks away, unsettled by the discovery of being found out in his own game. He's grateful to concentrate again as Thena picks up the theme of adolescence.

Holding the paper away from her, she demonstrates the enormously complicated stage of separation that happens as children grow up.

"When we realize that we are not accepted just the way we are, we begin to wall off our innermost selves, especially the more fragile and vulnerable experiences of being human. These become dangerous for many reasons—it's dangerous to expose yourself in the public eye and even more dangerous to remain anxiously conscious about your messy self. The wall is a wall of separation, a barrier to anything that is inner for many people for a long, long time. For many reasons, masses of people live outer-directed lives forever."

She grows pensive again. "I remember the day my mother told me not to be sad anymore about dad, that

120

I must grow up and be strong like the iconic Athena. That statement clearly shaped my life; it walled me off from many difficult emotions and set me on a tough and lonely course as a teenager.

"How about you? What memories surface for you from those formative years of adolescence?"

The room is so hushed that Dylan hears only pens scratching the paper; each person wandering alone down the rabbit holes of their adolescence. This time, he draws inward and is surprised where his mind immediately lands.

Carla, my first private love affair. What a nightmare— my first real dance, middle school prom. Near the end of the evening, tired of goofing off and joking with all the guys propping up the wall, I summoned up my courage and asked her to dance. Then, after fumbling across the floor as best as I could, with my wooden feet and sweaty hands, she pronounces, "Where on earth did you learn to dance? Next time—why don't you really learn how?"

Dylan reels in the memory, feeling angry, then sad, and surprisingly pensive. Eventually he is able to ask himself, *I wonder why this is surfacing today? I haven't thought about that incident for years.*

Thena holds her paper up again and bends it into a circle. "As the years go by we try to reconnect with ourselves in different ways. We gradually become more honest with ourselves and recognize the disparity of our lives, attempting to find congruence with inner and outer. Many of you have come to this retreat for this very reason—you are aware that you long to live more authentically from the center of your lives.

"Years ago, I remember sitting in a circle much like this one, and becoming conscious of many parts of my divided self. I felt torn up, primarily between being a good mother and living as an ambitious career person. It felt like a battle between one and the other; doing what I was supposed to do or doing what I wanted to do. Do you know that feeling?

"Unless we begin to identify some of these inner and outer conflicts, it leads to untold personal misery and difficulties in our relationships to others and the natural world."

Then Thena says something that takes many of her listeners by surprise. "There is a hidden danger in this position, in holding firm to this centered circle of faithful living." She describes it, "like the settlers in the West, when they used to circle their wagons and fight from within their circle of defense. Being centered within our own belief and moral systems can lead to exclusivity, an 'us/them' mentality that stands like a concrete pillar of truth for our lives. Unfortunately, this becomes a position from which to do battle against any idea or anybody that is alien … like what actually did happen in the tragic history of the West."

Sam grimaces. He shifts around in his chair, his body churning. Up until now, he'd been working with Thena's questions with intensity, grateful for her challenge.

This is me: *Questioner, Intelligent, Serious, Deep Thinker. Definitely my persona, the main ways I show myself to the world. And even a Joker, too—that's what my family would say about me.* Inside I am *Spiritual, Colorful, Odd, a little Crazy* … and then, he slid his hand over his writing for fear someone might glimpse the next offending word. Cautiously, letter by letter, *Deaf* had appeared on the inside. He had not realized how deeply ashamed he was of his hearing loss. As Thena speaks, questions keep popping through his brain.

Why? I know this has always been a painful reality,

but it also has been my life's passion to understand what goes on inside a human brain. Why is it so difficult to admit my physical condition? How can I be open and understanding to those who are different from me, if I can't care for all of myself?

He wraps his paper together into a circle. Now he sees the full picture, the "us and them."

I never thought of it before, but it is like I remain deaf to them. Even though I like to think that I am hearing, I do not really take the time to listen ... like to Jack, my Republican neighbor, or even my wife. At times I can't stand their choices in politics, in music, in TV shows ... and they both want me to listen, to be interested in their latest discoveries.

Maybe my deafness could teach me something about how to change ... His mind churns on. Sam is disengaged from the group, lost for a while inside his peripatetic mind, his thoughts circling at warp speed. When he focuses on Thena again, her mouth is moving and in her hands she holds a Möbius Strip.

Thena had taken her strip of paper and given one end a half-twist, creating what looks like an infinity symbol. *This is incredible*, Sam thinks, *my own personal symbol.* For years this exact object had been the philosophical backbone for his research in psychology. He had taught from the supposition that what goes on outside in the world is a complex mirror image of what is going on inside the brain. "*We just don't understand most of it yet, but like infinity, there always something new being created in the present, something that gets formed out of the multitudinous links of the past.*" He'd even requisitioned a copper model of the Möbius Strip to be built as a graphic reminder of this underpinning truth.

So what is she saying about this?

Thena is running her fingers along the curving form

123

and encouraging the group to do the same. "Note how there is no inner and no outer. If you start to draw a line, and never take your pen off the paper, you will come back exactly to where you started. One seamless form. The two flow backwards and forwards into each other in a continual sequence of co-creation. This is the state of the life we live: *This is how it actually is,"* she declares with more passion, like an orator suddenly flowing with fresh energy.

"What is going on inside of us, whether we know it or like it, or feel it, or not—that is what we end up being and doing. What we are gets lived out in our relationships. Unfortunately, it is mostly unconscious for many of us. We no longer shine with the simple authenticity of children, but we can make clear choices to live consciously, learning from all that we do, know, and experience. This is the wholeness that Thomas Merton speaks about in his writings." She points to the flip chart:

"That in all visible things there is a hidden wholeness."

After a thoughtful pause, she sets aside the next twenty minutes for the group members to take time to journal, or to reflect with their Möbius Strip. Thena asked that there be no talking, that this would be a time for personal reflection. She leaves a few questions on the board.

"Use these if it's helpful," she states again.

Sam remains stock still in his chair. He can't move a muscle. He is afraid that if he moves he might miss the full wonder of this moment.

During the session, George had not been able to

124

bring himself to write much, but he had reveled in some of his earliest memories. *Riding my bike ... alone ... that first Wheelie Bike I begged for for my birthday. How I loved hurtling as fast as I could around the roots and rocks of the forest trails nearby. I was terrified, but it was so much fun. Fighting against my fear of falling. Pushing on, knowing that if I fell, only I would know—there would be no one else to laugh at me. I was one bold, crazy kid then ...*

Now even George receives Thena's invitation wholeheartedly. As people move quietly out of the circle to find some secluded corner for their reflections, George drops his head into his hands overwhelmed. He knows this is why he had been drawn to the brochure originally. *Who I am, is mostly not what I am doing or saying. And, it sure makes me feel awfully anxious to even think about it. This is scary stuff.*

At last, out of the corner of his eye, he warily glances at the questions, as if they might leap off the chart and bite him.

> **Where in your life and work do you feel a seamless relationship between inner and outer, personal and professional?**
>
> **Where would you like to find greater congruence in your inner and outer life, and how might this occur?**

125

CHAPTER ELEVEN
THE SACRED LOTUS

Slowly the group regathers, many of them holding fresh cups of coffee and munching contentedly on one of Charles's humongous cookies filled with everything: oatmeal, coconut shreds, pecans, chocolate chips, raisins, and even a hint of orange peel. Dylan comes close to loudly exclaiming his delight to the silent room. It passes through his mind that this might have been appropriate.

Are we taking the silence thing too far right now? The atmosphere feels a bit heavy for me. I want to tell a joke, get people laughing. Isn't soul work supposed to be fun? Is it just me, or is Thena overly intense this weekend?

They each find a copy of a poem on their chair. "Summer Day" by Mary Oliver had long been one of Thena's favorite poems. She had decided that even if summer had officially passed, today was truly a summery day. The glory of the summer season needed extolling one more time this year, and surely the group was primed to respond to the last line:

Tell me, what is it you plan to do
with your one wild and precious life?

Dylan reads the poem with great enthusiasm, and after Thena rhetorically repeats the question, she continues. "We have just spent time considering how to live undivided, how to tap the deepest passion of our lives and find ways of flourishing from there. I'd like to leave room for your response. Before we move on, is there anything you'd like to share from your morning's reflections?"

The group is curiously quiet. Over the years, Thena has learned to be mindful in deciphering the many moods and hidden voices in silence. Sometimes a silent group means a resistant, frustrated, or even angry group. Possibly silence might call out bleakly as a dearth of understanding, everyone rather lost, waiting for a voice to show the way in the wilderness. Some silences embrace rest, like a hummingbird perching on its feet, like the space between musical notes—this was the pause that enlivens a timely rhythm of response.

In many circles, Thena often experienced the awe of a silent group; the stillness of souls caught open-mouthed and dumb before mystery—those times when words are entirely unnecessary. Today none of these fit. She feels unsure, tentative. *What is needed from me? Shall I continue on, or wait longer to see what emerges?*

She also knows that silence for some people becomes so anxiety-producing that like pressure on an infected abscess, it squeezes raw emotionality out of the more unconscious members of the group. This is not psychotherapy; she has no desire to pressure any ripening response.

I know I am full of my own floating insecurity this

128

weekend; but, I must be clear—is this about me or about them? Am I reading an outside text or an inner one? It seems all mixed together.

*   *   *

And so it is! A silent hiatus like this can be remarkably disconcerting to humans. Silence for us is the air we breathe, the ocean we float in, the bread and butter of spirit life that so often terrifies those who walk on two legs. This "space-between" is ripe with generative power, a veritable treasure trove of rich and textured life that waits to be discovered by those who can bear the emptiness of silence. We like to think that in these moments our work is to shore up those sturdy human souls who are ready to listen in the void, to serve those who are learning not to crumple with some vacuous response.

Yes, Thena has this type of fortitude, but today what she cannot see is that her uncertainty is an accurate read of the group. She is experiencing the symptom of emotional backwash from very distracted people. Each group member sits present in their body, but most are cocooned off in their private zones of experience leaving her to sit alone in community. One by one we note their absence.

Our thoughtful friend Sam would have gladly spoken but remains speechless with his recent understanding. Maria, the grieving singer, sits consumed with fresh terror, thinking only about her Grace and the tragic fact that her "one wild and precious life" is dying. Leona has been lying on her back for the past half hour in the far corner of the room communing with her Möbius Strip; now she uncomfortably wishes she had gone to the restroom before the session started, and can think of nothing else.

Jean, the therapist in the room has abandoned her inner process to become a professional observer of Thena, wondering how she will deal with group silence. The teachers are listening faithfully to Thena, but are so concerned—as good students always are—about making the right, helpful response, that they have wedged their spontaneous selves into the noose of their altruistic caregiving. Mei is aghast. She certainly will not utter a peep in public about something so entirely private as her "one wild and precious life". George is busy hoarding the last crumbs of his cookie, wishing he had the gumption to get up for another one.

Finally, Thena tries to catch Dylan's eye to get some sense of direction from him; this was where having a co-facilitator often helped. He too remains curiously absent, his eyes focused downward to his right. Dylan is swept-up in heartfelt admiration of the shapely legs of Raquel, who sits beside him. He appears suddenly attentive to more of the wild side of his precious life.

Thena decides—most appropriately to us—to move on. We know with assurance that when something is important, when the time is ripe, truth always will emerge. She begins again to speak, this time more personally, breaking into a fresh, soft layer of vulnerability that brings the group members back into cohesion, not unlike a flock of geese that rise off the ground, flapping and honking, and eventually moves into fresh formation as a leader rises out of the group and points the direction home.

She reaches into the center of the circle and holds up the lotus pod, takes a huge breath, almost as if the feather-weight object has become too heavy to carry.

"This question '*What do I wish to do with my one wild and precious life?*' has worked its way into my heart and out again, in all sorts of actions both personally and professionally. I am not here to tell you all about that, but want to share one personal story about how my life has been radically altered by identifying my desires."

We bear witness to the power of story. Immediately Thena's words delve under the surface radar of Zach's life. He has been slouched in his chair, off wool-gathering, thinking about the Strip of his young life. … *all the conservative wagon-circling that I've absorbed during my early years. How I need to unravel the tight knots of family.* Suddenly he sits bolt upright, attentive to her every nuanced word. *Look, it's my magic symbol from last night!*

"Listen as I speak. Let the pictures tell my story. Above all, pay attention to each of your individual responses." Thena reads aloud while a kaleidoscope of pictures wrap colorfully across the screen.

THE SACRED LOTUS

My love affair with the lotus began the first time I laid eyes on this awesome beauty on vacation in Barbados. I all but fell head-over-heels into the pond, attempting to capture the essence of this divine flower for a photograph. How I longed to live in a more tropical place! My mixed heritage often left me feeling like a tropical transplant. Where could I grow lotus for myself?

Shortly after my trip I was shocked to learn that this majestic plant could actually grow in my gardening zone. First, I needed to build a pond—certainly no small venture. After two years of unrequited desire, quiet faith, and painstaking research, my family was sufficiently inspired to join me in this major do-it-yourself undertaking. I could never have done it alone, nor could we have imagined the immensity of our commitment.

With a rented backhoe, my son started to dig the cavernous hole. It rained the second day, and when he almost tipped the backhoe over the slope, we realized we had effectively created an enormous, slippery mud pit. That night at 3:30 AM, I was awake, mortified with embarrassment, panicking over the destruction I had unintentionally wreaked in our peaceful garden. Nevertheless, there was no turning back—desire is a siren's call.

Over the next weeks, we hauled concrete blocks, scavenged materials from demolition sites. We erected a thirty foot-long retaining wall, and grounded the waterfall corner in tons of dirt, re-bar and rocks, most of which were hauled out of our creek. By necessity, instead of gardening that summer, I became the stone mason, the designer, and the chief laborer, but my family consistently pitched in to help. The design for one pond morphed into a series of three ponds with two waterfalls and a bog garden. All my careful plans kept changing.

Finally, on Labor Day we laid the giant sheets of plastic and filled the ponds. I was the first to splash in! Fall was joy-filled; but planting my lotus had to wait until spring. The tender growing shoots of the tough, sausage-like tubers are extremely fragile and must be handled only in the earliest stages of the growing season. One frigid day in March, one year after beginning the project, I planted two mail-ordered lotus in large pots, in rich clay dug out of the creek, added fertilizer tablets, and then expectantly placed them below the surface of the water.

Two months later I could not have been more entranced. Large circular leaves rose on thick spongy three- and four-foot stems. Nelumbo nucifera grow bountifully out of a bed of muck and mire deep under the water; they need abundant sun and fertilizer to bloom. These plants are a marvel of science. Their leaves are extremely hydrophobic; when a drop of water lands on a leaf, it rebounds into a spherical shape and quickly rolls away, staying dirt-free despite their muddy environment. In a rainstorm you can enjoy water dancing off the leaves. Lotus plants have the exceptional capacity to regulate their temperature, staying between 86 and 95 degrees, just as mammals do. No wonder that for Buddhists, the lotus symbolizes the most exalted human state. "A head held high, pure and undefiled in the sun, with feet rooted in the world of experience."

After the leaves, we watched the flower stalks rise: the buds swell into flower high above the canopy of leaves,

133

exploding into a crown of color. The flowers only last for three days. On the first day, the perfect majestic bowl of closely packed petals, a chalice of pale white and yellow-pink heavenly delight, can be as large as eight inches across. On the second day it becomes a saucer of lacy ruffled glory, open and inviting, a magnetic fragrant attraction to any insect or bee in the vicinity. On the third day, the head droops and the now-pink petals fall, leaving a distinctive seed head that continues to enlarge, embedded with life-producing seeds. These seeds eventually drop down and bury themselves in the mud below. The peculiar seedpod which graces the plants for months after the flowers are spent, looks like a wrinkled chocolate watering-can spout. It is often used in dramatic dried-flower designs. The entire plant is edible, rich in dietary fiber and vitamins, and has been a staple in diets around the world for centuries.

As an evocative symbol of beauty and purity, as a manifestation of the divine, and as a practical food for life, the lotus flower remains unsurpassed. Revered as sacred in all Asian cultures, in Buddhism it represents purity of the actions of the body and the mind, and floats buoyantly above the messy waters of attachment and desire. According to Hinduism, within each person on the earth there is hidden the spirit of the sacred lotus. Hindu deities are pictured sitting within lotus flowers in the yoga lotus position, holding blossoms in their hands.

The Baha'i Lotus Temple in New Delhi, magnificently designed in the shape of a lotus flower, is a magnet for spiritual pilgrims. It is said to be a place where "one feels one is at last entering into the estate of the soul, the state of stillness and peace."

As I sat one hot summer day beneath the waterfall, surrounded by the lotus and all the pageantry of life and color that flowing water brings, the chalice of my soul was rich and brimming over. The lotus had drawn me through hope and fear, through all the muck and mire of years of hard work, into new depths of my own inner sacred temple.

Finally. Thena is relieved to get to the end. She has been feeling increasingly raw, as if with each word she is slowly undressing in the circle. A stream of inner doubts march through her mind as though she has just put her naked self on display at the front of the parade.

Is taking a risk like this worth it? Why did I ever imagine I could offer something so profound, so personally sacred, to the public? Will anybody understand this metaphor about my desire to grow the lotus? Are the psychologists in the group judging me, thinking this is all about my narcissistic self-objects? Why is this plant so important to me, anyway?

Thena glances helplessly across the circle to Dylan, knowing that if she says one more thing, she might burst into a confusing mixture of emotions.

"Dylan can you lead us next—into our 'walk and talk?'"

He is right with her this time.

CHAPTER TWELVE
THE WALK AND TALK

Without missing a beat, Dylan gets up and flips over the chart to two new questions.

Is there a specific image or idea from this presentation that captured your inner attention?

If you think of yourself like a lotus, how does the plant speak to you at this season of your life?

"Let's take a few minutes as a group with these questions. What images or ideas from Thena's presentation resonate with you? If you would like, briefly speak them out into the circle. You don't have to describe why or give any kind of explanation; we'll have time to process more personal detail later if you wish."

Then, after a thoughtful pause, he continues. "Maybe I'll start. I found this presentation very insightful. I had read the text before, but today it came alive. Thena, the pictures really capture how long and arduously you worked before you saw your first lotus flower. The drudgery, energy, and time you put into this labor of love impresses me. I want to think more about what this means, especially for my day-to-day work. I wonder how much time and work I am willing to sacrifice for the sake of my deepest pleasures?"

Zach bursts out next, barely able to hold himself on his chair. "Last night I came back into the room after all of you had gone to bed. That lotus pod, Thena, the one you have there in your lap, was in the center display last night. Like … it totally grabbed my attention. I spent an age just sitting with it in my hands ... like …"

He takes a big gulp of air, then grinds to a halt, realizing the futility of words; even attempting to make sense of his transcendent experience last night feels hopeless. For the moment, Zach is beyond speech.

Michaela gently whispers how awesomely beautiful the lotus flower is and the contrasting fact that it grows out of such muck and mire. "It seems like such a paradox ... kind of like life, I guess."

Maria chokes when she begins to speak, but is able to eventually say, "Initially it made me sad, to think that such exquisite blossoms only last three days before the petals fall off. But when I saw the wrinkled pod, it came to me how beauty reveals herself in so many varied forms. The petals had to wither away before the resilient, eternal nature of the pod could be revealed."

Thena feels her eyes glaze over with tears, in recognition of the depth of Maria's words. She feels more centered again, her wave of self-doubt receding into some corner of herself. It never ceases to amaze her how this work of facilitation is, at its core, her own character work, too. The more she remains open and attentive to her personal growth, the more deep wisdom discovers her. Sometime later it will be important to sort out the unease inside of her, but once again she can listen clearly to the group.

Out of the blue, George shocks everybody. It is his first public statement. Wide-mouthed, he blurts at Thena, "How the hell did you ever get the whole family working with you on this project? I am astounded that you all cooperated, working so hard together for a vision that only you initially grasped. It was your dream in the first place."

Thena laughs gently, along with many in the group, but doesn't reply, even though her impulse is to volley back with some clever retort. She senses that George is searching for something significant, and to reply too quickly would sidetrack him from the heat of his searing question. Anyway, it would have been her answer— not his. So instead, she responds to him warmly in encouraging body language, breathing silent energy in his direction.

George's agitation subsides a little when Gerritt, who is sitting beside him, immediately responds. "I was thinking the same thing, George. How is it that I get left working, all by myself, so often? Nobody seems to be interested in my good ideas."

Thena notes that eventually most in the group have spoken at least once, some of them more. To her delight, she watches Zach as he keeps spouting a phrase here and there. Like a newly tapped geyser, he attempts to find words for each bubble of insight that breaks to the surface of his mind. His infectious enthusiasm viscerally inspires the group, so much so that Dylan has a hard time giving the next directions.

"It's time," he says, "to get outside, to go for a walk. I don't know about you, but sitting in long meetings makes me edgy. Our bodies desperately need activity. I encourage you to find a partner and take the next half-hour to walk and talk together. I'll leave you some questions to guide your conversation. Try not to have a normal chat session, even though I know there are many helpful things to talk about, but this morning please consider trying a different way of being together. Every time I have faithfully adhered to this simple practice, it has clearly been helpful.

"You will each have fifteen minutes. Listen deeply and openly to your partner; this will also be good practice to prepare us for our Clearness Circles this afternoon. We want to learn how to listen in respectful and trustworthy silence to one another. Each of you will speak for up to ten minutes without interruption. You'll need to keep your eye on the time, and even if you run out of things to say, just walk and be quiet together; more thoughts may come up during the quiet. If you like, for the last five minutes, feel free to ask open and honest questions to help your partner dig a little deeper. We want to inspire one another to hear our individual souls speak with more clarity.

"By the way, an open and honest question is a kind of question that you do not know the answer to. It is not a question that satisfies your curiosity, nor does it impose your idea of what the answer should be. Have you noticed how many of our conversational questions are 'clever'—ones we already have answers for, or ones we have some personal ego-investment in? That type of question says more about us than about the one we are listening to.

"Don't worry if you don't have any questions. My experience then has been that it's better not to speak. Walk in thoughtful silence together rather than dissolving into chit-chat and losing the thread of what your hearts have been noticing today. Remember, this *is* the purpose of our time together. The primary goal of this weekend is to listen to our inner voice speak."

As Dylan beams at the group, Thena listens with satisfaction. *What a great music teacher he must be— coaxing all that buried creativity out of the shy sanctuary of childhood. He's so enthusiastic, even George seems fully engaged.*

"This process is not necessarily easy; it's different than most social conversation. But please enjoy this time," Dylan concludes. "Remember, each person will have fifteen minutes, so after half an hour, take a break and be back here promptly for our last wrap-up session before lunch.

"Oh yes ... an important reminder. We need to know if you want to volunteer to have your own Clearness Circle today. Come and talk to Thena or me before lunch. Maybe just walking and talking now will help you decide. If you wish to be a focus person, or aren't sure yet, come and join us at lunch so we can give you more direction about the process of Clearness Circles for this afternoon.

"Here are some questions. Use them as you wish." Dylan hands out another paper to each member of the group.

What work inspires you? Is there a project or work of love that you do or have done, that energizes your life with longing?

What is the muck and mire that your roots are growing in right now?

What are your 'tender growing tips' stretching towards?

*   *   *

The room is suddenly humming with activity, but

141

from our vantage point we see time reeling out in slow motion; each thought propelling some bodily response, each individual completely absorbed in decision-making. We laugh as Zach, still in his fever pitch of excitement, rushes across the room to Dylan, breathlessly inquiring if they could walk and talk together. Surely he exemplifies the "tender growing tips" of youthful transformation.

Evan, now more firmly planted in the group process, timidly smiles at Vanessa, and invites her to walk with him, as if in a delayed response to her warmth earlier in the morning. Vanessa bustles out the room beside him, a pink flush of excitement creeping up her neck into her already animated face.

By accident, Raquel and Sam once again find each other—at least that's what anyone else would say. Unsure of whom to pick, both of them stand up simultaneously and catch each other's eyes across the room. Clearly these two are predestined to share their lives more intimately. The embarrassment of their previous truncated conversation definitely calls for some kind of closure.

Mei glances around the room somewhat apprehensively. We see her mind analyzing, deliberately taking stock of the situation. *No definitely not George, maybe Maria, no ...how about Michaela? There is something more about her than that tough exterior. I like her gentle spirit—I think I can trust her as a partner for this activity.* She glides across the room toward Michaela and in a soft voice asks, "Would you like to walk together?"

Grinning broadly, as if quite relieved to have been asked, Michaela gives Mei a big hug, promptly knocking her off balance and back onto a chair. Mortified, Michaela helps her back to her feet, and the two of them peal with laughter in the hushed room.

The couple draws our attention; curiously they have been sitting beside each other this morning, whereas all day yesterday they seemed to make a point of keeping their distance; almost as if they didn't know each other. Leona and Gerritt had looked at each other when they heard the word "partner," both aware of their longing to speak uninterrupted, to be listened to by the other. They don't know it, but both are desperately hoping for the same thing.

Imagine! To talk about the things I most care about— for ten whole minutes. Obviously we have a great deal to "walk and talk" about. Maybe having clear questions and a frame with solid boundaries will work for us. I guess I'll risk it. It appears that both feel safe, if not a tiny bit hopeful, as they step out the door together.

Slowly the group filters outside, as if let out of the ark by twos to wander down the pathways, into the nearby conservation area, and out into the familiar sounds of a warm Saturday morning in suburbia. A lawnmower buzzes nearby and several neighborhood kids racing each other on their bikes around the curving drive almost career into Sam who had not heard them coming.

Somehow, Maria and George had ended up together which appears like a disastrous combination. We often marvel how groups of two or three are formed during these retreats. Inevitably, they seem guided by the invisible right hand of loving compassion and the divine left hand of the eternal trickster. We all know better than to get in the way of that powerful influence.

It did seem strange though, when Thena notices that the Canadian therapist is sitting at the art table by herself. "Are you happy by yourself, Jean, or do you want a partner?"

"No, I am great, thanks Thena, all I want to do

right now is draw or paint. I haven't decided which. I remembered this morning that as a child, my happiest moments were with my Jumbo Crayola Art Box. It's been too long since I let myself play with color. I am quite delighted to be alone. Thank you, though, for asking."

Thena chuckles to herself when she sees Zach slowly inching backwards down the hall, pouring out his heart to Dylan, who evidently already has his hands full. *At this rate, they won't make it out the front door!*

Thena remains for a few minutes, mired in uncertainly at the door of the meeting room. It is her custom to place herself in the middle of the action, fully taking part in the activities of the group; usually she loves the fervor of participating as a member rather than just an observing guide. Relieved of this duty now, all Thena wants is a good cup of coffee. She heads for the kitchen, hoping to find her friend Charles.

CHAPTER THIRTEEN
THE KITCHEN

Charles is brewing his second very potent cup of espresso when Thena arrives. It has been a difficult night, awake for hours around four, then finally getting up to make himself a cup of chamomile tea. He'd sat outside on a garden bench, wondering how it was that once again, he was up, wide awake for the morning watch.

Morning Vigils at four o'clock had never been easy for Charles during his religious life: all those dark, silent shapes moving on padded feet, sitting and chanting the Psalms, waiting for the light to arrive, committed to being in the act of prayer as the new day began. He had understood intellectually the power of rising early and entering the mystery of darkness, but it had rarely been an action borne out of desire—one of the many challenging acts of obedience expected from him.

Obedience: this had been the most difficult monastic vow for Charles, the one that finally he could no longer tolerate as a maxim for his life. For years he had struggled, caught in conflict with what appeared to be the authoritarianism of the church but recently he has become aware that his issue with obedience is at the heart a struggle with self-reliance.

How is it that once again, I am learning to trust that darkness will be the light I need for the day ahead? he'd thought. *It's all so backwards. Nighttime has become a mystery for me.* After all those years of dragging myself out of bed, I now have no choice but to attend my own private school of prayer. Maybe if I can see this as a gift that gives me time to search for insight.* He'd bundled himself in his arms trusting for solace, and as dawn appeared, he was ready to fall back into bed for a few more hours until work responsibilities called him.

Now he is rather pleased when Thena arrives, looking for company.

"It's been a good morning, but this retreat business keeps me on my emotional toes. How about you, how are you doing? I must say I'm already looking forward to the feast you're planning for tonight."

Charles smiles. "Yeah, I'll be happily in the kitchen most of the afternoon. But it sounds as though we're both on the same page today: both keeping on "keeping on," but inside finding everything more complicated than we show." He sighs. "I was up half the night, feeling like I was back with the monks in an all-night vigil. Despite the gloom of my solitary life, I miss the old boys more than I ever thought I would.

"Here, let's share a good cup of coffee to raise our serotonin levels. I need good company like you—way better than the shadows of the monks any day."

They talk easily for a few minutes until Charles asks Thena what she had been learning that morning.

Thena furrows her brow, slowly and methodically

combing a black curl through her fingers. "I arrived here yesterday, rather unaware how dried up I was. You know—like a wrinkled old lotus pod." She screws up her nose with a wry twist in her face.

"So there I was today, giving a rather energetic presentation about the wonders of the lotus plant and, if I am honest, all I can hear are these debilitating questions rattling in my ear. *Whatever made you think you had something important to say? Why are you parading your private life out in public?*

"The interesting thing is that I didn't realize the extent of my depletion until the middle of the session with the group. It was hardly the appropriate time to call attention to my needs—that is not the job of a good facilitator, right? We may be continually doing our work, learning on the job, but ideally we do try to sort through our own rough edges before a retreat begins."

"Ideally, huh?" Charles laughs. "Since when is the work of professional caregiving ever ideal? My life experience has been more about learning in the most inauspicious situations. When I least wanted my personal drama to erupt—it did. Incredibly embarrassing at times. I remember the day I was asked to present a teaching to new postulants on the monastic vows. I was so familiar with this topic that I assumed I could teach it off the top of my head. It wasn't until I started talking that I realized, with a new certainty, that I could no longer adhere to the vow of obedience. Can you imagine how totally disconcerting that was? What an ass I felt like. I begged off with some flimsy excuse.

"I think this is the price of leadership. We make the choice to live our lives in the public eye and imagine somehow that we'll never be caught with our emotional fly unzipped."

Thena snorts with laughter. "Funny you say that,

because today I had the sense of being totally naked, parading in front of the group. All I did was bare a tender part of my soul, and *wham*! I may not have been stripped of my clothes, but the dark sensations stripped me of my power. So, Charles, I wonder, when does personal disclosure become too much? I long to live an authentic life, but in this age of so many god-awful reality shows, where is the fine line between offering a core part of yourself as a gift, and giving away the whole sacred jewel of your precious, messy self?"

She stands and paces. "This work of facilitation is not for the faint-hearted—but it sure is essential that we set the example of being alive and human. I guess most of the time we don't get to choose how to do this. Being a leader is all about living on the edge of falling, and balance is impossible. Why do I keep on assuming that I am balanced, and then get punched in the gut by some chaotic product emerging from my shadow life? I know that all of us grow out of the muck and mire of our lives; still, a leader should not drag others through their personal stuff."

She cups her hands and unfolds her fingers like petals. "I think I'm learning that, like the lotus, we take one growth step after another, but there is some mysterious sequence and order to everything that happens in our lives. Even the dirt that emerges over time—this is all about being human. Like the night, the dark side looms suddenly on time, on some mysterious schedule." Thena groans, trying to bulldoze her way through the morass of her discomfort. Charles waits, patiently attentive.

"So, how about God, Charles?" she says abruptly, sitting opposite him again. "You used to be in that business. Is this all part of naming the mystery that surrounds us? How about the sense that something, let's call it God, is there as the 'ground of all our being?' Is this messy bog of humanity right where divinity lives? Is *'I Am'* here in the midst of dirt and darkness, holding the essence of our lives together, bringing fullness to life?"

She stops and catches her breath. A frustrated tear squeezes out of one eye, which she wipes away in an impatient move. "I thought living and working in community was supposed to feel like a divine holding experience ... real presence ... comfort, from which we grow and feel supported. Today I am more aware of all I don't know. These hopeless existential feelings are swelling inside of me, like energy-sucking black holes."

Charles nods, pensive, and then says, "You know, Thena, this is the exact thing that eventually brought me to the end of my role as a priest. I spent all my years of postulancy and through my novitiate, learning and training wholeheartedly. My life was incredibly public; busy studying, then eventually teaching in the boys' school. But even though we had daily prayer services, I had the rare opportunity to empty and refuel privately, to let myself be raw and entirely human.

"The more I was schooled to become the voice of authority, the one who spoke with assurance and clarity to the younger learners, the more I realized how little certainty I actually experienced. I spent years wandering in a haze of questions. Each year, when the time came for my final vows, it was clear that I needed to defer once again—I was not ready. Even my spiritual director seemed unable to support the need I had for intimacy. When I lost myself in a puddle of angst or a storm of rage, especially against the hierarchical institutional leaders, he would unconsciously deflect my emotion and leave me feeling chastened, guilty for 'challenging God's anointed.' Even though I still honored him and the wealth of wisdom he represented, I had to move out of that closed loop of doubt, frustration and fear." Charles closes his eyes, remembering.

"I really miss community. I can't begin to express how hard it was to go it alone in the outside world." He feels close to tears but notices their coffee is getting cold, so he gets up to heat the mugs in the microwave. He sets them down on the table and sits again, continuing.

"We as people need a community to encircle us, especially when we are most vulnerably authentic. We need the grace of being held by real human arms. God is not enough when all you see is a row of backs at a Sunday morning service. This is why you do your work with groups, Thena. The church as an institution has so few communal systems for truly embracing humanity in our complicated, deeper issues—or frankly, in our most outwardly successful times, either. This is good work that you do. I hope this encourages you. I don't know what else to say other than tell you my own story."

They both sit quietly for a few minutes, listening to the hum of the ancient compressor of the walk-in cold room.

"You know, Thena, the reason I came back here to cook, back to this place that is full of bittersweet memories, is precisely to do what I see you doing in your groups. I am called to be a compassionate witness to others, and I need a community to find that mutuality. I stand here on aching feet for more days than you can imagine, and wonder the same thing. Why am I doing this? Why don't I take a simple retirement and disappear out of active service?"

Charles met Thena's eyes. "Because until the day I die, I want to continue the work my spiritual ancestors began over a century ago. I feel them in the walls these days: their eyes, their ears, and their hearts moving with me as I serve food, nourishing hope and offering a few joy-filled moments of communion, that will inspire these pilgrims to get back into their messy worlds.

"Mostly, I have no idea what is happening in their lives, but I am assured that anything I do in love becomes fertilizer for their souls. Thena, as I watch you, I know God, or whatever you call this Mystery, is in you and working through you in ways you will never understand. Just be faithful to yourself, faithful to your calling from inside. You'll never go wrong with the goodness and compassion I see in you."

He reached out and hugged her unreservedly.

Thena speaks with tears streaming down her face. "One day before she died, my grandmother took me aside and gave me a treasured cameo locket, and then said something very similar—something I 'must never forget.'

"She told me, 'Yahweh loves you more than you can imagine. He desires good for you and not evil, He is going to open doors for you to be a blessing to this world.' She blessed me, probably knowing it was the last time we would sit privately together. She prayed for 'the oil of joy to pour over me, from the top of my head to my big toe.' She even used those very words you did today, Charles, isn't that something?"

Thena's eyes widen. "Oh! Remember yesterday, my memory and image of Bubbie, here in the kitchen? For an instant you reminded me so much of her. I think it's not just that both of you are amazing cooks, but it's about your role as people who are there for me, so serendipitously, exactly in the right place at the right time.

"You know, I just realized something … maybe my lotus presentation had so much positive energy in it, that it highlighted something dark inside: Just like my lotus plants, I am partially root-bound. I am flourishing in the container of my secular life, and yet have resisted growing as a traditional Jew, like Bubbie. As if I could turn my back on my spiritual roots. Like the lotus, my Jewish roots are fat and fleshy and full of life. I wonder—maybe this 'fatness' is waiting there for me to discover. I clearly remember a visit to the synagogue with Bubbie, and hearing a talk on the verse that we should '*delight ourselves in fatness.*' At the time I thought it was 'old folks' nonsense, but interesting how it did get buried deep in my kishkes!"

She laughs. "Now I think I might be ready to nurture that seed of spiritual fatness—ha!"

Charles grins, staying with her as she keeps plowing forward.

"Sure, I've enjoyed all the annual ritual celebrations, the holidays with family, but I am not a true worshipper in spirit, like my Bubbie exemplified. She was always overly conservative, almost orthodox, and being from such a different generation, I knew I never could be like her, so like my hippie mother, I gave up even trying. Being religious was something we both left behind in the dust of tradition.

"Isn't it odd, Charles, that you, a Christian have given me a taste of what I might be lacking as a Jew?"

Charles chuckles. "Well, Jesus was Jewish—completely and entirely. He got thrown out of the fold because he sided with the poor and became a threat to powerful people, both the religious and the political. He was one radical rabbi. I feel sad how, for years, I would extol the value of salvation instead of just following the simple way he lived: a person of love, doing his best to live out his calling in the world instead of all the rituals of sacrifice and atonement…"

They fell quiet again, digesting their deep dialogue, until Thena bolts to her feet. "Eek, I'd better get back to the group, I'm almost late. Thanks, Charles, you were the exact partner I needed for my walk and talk!"

CHAPTER FOURTEEN

SAM and RAQUEL

Side-by-side, Sam and Raquel now stroll back toward the front door. They have meandered the paths for the past half-hour, and of all the conversations we are listening to this afternoon, these two have used their time exactly as suggested. Each have found it refreshing to both talk and listen intently to one another. We note that unlike most conversations we hear outdoors at the Terra Center, they offer each other three uncommon gifts: a compassionate heart, an authentic witness, and the spaciousness of shared silence.

We sense their bursting hearts—both overwhelmed with a sense of gratitude to each other for the past thirty minutes and yet overcome with a sudden shy reservation. Both are struck by how much has been said, how honest they have been, and how suddenly it is now over.

Impulsively Raquel turns to Sam, her hands reaching towards him, as if she is still in Africa, communicating with a much-honored friend. She bends her knee slightly, in the traditional way, but catches herself, realizing this might look inappropriate—more like a corny curtsy. She squeezes his right hand and while holding his forearm for a few seconds, looks deep into his eyes.

"Sam, thank you so much. You have no idea how meaningful this time has been. I've decided to be a focus person this afternoon in a Clearness Circle, and have been worrying about it, wondering if I have the emotional capacity for it. This time together felt like a first step, almost a trial run. And even more than that, you helped me realize that under all my exhaustion, my soul is calling to be named, to be greeted and spoken to.

"Now I'm certain that this afternoon I want to give myself more time to continue the conversation. I am amazed how helpful your questions are, especially trying to work through my dream from this morning. I was so confused, and your questions opened me up, revealing layers of meaning I would never have *dreamed* of. " She smiles at her joke, then ends her speech soberly.

"I can take all the time I need to bring this baby to birth. She does have a name—it is Raquel."

Sam, choking on his upwelling emotion, releases his arm from her grasp and fiercely hugs her, whispering in her ear. "Thank *you*, thank *you*, Raquel."

As she steps into the building, Sam does an about-face and wanders back down the path into the garden. He appears dazed, having no idea what to do for the moment. We watch him pass by the strong handsome woman talking on her phone quietly, and then past the black woman with the tattoo on her arm. She too was holding her cell phone to her ear, laughing and conversing in a voice that parents do with older children, as if they are still giddy teenagers themselves.

"What a good idea," Sam thinks. *"I'm going to call Sheera and tell her how much I love her. I need to remember to do this more often."* As he dials home and chats with his wife, his gratitude spills through the airwaves, filling the space around us.

MARIA

"Hi, Grace. It's me … finally. I haven't had a moment this morning to call you, but I have a fifteen-minute break before we have to be back in the meeting room. How are you? How was your night?

"Pretty good, nothing more unusual than normal. You can stop fretting now. The question is how it's going for you at the retreat?"

"Well, it's been really good and also hard. Both. I just came back from half an hour with a man who probably is the most difficult person in the group."

"How did you end up with him? There must have been more pleasant people around."

"We somehow ended up together, kind of like being the leftovers once everybody else got first pickings for partners … don't laugh, it really was unnerving. You know how it is for me with people; I can figure them out, keep calm and steady, not rock the boat too much. Well, this guy would push all my buttons in a normal environment, but there we were, asked to talk honestly and openly about our deepest stuff. Asked to think about what inspires us about our work, and then—imagine this! We were asked to describe the difficult things in our lives that are helping us grow."

"Good God woman. How did you endure that?"

"No, no, he's really not at all mean, or nasty, just rough around the edges; he doesn't have a lot of social graces in a group like this. It's easy to see there's a whole lot going on just below the surface..."

"…sort of the way I am, huh?"

"Yeah. You've got it. Now you understand. … Actually I talked about you, how you're the rock star in my world. How you've been my anchor to home, no matter where in the world my work took me. I hadn't even planned on mentioning the fact that I was gay, but

155

needless to say it became obvious."

"Did he instantly despise you?"

"Of course not silly. He just remained silent and listened to me. We were supposed to be listening to each other's stories. But, he was kind of jaw-droppingly silent. Initially I felt a little of the zoo animal feeling—you know, the one we hate the most ... exotic curiosity, the stare-at-me-wonder-what-we do-in-bed-routine ... but then I realized that actually this was not what he was thinking. Those were my fears. He really was listening to me, hearing our painful story and the awful medical prognosis you have."

"Please don't go there Maria, not now, not ever."

"I know Grace. It's hard to talk about this with you, but we have to face it. I had to talk about this with him. I had to verbally process our lives right now ... how much uncertainty there is in ... in everything...

"...Okay, maybe this will make you laugh—you should have seen his eyes bug out when I said I was an opera singer. I think that really took him by surprise ... Grace, are you still there?"

"Yes, I'm here. I'm not going anywhere, remember?"

"I'm glad. You got very quiet, I thought the connection might have been broken ... I know this probably doesn't make sense to you, but it's helpful to let my heart run and speak the plain truth. Frankly, it rather helped that he wasn't a gushy emotional woman, drowning me in her sympathy. That would have shut me down real quick. I would have come unglued and lost the opportunity to talk through everything. His cool manner literally helped me stay calm."

"So how did he help? What did he say?"

"Good question—can you believe it? He only said one thing to me. He asked a question. It bowled me over though. Such a simple question, but it provoked me in a good way."

"Maria! What did he say?" begs Grace.

"Ha! I bet you want to know. No, I won't tease you and leave you hanging—it's way too serious for that. He asked me, 'Why did you choose to be an opera singer? What is it about opera that you love?'"

"Great question, what did you say?"

"I didn't have much time after that, but I still think it might be helpful to sort out my answers."

"Answers?"

"Yeah, answers. I know it's plural, like a whole lifetime essay, I think ... maybe a whole opera!"

"That sounds like you, the opus of your life. These sound like interesting people—not weird like you feared."

"You'd like these folks, Grace. They are all quite different, characters from all over the country. The more I hear each person speak, the more I realize how shallow many of my assumptions are. It was like that with George."

"Who's George?"

"Sorry, the guy I was talking with ... George is his name. I had such negative assumptions about him initially, all the worst things you could think about a person. I'm not supposed to say what he talked about because it was stressed that we keep what we hear confidential."

"That's cool."

"I know ... it really helps to know that someone isn't blabbing to their friend about me right now or won't be doing it tomorrow. Telling my private story to some stranger when they get home. It feels safe and sacred, like an old-fashioned covenant of truth, without all the blood-letting and ritual. Oops—there goes my operatic, high-drama mind. Anyway, it's okay to say that he talked about his family, too. He told me he was awe-struck by the love in our relationship ... how I talked about you, that I would give my life for you if I could. He said he was staggered by that. He said it actually made him jealous to hear my story. How about that!

"Oh shit ... I have to run; I'm going to be late. I'll have much more to tell you tomorrow when I see you, but I'll try and call again before then. Bye."

"Bye. And for the last time, daahling—puhleease don't worry about me."

"Okay, I'll try. Love ya."

DYLAN

Grateful to find a few minutes on his own, Dylan strolls the perimeter admiring the ancient stone walls. *There is nothing holding these stones together—no mortar, just dry stacked rocks. I wonder what holds me together? I feel somewhat disabled by this last conversation, shattered by Zach's newfound freedom. I can't believe how exuberant he is, enjoying the novel opportunity to speak openly. I guess he needed that— someone to accept him fully. Experimenting, expressing whatever landed in his brain. It was like listening to someone on speed—wild, free association, a lifetime of buried thoughts shot out of a fire hose. Phew! No wonder I'm struggling finding my emotional feet. Hosed off by rampant, unbridled energy. How the hell do therapists do this, day after day? Teaching music to city kids is a breeze compared to this.*

Dylan slows his pace, the heat of the sun warming him.

Why am I so wiped out? I have a natural capacity to be present with people. Where has that gone? Maybe it's because I didn't get a chance to speak. I have lots to sort through, but I said practically nothing. Of course,

158

Zach was likely unaware that he used up most of the half-hour. But I could have interrupted—I know how to do that. I knew he was going over time. Maybe I didn't want to express the more private feelings that emerged from Thena's lotus presentation. This idea about how much time and energy I am willing to sacrifice for my deepest pleasures—I didn't want to go there.

Ha! My therapist would say that I was unconsciously colluding with Zach, keeping him engrossed in this manic flow. I could have laughed with him and helped him to self-observe ... casually, to point out his intense energy. But ...hmmm, that would be a therapeutic move, something she would do. That's not what the work here is all about.

Oh well, whatever happened, happened. If it is important, it will come back to meet me again. Relaxing, he sits on a nearby bench and closes his eyes, then stretches out, extending his long legs up over the arms of the bench. All at once, he hears voices all around him. Sitting up, he witnesses several group members laughing and talking, huddled off alone in various corners of the garden.

What the hell? Cell phones? Are you kidding? Can't they give them a rest, for God's sake? This is supposed to be a retreat, a place to stop, to be unwired. I'd like to add a new Boundary Marker to the norms list: 'Leave your iPad turned off, hide your cell phone, do not even think of activating the Web.'

Then he winces. *What is my problem? It's not like me to be so instantly judgmental. How moralistic—to dress up as the group superego. What am I struggling with?*

He pauses, his body frozen in place, half-sitting and half-lying down.

I'm jealous, just plain jealous. I wish I had someone

159

to call, someone to relax with for a few minutes. I'd love to joke around right now, I need that. I have nobody that close, no intimate partner to call. I've dated wonderful women, but none of them was the one I want forever. What is wrong with me? Why can't I settle down? Why is it taking me so long to find a life partner? Maybe marriage just isn't for me.

"Shit—double shit," he grunts very loudly, scaring himself, as he bolts to his feet, compelled to move his body; relieving the tension of this inconvenient reality show scrolling behind the curtains of his inner world.

No wonder the allure of the beautiful lotus inspired me, then dropped my spirit into my boots. I long for a woman to love. I have denied myself, and now all I can think of is finding a partner. Surely, it's not that simple— but, it has been a self-imposed limitation. Why have I chosen to remain mostly celibate? The older I get the more I want real intimacy: the kind when body, soul, and spirit are all united. Maybe I'm a crazy idealist, maybe I'm scared, maybe all of the above churned together with my neurotic fear—but at least now I'm more conscious of what has been plaguing me, leaving me bereft and depressed on and off for years.

Intensely animated, Dylan marches around the garden, attempting to marshal his thoughts and feelings. He laughs darkly. *My therapist will be delighted. She has been alluding to this struggle forever, but I've never been ready to hear her. Now I get it. Finally I've tapped the energy of one of the most dominating, infuriating, and delightful aspects of my being.*

His footsteps mark circles on the grass. *How is it that some people just fall in love instantly and know it's forever—staying loyal, even when it gets rough? Recently, I've given up looking. Where did my passion go? It's curious. I forget my singleness in groups like*

160

this. Maybe being in a group takes my mind off this uncomfortable part of myself. Is it possible that groups have become like a series of lovers to me—the more the merrier? Shit, that's a challenging thought. I've never, ever, thought about myself as being promiscuous in a communal sense. No wonder I stay busy facilitating, drumming, teaching—the center of attraction for everybody, other than my deepest sensual self ... and, sadly, shut down, not attentive for her, the other, who is still out there—somewhere.

With a start, he looks around, aware he is alone in the garden. The cell phone talkers have disappeared. *The group has started without me. What will Thena think?*

Uneasily, he slips into the circle with his eyes averted. Thankfully, she is leading this last wrap-up session of the morning.

CHAPTER FIFTEEN
THE CIRCLE

Thena couldn't wait for Dylan any longer. She finished writing on the flip chart, puts down the red marker, and rings the bell. She begins by reading a quote that had just surfaced in her memory.

There came a time when the risk to remain
tight in the bud
was more painful than the risk it took to blossom.
~Anais Nin

"It's curious that a few minutes ago, I was reminded of this quote. Since it seems significant, I'll share it with you. These words inspired me years ago, during a difficult season in my life; days when I felt stuck, almost powerless, feeling as if I had few choices. My kids still were dependent on me, but I needed space, freedom to grow separate from my family. It was then, during those fragile days, that my favorite person in the world died—my grandmother Bubbie. She was the only consistent person in my childhood.

"She left me a small inheritance, and after much thought, I risked investing in a personal business. It was a painful decision to make, but I had to break out of the enclosed bud of my life. I remember how my friends and family were aghast, but eventually I worked my way through graduate school, and started a completely new career. Unexpectedly, this old quote comes back to me today."

Dylan appears at the door, quietly sneaking into the room while Thena continues uninterrupted. "It's challenging to live through the pain of life's passages; it's complicated to live mindfully in my own skin. But the more I understand that the flower of hope is contained in the bud of pain, the more I am propelled to keep on growing. I just came back from a remarkable conversation that gave me new insight as I wrestle with the present restrictions of my personal life. I find that I'm often my own worst enemy. It still surprises me that some of my past choices are now precisely the ones that are squeezing me dry. Like my pot-bound lotus, my roots are cut off from critical renewable resources. Today, a kind person on the journey helped me examine this tender area, giving me time to think and hopefully break out of old patterns that are no longer useful."

Thena chuckles a bit, breaking the tension of her little confession that had arrived unexpectedly. "How about you? How was your time on the walk and talk? We have half an hour before lunch. Remember, when you speak, remain focused on your personal learning experience, and if your partner wants to speak for themselves, they will."

Michaela jumps right in. "Thena, you're speaking about me right now, right where I am in my life. I was processing a similar situation with Mei while we walked. I'm trying to figure out, if and how, I should go back to grad school, and why I am so afraid of change? Seeing the petals fall off the lotus just about killed me emotionally. That's how I've been feeling ... like all the zing of my youthful teaching career is gone. I've been so afraid of being a brown, crusty old pod—as if that were the end of the world." Her laugh has a hollow ring to it.

"But I am drying up ... feeling shriveled in my school district. Nobody, nothing is fertilizing me. I realize that teachers need fertilizer just like plants. I'm stuck all day in the same old classroom, without anybody admiring me and telling me I'm doing a great job. Nobody is appreciative of me like that beautiful lotus flower. I've been working incredibly hard, and I'm just plain tired."

Thena feels herself jolted by the clarity of Michaela's words, quite aware that she had expressed almost the same sentiment to Charles less than an hour ago. This time though, she can tolerate the force of her own feelings, and also continue to empathize with Michaela, knowing that the stinging reality of truth is a complex and most demanding companion, but in the end leads to fresh resolution.

Michaela frowns as if with cynical disappointment, then her eyes light up, and to Thena's delight turns a significant corner. "But I have to trust that if I am like a dry seed pod now, if I accept that reality, there is still hope. Soon my seeds will ripen and emerge. Maybe I'm learning that I don't need to be afraid of the fear of change itself. I've managed before, and I will find my way to grow into a blossom again."

A profound silence lingers over the group until Sam speaks, his face glowing. "I am so encouraged. Walking and talking with Raquel brought me back to the realization of how much love hides in the world. It made me return to some basics, to the core of what is utterly important in my life. As an academic, I get lost in my head, mostly attempting to resolve significant world issues. I don't know how it happened, but our conversation opened me up to new ways of being in love with this messy world. I am so grateful."

Dylan, sitting beside Sam, could have broken down and wept. He wants in that moment to lean against the older man, and like a sponge, soak up his joy; drinking in the hope and promise of love. Instead he closes his eyes and wills that some osmosis in the spirit would take place.

He's able now to pay close attention as one by one, others speak of their learning: how listening to their own words has taught them new truths, and how insightful questions from their walking partners helped them delve deeper into the murky waters of their conflicts. A few speak about the process itself, especially about how hard it had been to maintain silence, and not respond with social niceties that often mask uncomfortable moments in the listener's psyche.

Eventually Thena asks, "Before we wrap up for lunch, is there anybody else who wishes to speak?"

He notes that neither Gerritt nor Leona have spoken a word during this group session. He had been surprised when they also arrived very late, coming in well after him. Both appeared grimly sober, and little had changed in their demeanor during the session. They remain silent and deadly serious. Tugged by their misery, he recognizes a piece of his own isolated suffering, and longs to help them, to release them from whatever hell is going on in their relationship. But it is clear that Gerritt and Leona will say nothing this session.

Dylan is surprised by the measure of his relief when Evan closes the circle with a statement about "how difficult it was to only listen and not react to my urgent need to fix my partner. I wanted so badly to give her advice, but I'm happy I kept my mouth shut. It made me wish I could do the same for members of my family."

Dylan is still looking at Evan, hearing some echo of recognition of his own conversation with Zach, when he sees Evan smile warmly at Vanessa. He doesn't see that Vanessa up to that moment had been basking in how special she felt while walking with Evan. She had re-entered the circle feeling serene, not riled up about anything—good or bad. But when Evan spoke of his personal struggle to not "fix" her, she recoiled with a pang of anxiety. *I wonder what part of me he thinks is broken? He didn't tell me that. What advice do I need? And why does he bring this up in the group? People know he's talking about me. Oh dear, why must I take what everyone says so personally?*

She had been staring fiercely at Evan while her mind whirled, frantically trying to regain her equilibrium. Fortuitously, he acknowledged her with a most angelic smile that embraced her across the room. It is almost as if Evan had mouthed the words, "I love you Vanessa—just the way you are."

When Dylan saw that smile he couldn't help but wonder what had just happened, but quickly has to move on with wrap-up announcements.

"Raquel, Mei, and Evan have volunteered to be the focus persons this afternoon." He thanks them and says, "I am aware of the courage it takes to step out like this. Let's remember to hold them in our hearts over the next hours as they prepare, and as we meet together over lunch to go over the process. Remember, after lunch, there will be free time to do whatever your body and soul desires, but make it a time for solitude. We'll return here at three. Enjoy your quiet hours."

The group disperses quickly. There is little talking. It appears that each person carries out more than when they entered. Dylan sits still, not ready to engage anyone in conversation yet.

I feel as if a load of dirt has been shoveled off my soul. It's been a long time since I felt so free. Not that much has been definitely settled. In fact, I feel my sexual frustration and my singleness even more acutely, but just naming it helps me find more grace for myself. Uh-oh, here comes Zach.

Zach sidles up to him tentatively. "I know it's probably way too late, but is there any possibility I could be a focus person, too? I have so many questions, so much clarity I'm seeking. I hate to miss this opportunity."

Dylan stalls, searching for the best response. In his gut, he didn't think that Zach was emotionally ready for two full hours of undivided attention; he sensed he was vulnerable at present. His enthusiasm, although infectious, might come back and bite him. Dylan had seen it once before: a young woman, just recently out of a frighteningly abusive relationship, was unable to tolerate the intensity of the small-group process. Her ego was too unstable, not solid enough to hold the spotlight and receive such extended care. She'd fallen completely apart during the session, and the group leader needed to step in to refocus the whole process.

It's a weird thing how too much attention, too much love at the wrong time, can break someone apart. We talked about things like this in facilitator training. Yet I know how solemn Zach's question is, I want to honor the extraordinary light that's bursting out of this passionate young man. I think I understand a little more about how he feels today.

All these thoughts flash through his mind like a quickly changing stoplight. He is not sure whether to go, or to stop, or to proceed cautiously. So he waits; then it comes to him.

"Zach, why don't you come and join us for lunch? Listen and ask your questions. And once the others have left, we can decide together if the timing is right for you. To be truthful, it does seem rushed, but you need to know clearly. Plus, as the leader, I feel like I need more time to be discerning."

As the two of them companionably leave to find a table for six, Dylan breathes grateful thanks. *Once again I've encountered the absolute truth—that if one stops long enough to pay attention—there is always some middle way.*

CHAPTER SIXTEEN
SOLITUDE

They are the last two in the dining room. As they pick up their plates and walk to the kitchen cleanup counter, Dylan asks, "So, what do you think, Zach?"

Zach answers immediately. "I'm going out for a very long walk. I'm sure it's not the right time for me to be a focus person. I have too much going on. Just formulating a clear question is next to impossible. I have too much catapulting though my head, it's a wonder it stays attached to my body. Thanks for helping me find my way. I know I can be impulsive at times."

Dylan laughs. "Well that makes two of us. I've spent much of my life chasing my butt around after my last wild decision. It sure has kept me busy! Enjoy your walk. I'm heading for a nap."

As Dylan moves to the door, he spies a very red-faced Charles, sweating and stirring something hot and savory on the stove. "Charles," he hollers affectionately. "I hope you're not working too hard on our behalf. Hot dogs for dinner tonight might be a hell of a lot easier. Go take a break—look after yourself."

Charles grimaces at the mention of ever serving hot dogs from his sacred kitchen, but laughs with Dylan. *I like this young guy; he reminds me of myself as an ardent young man. I wonder if he has a partner? I sure hope so. I wish I hadn't waited so long to figure out that sexual relationships are not a mortal sin.*

Charles's feet ache. His ankles are swelling, too. This hot and humid Indian summer weather is delightful for many people, but strenuous on the cook. The espresso machine splutters, volcanically spewing more hot steam into the kitchen. Charles pours coffee over a glass full of ice cubes, adds a touch of half-and-half, and then unties his apron.

I choose daily to don this work symbol, but how grateful I am not to be tied to church apron strings anymore.

Smiling, he ambles over to the water garden, then squints at darkening sky. Determined, he pulls up a lounge chair, brushes off the colorful quilt of autumn leaves, and falls heavily onto the plastic webbing.

Hello, dear place. How I adore you—every intricate detail. You've always been an oasis of peace for me, full of so many memories. Abundance flourishes in him, around him, and through him. Dozens of giant tropical leaves arch their way into the sky, competing for light and air. Striking burgundy banana fronds weave through the thick foliage of black and green elephant ears. To his right, hundreds of red and pink cardinal-vine flowers cascade on an arched trellis behind a tumbling bed of lavender: all fragrant magnets for hummingbirds and giant bumblebees. On his left, the waterfall is crystal-clear; zillions of friendly bacteria as algae cleanup-crew are decomposing the falling leaves that are still settling into the ponds for winter. Under the falls, he spots a plump green frog nesting in the clump of forget-me-nots that an ambitious young gardener had transplanted earlier in the season from the wild creek bed. Behind the water, fronds of twelve-foot-high variegated grasses blend seamlessly into purple fingers of hibiscus and yellow Japanese maples. The rich nut-brown bark of the Heritage birch curls in ribbons, hanging in a crusty display that will soon explode into full view once all the surrounding leaves are gone.

Look, another fig. Charles reaches up and picks the hidden fruit—it is dark and juicy. He smacks his lips, reveling in its texture and earthy flavor. *I wonder how the new gardener is going to protect this tree over winter. If this were Nonna's tree we would be burying it soon, layering it down on the ground before the first deep frost. What a funny family ritual—the burying of the fig tree. At least that wasn't half as tasteless as the neighbors' method. They encased their fig tree in old windows and sheets of plastic.*

A flock of migrating robins settle for dinner on the lawn, calling cheerily in cascading bursts of bird gossip. *So much energy everywhere. Look at those tiny goldfish; they seem to be multiplying by the second.* Charles sighs with recognition. *"I wish I could keep going forever…"* He closes his eyes, resting, as the past twirls in his head.

My first days here—next door at the diocesan high school, barely a teenager, a city transplant dropped into that colossal, drab school complex … before the big fire gutted it. I remember playing basketball in the concrete courtyard … the entire wing of dormitory space that housed all of us male boarding school students. That was the year not one student was refused, one hundred freshman students in overflowing dorm rooms…

Charles shudders, fiercely swirling the ice cubes in

his glass. His mind whirls, clashing as the present and past collide. *The terrible nightmares ... the horror of being tormented by the senior prefect. 'Like a mighty army moves the church of God.' ... The laws of reward and punishment ruled my life then. My youthful wildness tamed and ruled by a system of order, galvanizing the imprisoned adolescent inside me.*

But, aaahh, my only freedom—this daily work assignment, assisting Antonio, my Italian mentor. What back-breaking work. The more he aged, he sat in the sun and talked—while I sweated. But what I gleaned in return—nuggets mined from his deeply worn life. It was in this garden that I learned how to live from the inside out. I learned to speak the language of the earth—the language of my soul—in my mother tongue. Transformed by unearthing this deep mystery through digging, weeding, deadheading, watering, and harvesting.

Here, Nature distilled her essence into me. It became increasingly clear that much religious worship, out of ignorance, repressed native, natural spirituality. Gardening taught me about the creativity in my soul. As I learned the skills of tending the earth, I realized there was not one right way to garden—rather, it is a natural, organic process.

Religious life was taught me mostly through a series of moral rights and wrongs. Eventually I discovered God again, not in doctrinal creeds or statements of belief, but in my experience of life: a wandering, circuitous, most convoluted journey. I needed to get rid of the straight edges. Plant new flower beds in the bare square of the formal front entrance. I intuitively softened the lines, adding flowing new borders, the sunshine invited masses of spring bulbs along the curving walk up to the main house.

I remember starting work on this pond during my

last year in the mission house. Each stone, each daub of mortar, a remembrance of tears and joy, mixed with buckets of sweat; I felt compelled to close this chapter of my life with a final creation. It was clear to me that the institution was struggling to survive. I mourned the loss of my old friends, the priests who were slowly dying, and wondered why younger men were not replacing them. Tirelessly I worked, prayerful that, like an alchemist, I might transform this suffering into something precious. I understood this was my true worship.

He recalls the day he left, and the great fire shortly after; the school building destroyed, and the mission house forced to close its doors. *Then I truly was a tumbleweed, adrift without earthly roots. Transitory, always feeling out of synch, being neither here nor there, but in between. My birthplace has haunted me. Born on Ellis Island, not quite in America, and yet definitely not back in the old country. Wandering, teaching again, looking for love, searching for home, for a place to put down my roots. Yet all the freedoms in the world couldn't fill me. I knew I was missing something. It took a while, but I came to see that despite their human failings—I am, and always will be, one with them. My heart is the heart of a priest. That was why it was so hard to attempt to rebuild my life on the other side of the garden wall.*

And, last year, like the prodigal son back from my wanderings, being warmly given a place of honor in this small community. No more gardening now, but I can still revel here. The garden shines today with a bold and brilliant energy. What a faithful reminder—from death, life will come again. Death and resurrection go together, side by side, a constant theme in gardening, as in life. I cannot experience one without the other. Suffering and love are woven inexplicably into the fabric of humanity. Truly, this is the circle of life ...

The sky darkens. The temperature plummets. Disrupted, Charles' reverie ends with a shiver. The wind blows him back into the sheltered circle of stone and water as he witnesses summer exit and fall arrive with a blast.

Images of inner change whirl in his mind as the wind throws everything crazily awry. A potted pond plant overturns sideways, spilling across the current. Leaves cascade into the water, and acorns and branches from the oak tree shred the tropical banana leaves, knocking off the delicate canna flowers. The birds vanish with the first sign of rain. The fish and frogs had already disappeared into the depths, and the last remaining water lilies close for the season. Only the shining blue poisonous monkshood glistens in the shadows of the bog garden.

While hunkering down in his chair Charles ponders his place in this drama. *What am I witnessing? What is my heart saying about this? Of course I'm repelled by the idea of winter. Emotionally I'm not ready. Of course, autumn is long overdue—but I am still soaking in the bounty of summer. Today I finally received her warm abundance inside me. It's a hard-won victory after grappling through this year of transition. Finally I am here—fully and abundantly alive. Summer lingered this afternoon, and I'm going to treasure that wealth with all the joy-filled tenacity I can muster.*

It is growing darker and wetter, and the dinner hour is fast approaching. In an act of priestly ritual, as he walks along the path, Charles picks a dazzling bouquet of blossoms: huge white-dinner- plate dahlias, smaller, rich-red Bishops, and willowy stalks of yellow grass. Inevitably, all would be flattened by winds and rain that night. What bounty he heaps on the kitchen table.

With Zen-like composure, Charles arranges a

bouquet. *It matches my inner picture of summer, glowing and still alive.* As he starts to sauté the onions and garlic, Charles, the cook, breathes a prayer of deep gratitude to the garden Mystery that has once again brought him back full circle, into himself.

CHAPTER SEVENTEEN
THE STORM

The weather change catches Thena unprepared. She had planned a relaxed outdoor fire for later that evening. *Now what will we do? What could we plan that is low-key and creative?* Her brain charges into overdrive, spinning out assorted ideas, but nothing jells. *I should have known better and been more prepared to be flexible. Oh, come on, lighten up. This is really no big deal. Relax. It will all work out.*

She had enjoyed a short walk after lunch and then, for a while, tried to read. But her mind couldn't rest. She found herself wandering into the quiet kitchen, looking for something, unable to specify exactly what, but grateful to find cookies and an inviting urn of iced tea on the counter. *What a dear man Charles is. Even at his age, he would certainly make a great partner for someone. I wonder who I could set him up with?*

Thena's pleasure evaporates as quickly as it arrived. Maybe it is the oppressive clammy weather, or maybe she is getting sick, but when the rain starts, a flood of dread sweeps through her. She bolts down the hall to

Dylan's room, forgetting the silence of these quiet hours.

Dylan, on the other hand, has been blissfully fast asleep. He comes to the door in his boxers, clearly dead to the world, and confused by her sharp knocking. His inertia launches Thena into a furious mental attack on his lackadaisical approach to leadership. *How can he be so unconcerned? How could he leave me with all the work to do?* As this wave of silent recrimination lashes at him, she yearns to set this young leader straight. Like the roiling storm outside, her exhaustion trips the bottled-up neuronal circuitry of her mind, leaving her emotionally flooded and unable to think.

She reaches out to steady herself, teetering with the force of being physically off-balance. As she thrusts out her arm, she briefly touches him—a complicated move that involves self-protection, reactive anger, and ending in a gentle touch of surprise. *Good gracious.* Thena closes her eyes and takes a deep breath.

"Let's meet. We have to talk, earlier than planned. Can you please come to the meeting room in a few minutes?"

Shaking, she backs out the open door while staving off a rush of tears. *Oh God, another storm whirling through the fragile ecosystem of my inner world. I can't believe how high-strung my nerves can be at times like this. Tuned like a delicate violin ... not like the old beat-up guitar Dad used to play.*

I really am on edge. Probably nobody else notices; I hope not. I naturally cover it up so well. Poor Dylan, I wonder what he thinks. I hate how judgmental I can suddenly become. He doesn't deserve it. What's happened to my empathy? Dylan is doing a great job. Chill out, Thena.

A few minutes later Dylan appears, boyishly ruffled from his recent siesta, and enveloped in a delightful haze from some sexy spritz. *This man is quite a hunk. How is it that I keep missing that fact?* Thena laughs to herself, feeling more composed as the two of them settled onto the sofa to formalize the plans for the rest of the day.

"We need to select the three groups for the Clearness Circles this afternoon—this is always an interesting task to navigate. Let's see what is going to work best ..."

GEORGE

George is lying on his bed, listening to the wind outside and the dilemma roaring within him. It's two-thirty in the afternoon, but it already feels like an excessively long day. *I can't believe I arrived here yesterday.*

Despite all initial misgivings, he knows he has learned something significant today. It has been strangely eye-opening to uncover a possible key to his distress.

If only ... if only I could build a solid, working relationship with my family. This is the missing link. If I could accomplish this, then all the other broken facets of my work might fall into place more readily. I have always felt like it's "me against the world." Having three daughters makes it harder to be close to them. They more naturally turn to my wife, and realistically, I've been traveling almost all their lives—forced to be on the road.

Maybe I should set this as my next working goal. 'Build new bridges with family.' Now, how can I possibly achieve this?

His mind marches on, attempting to strategize, plan, and set attainable steps toward this goal. This was how George did business. He had seen the light this morning, and now he was determined to climb toward it.

During the group sessions, he'd been stunned to realize

181

how most people in the circle lived firmly connected within a web of relationships. After a while this was all he heard, all he saw—"everybody is connected to somebody." Family members or special friend's names were casually dropped into conversation as if it were the most common thing in the world—real networks of love. It staggers him to expose this hole in his life, this gaping deficit in his relational world.

What a relief to find something I can focus on. Now, if only a solution is actually attainable. Maybe when I get home I'll start by talking this through with my wife.

A pent-up surge of longing passes through him … *to be with her, to take time to be close and real. Work has dominated our lives for far too long.*

Relieved suddenly, he thinks aloud. "I know—I'll leave now. I can go home tonight and surprise her. Maybe I'll buy her flowers … let her know how badly I feel for not focusing on the two of us." George feels excited, as if it were possible to learn how to fall in love again.

Another thought pokes his uneasy conscience. *I have to admit that every time I sit down in the group, I am afraid. What else might jump out to grab me unawares? It might be good to leave now, while I feel so relatively positive. I hate the anger that keeps erupting. And … God have mercy … next session they might offer us all those damn art supplies.* George had been eyeing the back table with dread. *Gerritt, one of the scientist guys, said that the idea of doing art has enraptured him. He actually said out loud, for the entire world to hear. "I'm looking forward to finding myself through creative play with color and design." What the hell does that mean?*

And … I have to admit, I am not looking forward to this Clearance Circle thing, whatever they call it. It sounds perfectly overwhelming … to sit and listen to a person struggling with their issues for two hours? I can't tolerate my personal stuff for fifteen minutes. Look at me, lying here, sweating it out....

But, this morning, I did try it out—that half an hour together walking with Maria. What a fascinating woman. We had a great time. I had no idea I had been talking so intimately with a lesbian. Another first for me ... her partner is a woman! It floors me to witness the outpouring of genuine affection that has evidently sustained the two of them for years. I hate to admit it— feels weird to even think it—but I desperately want that kind of relationship with my wife.

As he lies on his bed, debating whether to get up and go, or stay and endure the consequences, George chuckles to himself. *Aunt Bertha! Crazy old Aunt Bertha just channeled herself into my mind. Where did she come from? I haven't thought about her for ages.*

The only artist in the Whittaker clan, and man, was she off the wall. One of those classic souls who spends their life collecting; recycling from thrift stores and garage sales, her yard awash with gnomes sitting under mushrooms and squirrels with pants on. Ha! Her herd of plastic deer was a hilarious source of glee in a neighborhood that spent inordinate energy erecting deer fences and spraying coyote urine over their precious shrubs. Still, I have to admit, she was the warmest and most welcoming relative I ever knew. The rest of the family measured up as interminable bores and perpetual stuffed shirts.

George remembers wandering absent-mindedly to his aunt's as a kid, riding his bike to see what stories he might come home with, not quite sure how or why he got there. Without fail, he found himself pampered with snacks and sweet black tea served in the latest addition to her ghastly mug collection. Bertha would prattle on,

183

doing her best to engage this big surly youngster, but eventually he'd get up, politely thank her, and rush out the door before she could wrap her arms around him, bathing him in the nauseating scents of rosewater, lily-of-the-valley, or sickly sweet jasmine.

"This is hopeless," he says loudly. *I'm regressing back into more frustration by the moment. I have to leave—now! What a relief I have the rental car. I can get out quietly without having to call the shuttle, drawing any more attention to myself.*

George stops; his head halfway up off the pillow, then lays down again. *Well, it's kind of relaxing here, and ... I'm feeling hungry again. "Peckish," Aunt Bertha would say.*

I heard someone say there is a feast planned for tonight. His mouth waters at the thought of what the cook was preparing right now. *I have paid for it, so how about waiting till after dinner? Then I can sneak out and catch the last flight home. I think there is a nonstop and I'd be home by midnight. Maybe I need that gustatory energy to send me on my way... no, I should leave now, I can get back home earlier and be with my wife.*

With resolve, he gets up and quickly packs his few belongings, zips up his carry-on, and then flops down in the armchair. Abruptly, he feels spent, drained of life force. It was as if he'd lost the energy to run. He doesn't even feel angry—just plain empty.

The hollow void swells in his gut, and he feels himself sinking into despair. As sensation leeches from his arms and legs, leaving him truncated, the abyss wells up to suffocate him. Terrified, his heart races and sweat pours through his body, soaking him to the skin. Certain he is having a heart attack, George lurches to the door and staggers down the hall.

His room on the main floor of the building is close to

the dining room and he propels himself onto the paneled swinging doors, erupting into the room, almost knocking over the surprised, ample figure of Charles, who had been setting tables for dinner. For a moment, the two men hugged each other like circus bears, grappling for their lives. Slowly, the cook manages to gently extract himself from the terrified man and leads him to a chair.

After George calms down enough to relay his worst fears and describe his physical symptoms, Charles gently suggests this might be a panic attack. Still, he quickly calls for medical help, and the doctor recommends that George rest and that someone keeps a close eye on him, and takes him immediately to hospital if the symptoms reoccur. Charles kindly offers to watch him for the rest of the afternoon.

George remains seated, still scared, yet oddly relieved. *I have no choice. I can't leave the building—doctor's orders—so I'm forced to stay to the end of the retreat. It's surreal, like entering another life. Is all this really happening to me? My need for control and independence unraveling before my eyes.*

"Charles, do you mind if I stay in the kitchen and watch you work? I can sit and rest, out of your way in the corner. I can't stand the thought of being alone in my room this afternoon."

"Great idea, come with me. I have lots to do." He ushers George into the aromatic room.

"Here we are. Sit in the corner, in my big old stuffed chair. Push all those papers onto the floor. Here … this may make the afternoon go better for both of us." With a magical flourish, Charles triumphantly produces a cold bottle of Chardonnay from the back of the refrigerator. He pours two big glasses—a casual offering of another form of priestly medicine.

"Relax a bit, George, and when you are ready, tell

me—what brought you here this weekend? How did you get to this retreat?"

Oddly, it calms George to look back and begin to tell his story.

"A few months ago I was on my way to Hong Kong for a convention. A ten-hour flight, and I needed something to fill the time. My airline connection had been late, so I couldn't get to the bookstore in the terminal to buy reading material, and the two in-flight movies were frightful. I was stretching up to look over the seat to survey the magazine rack, when my wallet fell out of my pocket and wedged between the window and my seat. When I reached down, I found, not just my wallet, but a book. Crazy ... huh? A book found me.

"I read it from cover to cover that flight. I would normally not have picked it up as it was all about groups, and the inner life, and all that stuff. Still it made me intensely curious. Where could I meet people like this? Do groups like this really exist? It was like nothing I had ever seen or heard of."

Not surprisingly, the two men talk for the next two hours. George did not realize it, but he is now a focus person, unwittingly led into a private Clearness Circle with Charles, the priest.

CHAPTER EIGHTEEN
CLEARNESS CIRCLES

Thena is speaking in hushed tones to the group gathered around her. "If there ever is a time and place when I feel drawn to prayer, this is it. A Clearness Circle never fails to inspire me. It consistently embodies the sense of the word 'awe'. No matter what role I play: whether a part of the listening group or being on center stage, searching for inner clarity, it is as if I enter the Holy of Holies. Even though I am not a practicing Jew, I now understand more fully the significance of the historic Tabernacle in the Sinai desert.

"People need a place of sanctuary. Our modern tribes, in the midst of our arduous journeys into the unknown Promised Land, still need tents of meeting, places to honor each of our personal and communal pilgrimages. Somehow, these unique circles are a form of the same sacred space."

She articulates each word with intention. "A Clearness Circle offers a few hours of sanctuary, a center for holy listening to delve into the deeper questions of our lives. This is a safe house for soul energy to soar beyond the bounds of Google, psychology, or even sacred texts. For me it has been a deep dive into the depths of humanity. To be in a Clearness Circle is to glimpse mystery, to reach for the light while wrapped, sheltered in a cocoon of love. As groups today, it is your sacred duty to honor and build this safe place."

She can sense their curiosity now, as she commands the attention of the whole group. Zach is no longer doodling in his journal, and Vanessa has stopped waving a piece of paper she has been using all day as a makeshift fan. Thena's impassioned introduction has penetrated the classic mid-afternoon malaise, and despite the heavy air still trapped in the meeting room, Thena knows she is on target as the leader. She is well aware that other than Dylan, only Sam has been a part of this type of experience previously. It is essential for her to offer clear instructions, not only to communicate the parameters for how this time will unfold, but also to be a champion, a guardian for those who have willingly offered to be the focus of each Circle.

In the back of her mind, she gratefully acknowledges her renewed sense of peace. *What a lesson to remember: Speaking clearly and thoughtfully grounds my soul. It brings me confidence for my own life, and builds a platform of expectation for others.* She moves on with urgency and direction.

"These Clearness Circles are the bone marrow of our retreat. Everything we do converges and then grows from this experience. Taking this time to prepare is the most important teaching of the entire weekend. Mei, Raquel, and Evan have stepped into a place of acute vulnerability in being willing to open their inner worlds, exploring personal questions and stories that would most often be done alone, or in the company of paid professionals."

She repeats emphatically, "anything that transpires during this time is entirely confidential, never to be spoken of again unless the focus person chooses to do so.

*   *   *

Mei's shoulders release as she sighs with relief. It was this lodestone of safety that drew her. As an extremely private person enmeshed in a very public world, Mei yearns for her authentic voice to be heard. *I have so much to say, I must escape this silent box of confinement. I'm ready to explore, and I know I can't do it alone. And unlike most of these sitting around me, my communal culture deeply honors this value—I know that I'm a small part of a diverse whole. Still, how important to be in charge of this time, not to be forced by expectations of others. I need to be able to answer questions when, and if I want, and also able to remain silent as need be.*

Evan also listens intently as Thena's voice strengthens in intensity. "The focus person is the one leading your small group. They will lead however they wish. As listeners, your job is to walk compassionately and wholeheartedly with them."

As both a caregiver, and a businessperson in a not-for-profit setting, Evan feels grateful for an opportunity to process his work dilemmas without the fear of finding them return to him, distorted and misrepresented, by Monday morning. This afternoon he had formulated some clear questions about what was troubling him; it had been helpful to write them down. In doing so, Evan had uncovered the heart of his predicament: feelings of profound betrayal. This crisis was what had kept him away on Friday.

His favorite co-worker, one of the younger men who had stayed with him the longest in the organization, had staged an apparent mutiny that afternoon. It took Evan by surprise, leaving him unsure of most everything. Hurt and angry, he could hardly bear to think about the details, but kept asking himself. *What must I do? What is the best way to handle this?* He was both anticipating new questions and fearful of what they might uncover.

It helps him significantly to hear Thena define how to ask open and honest questions. *Interesting, it was a barrage of questions that undermined my leadership on Friday. My insecurity spikes off the charts when peppered with questions loaded with a personal agenda and not-so-subtle judgment.*

Thena seems insistent, deadly serious in fact, impressing everyone with the value of a quiet, non-intrusive role in this process. What have I gotten myself into? I had no idea how much there was to think about. She seems to dramatically safeguard this time ... and me. I feel so ... so honored and scared.

Unused to being treated with such kindness, Evan feels rattled. His mind still doubts the decision to step into these hours ahead. Then, as if in response to his apprehension, Thena offers a calming image that a beloved mentor had shared at the time of her first Clearness Circle. It has remained with her as a helpful picture of how to stay present during these hours.

"Consider the focus person as a young bird learning how to fly. The group's role is to gently hold that bird," she cups her hands softly, "... carefully, respectfully cherishing this precious living thing. Your job is not to force the bird to fly, nor grasp it too tightly, squeezing the life out of it. Your place is to give them room to flap their wings, rest, or take off for a while. As a circle of quiet, you may not pick at their feathers curiously, wondering what makes them tick, nor succumb to fatigue and drop them, letting go of your attention prematurely.

"This is true soul work. We are certainly not used to being so close and intimate with another for this long. Two hours is a long time to remain focused. What a gift it is—what deeply honorable work to be with another soul while they find their unique way. Each of you must offer appropriate distance, not being overly involved by pressing your energy on another. Rather, give them all the time and space they need, and they will find what their deepest soul knew all along."

Thena closes with an encouragement. "I assure you that you can trust this powerful process of being present as both an individual and as a small group. I know each of you desires to do this well and are able to provide an open, loving space for the focus person to find what they need today."

Reassured, Evan looks over at Raquel, on the other side of the circle, curious whether the others were passing through this visceral tunnel of doubt and hope.

Wow, does she ever look uptight. Glad I'm not the only one ...

Raquel sits with her eyes closed, her body rigid with anticipation. She has spent much of the past half hour focused on breathing deeply and silently wishing for Thena to let them get on with it. Although she appreciates the care, Thena reminds her of a great mother bear, lovingly protecting her dewy-eyed family from all the potential pitfalls of unregulated group process.

As a physician, she wonders: *Is this what people feel like while waiting for surgery? Those last miserable hours, waiting, worrying, and then trying hard not to worry—knowing that everything was probably going to be all right. The endless circling back, caught in the space between the need to go forward for healing and the gut-shaking anxiety of being cut open and injured once more.*

Maybe not a helpful image to ponder, but is there a missing link here? Patients could never know in advance how much I, as the doctor, truly care for them—love them even. It was that way in surgery in Africa. I often felt that love guided my fingers...

There in bush-country, pushed beyond the bounds of her medical training, Raquel had learned to trust that she *was* the doctor. If she remained solid and grounded, in an uncanny way, she found herself led through a multitude of emergency situations. She recalled the trepidation that some surgical procedures evoked. For assurance at times, she had even brought her medical textbooks into the operating room—just in case.

Now, on the other side of waiting, these past hours of preparation since lunch had felt close to torture. Time stood still. Finally, she had escaped for another long run just before the large group started.

Curious now, Raquel sees Thena get up and flip over a chart with three groups of names written on it. *Good. Dylan is in my group—I like his easygoing nature. His carefree air might relieve me of the burden of having to be so morbidly serious. Zach and Michaela too—more youthful zeal, very appealing. And Maria—she's an interesting enigma. I know so little about her, but I like the idea of her solid physical presence, close beside me in the group—motherly, without being too overpowering. And Jean—maybe it's a good thing to have a therapist in my group. God knows I need a ton of therapy.*

Mei is also looking at the list with interest. Earlier she had requested that Thena be in her group, so was relieved to see her name. The focus people had been given the opportunity to request certain people, or to even consider mentioning anybody they didn't want in their group. Mei squirms at seeing George's name. *He's not somebody I really want in my group. I should have told them, but I was too shy to ask. It doesn't seem right to clearly point out someone as undesirable. That definitely is not the Chinese way.*

As the large group silently disperses to all their different meeting places, Mei is pleased to be assigned the meditation room. *I have grown fond of this space over the past two days and feel right at home here.* She walks in, followed closely by Vanessa, Gerritt, and Thena. George is noticeably absent. Mei realizes then that he hadn't been in the earlier circle that afternoon.

Thank you. Mei smiles slyly to herself, grateful for another granted wish. She chooses her chair carefully, wanting to sit and concentrate on the huge crystal rock centered on the plain altar. For a prayer room, the space is surprisingly devoid of religious symbols: just one white candle surrounded by natural objects from the animal and plant kingdom and sweetened with the sound of water flowing over the rocks in the fountain. To Mei, the room brims with spirit energy, and she quickly feels calm and present, while the others take time to shuffle around and find their seats. Soon they too become still.

*   *   *

Sam is leading the way for Evan's group as they withdraw into a sitting room located off the main entrance, a secluded spot that most have not discovered before. Earlier Thena had asked Sam to be the timekeeper, to guide direction gently if needed. Thena and Dylan had placed him in this third group, recognizing his capacity and previous experience in similar circles like this. *Such a cozy room for a small group—lined with built-in shelves, full of musty books and relics of the past life of the mission house. I wish I had more time to prepare; to set a fire in the old stone fireplace. I would have liked to do that for Evan,* Sam thought.

I'm a little afraid that, like at Quaker meeting, I might not be able to hear clearly, but I'll keep my eyes open and lip-read if necessary. Thankfully, Evan has a strong voice. Women's voices are much harder to decipher. I hope Leona and the other women speak up clearly. Oh dear, I do worry about my deficiency excessively. Enough already ... it's time to devote all my attention to Evan...

*   *   *

Raquel's group remains in the large meeting room. Awkward at first, the six stay seated, left there, scattered among the empty chairs. However, Dylan quietly and efficiently rearranges a smaller circle in a private alcove off the main room.

"Raquel, would you like this candle in the center, or something else to focus on?"

She stares at him, blankly, unable to trust herself to speak. Cognizant this might be a plea for help, Dylan smiles at her, hospitably extending his arms to invite her to find a seat in this unfamiliar territory of intimate, communal ground.

Seconds later, she blurts out, "I don't know why I ever signed up for this process. I'm incredibly tense. I'm horrified how uptight this waiting is making me feel. I don't know what's come over me. I am not usually like this at all. I really do need help." She gazes at each of the five silent bodies in her group.

It is a precarious moment for everyone. Each group member reverberates with the power of her words, thrown so forcefully into the circle. Each becomes

194

conscious of their impotence, aware there is nothing to say, not yet. Instead, each person responds with a wave of tenderness, silently embracing her, as if each apprehends without a shadow of doubt, how scared she feels. In that moment, Zach, Jean, Maria, and Michaela are thinking precisely how glad they are not to be sitting in the focus chair. Several stifle the urge to get up and hug Raquel, to comfort her, saying that she will be fine.

Dylan, now certain that his first instinct was correct—Raquel is at an emotional tipping-point—gives her another gentle smile and closes his eyes. He finds his own centerpoint, taking from her the social pressure of obligation, that need to react to him or to any one of them in the circle. He hopes that Raquel will recall that at lunch, he had offered the same suggestion.

"Closing your eyes when you speak might bring inner attention, instead of the forced need to comply with the external world."

Dylan understands the intensity of being in the microcosm of group focus; even when it is loving, attention can be remarkably disquieting to the shy soul.

When Raquel eventually composes herself, she keeps her eyes on the floor, and her words flow smoothly as the group settles in to listen.

CHAPTER NINETEEN
BIRTH

"Since coming back from Africa, I have been confused, "Raquel says bluntly.

"I need to know where to go from here? How to restore hope, how to heal myself? Should I start a new job in this country, or find a place to serve somewhere else in the world? Maybe even go back to Angola?"

As she listens to herself articulate these questions, Raquel realizes again why she has chosen to be in the center of this group. She glances at the others with a wry smile, "Well, at least this part is clear—at least I know what my core questions are."

She puts her head back down and waits silently before speaking again. "Before I left Africa, I knew how overwhelmed I was. After almost ten years of intense work in very stressful situations, I knew I had given everything I had. But I love being a medical doctor, I loved living in Angola; it's an extraordinary country, it was almost impossible to tear myself out of there as there was still so much good work to do. But I knew I had to rescue myself, before I turned to stone."

Slowing down to catch her breath, her words pull her inside to listen. "Now, after being home for a few months, getting over the busy-ness of the summer, my heart and body feel weighed down, as though I've come to the end of my own strength. This morning while jogging, all my body wanted to do was to lie down and release myself from needing to keep going. I literally lay down in the grass by the side of the road, collapsed, waiting for the longest time before I could find my way back to breakfast, to join you all.

"I have shut down, stopped. This retreat has brought me full face into the painful reasons why I returned from Angola. There, I couldn't go forward any longer, and now it's the same thing here."

Raquel sits mutely. She has said it all, wrapped up in one word. She has *stopped.*

She is grateful the group doesn't abandon her, but instead, remain silently attentive. Nobody moves a muscle, each person seemingly aware of stepping onto holy ground.

Finally, out of this place of stillness, Raquel finds more words and plows on, her voice rising in volume. "In the midst of my fatigue, I am angry at my own naiveté, at those early years of blind trust. Imagine! Walking into a battlefield and magically thinking I wouldn't get hurt. Believing I was a modern day Florence Nightingale or a saint like Joan of Arc, called to lead the people into freedom. I am mad that nobody stopped me, angry that everyone believed in my own ideal capacity, too.

"My family needs a flawless hero. They loved reveling in my accomplishments. We've been through a lot of crap in the past, lots of family drama, so they were more than ready to embrace me as the ideal heroine, so all of us could feel better about ourselves. I guess I needed to get away from those growing-up years. Medical school helped; during the unending days of training there was no time to feel anything about anything.

"What nobody knows, what I am only now starting to see, is how battle-scarred I am. The creeping lethargy of Africa has sunk into my bones. The harrowing needs of that place sucked me dry and left me unaware of my own frailty. I needed to be a success; to make this mission my own personal Mount Everest. Conquer, and then die. So few make it to the top and get off the mountain unscathed. I knew that in my head. Medical work in Angola is no picnic in the park, but I didn't realize how hard I pushed myself.

"When you do humanitarian work you never have the thrill of reaching the summit. There is always more to do. Africans have been fighting for their freedom; suffering through centuries of domination by tribalism, slavery, and colonialism. Now the lure of capitalism once again pulls the strong to ravage the weak. Even with the increasing devastation of climate change, oil and diamonds are now the enticement for further exploitation. Political power is ravaging the country, as it has done for years. Greed rules. Greed is sucking the life out of the earth and her precious native people … like my life felt … like it was being sucked away.

"After all my hard work, all the dogged exertion that a body could muster, after all that energy spent serving, helping, and saving, I am left exhausted. I'm swimming in cynicism, caught in a riptide of compassion fatigue. The worst of it is that no one even knows that I am drowning. Hardly even me—until today."

Raquel breaks down, letting loose a flood of tears. After blowing her nose a few times and looking around, she is shocked to see that there is barely a dry eye in the circle. Nobody is crying like her, but the silent tears of witness, glistening on faces full of compassion, almost break her heart again. Instead she laughs.

"Here, you guys need these, too. Sorry to have made you all cry." She passes around the tissue box. For a few seconds the group relaxes with her jest, until Dylan breaks the group silence.

"Raquel, do you have a story about Africa that touched you—some personal experience that you'll never forget?"

Raquel, transfixed by his question, perks up. "Yeah! I sure do have stories, lots of them; I hardly know where to begin. Many stories of noble people who inspire me to find hope in the midst of the battle.

"I remember the day a young couple emerged from the bush for a medical consultation. Run out of their village, like most during the war, they had been living in hiding for years. Nervously the husband spoke for his very pregnant wife. He explained that three years had passed, but her unborn child would not come. He marked the time with quiet assurance in the native calendar of the earth's seasons. The rainy season, the hot dry season, the drought—three years of an endless waiting. I listened to him with a heavy heart, aware that he told the truth; it really had been three full years of waiting for their child to be born.

"It was difficult to set them straight, to clinically diagnose the problem. This definitely was not a living baby, but most probably a uterine tumor. We decided to schedule surgery for the next day. How heart-rending to consider the agony of these dear people, the torture of waiting years for their baby to arrive. Medically, this would never happen in our country. I ... I will never, ever forget what happened the next day.

"After opening her up in surgery, I was shocked to discover—not a tumor, but a full-term baby boy. Deep inside this woman's body, a baby had been conceived, and strangely wandered out of its uterine nest into the peritoneal cavity. Remarkably, it had been fully supported with all the resources for physical life, until the time came to be born. But then there was no place to go. No passage for birth. No way out. The baby died and turned to stone.

Raquel pauses, then repeats, "Literally, stone. What I witnessed was a very rare medical condition: the woman's body, in a remarkable capacity for compromise, had slowly encased this child like a precious pearl in an oyster shell. The hardening process of the years calcified every fleshly feature and crystallized this little one into a priceless object of beauty. He had porcelain features, like fine china: round knees and ankles, even fingers and tiny toes, a nose and eyebrow striations. God, what a beautiful, mysterious tragedy—a stone baby. When I placed him wrapped in his umbilical cord, in the metal surgical bucket on the floor, the little one clanged like a rock."

The group barely suppresses their gasps of horror and awe, as if the story feels too impossible to be true, yet Raquel, immersed in the unraveling of her inner mystery, continues. "It's uncanny, but I just realized this … last night I dreamed about another baby ..."

She proceeds to recount her recent dream and the talk with Sam that morning, which had clarified that maybe she was the pregnant person, giving birth to a part of herself that had yet to be named. "Maybe I am discovering my feminine capacity to give birth, but not in my usual role as a helper. Instead, I'm confronted with the need to attend to myself—challenged to become midwife for my own soul and body, which I have mostly ignored these past years."

Raquel muses. "Maybe this unborn part of me, like

the stone baby, has been waiting all these years. Waiting for me to pay attention and give birth to her."

Michaela sits frozen in place. She can hardly believe it; astonished to hear Raquel's story that in a multitude of ways, sounds so much like her own. As a mother, she knows what it is to give birth, so can identify with the African woman and the horror of interminably waiting for something that would never happen. Deep inside she realizes this is happening for her, too. *This idea that the baby has turned to stone ... is this also my private fear? Wasn't it just yesterday that I realized a part of me was hard—like stone?*

She is reminded of Thena's picture of the little bird. *What can I do here? How can I hold Raquel right now? I mustn't let her go, drop her, by withdrawing into my private world of questions. Maybe there is a question I can ask that might help her. Stone ... I heard Raquel say that she "needed to rescue herself before a part of her turned to stone." This seems important.*

"Raquel, what part of you is afraid you are going to turn into stone?"

As Michaela utters each word of her question, she senses it rises from a place of being that she has rarely encountered in conversation.

Softly, Raquel says the first thing that pops into her mind. "Being a woman ... becoming a stone woman. I was afraid I was losing my femininity. It's not easy to be feminine out there in the bush. Work never stopped—for men and women the same. Even when we had precious time off, it took work to play and organize the fun. We used to joke that 'it takes a lot of work to have fun.'

"I remember looking around at the mission people and the long-term NGO workers, so many living their lives dedicated to serve God or some good cause, devoted people with hearts of gold, but so many were independent loners, really better able to live by themselves, without the confusion of intimate relationships. The missionaries seemed to have God to be close to, and the expats found pleasure in adventure and personal risk. Family life was incredibly hard to sustain in the long term, so, not surprisingly, most problems we struggled with were relational issues. There wasn't time to focus in a healthy way on our private intimate worlds, learning better how to get along with each other.

"I've always wanted to get married and have children, but I loved my work and it seemed like it needed to be either one or the other. I must have slowly given up on the idea of intimate relationships. I'm close to forty now and can't really imagine ever having a baby. All these baby dreams and stories have been haunting me, though. I can't get babies off my mind.

"Sophie, my step-sister who was the 'mother' in my dream last night, is such a girly girl; she used to drive me crazy when we were kids. It still takes her an hour to shower, do her hair and make-up. I can be ready in less than ten minutes. Being my sister is not the kind of woman I want to become."

Dylan stares in amazement at Raquel. *Is this a responding echo of my own inner dialogue with intimacy a few hours ago? Is this the answering call? Like drumbeats in the bush, my heart-cry evoking a response from her? Is it remotely possible?*
Magnetically drawn toward this woman, it is as if his smudged eyeglasses have been wiped clean by some unknown hand. He gazes at Raquel with a desire that moves beyond that of the care of a special group member. He perceives her in vivid color, in perfect size

and in both inner and outer form. *What a profoundly desirable woman. How did I miss her up until now?*

He blushes at the wave of ardor that overwhelms him, embarrassed at being snared by a fantasy that has derailed him out of the here and now of the circle. Chagrined, he pulls himself back, honoring the Clearness Circle moment, supporting Raquel in her process. Consciously, he abandons his startling revelation and focuses rigorously instead on the verbatim notes that he has been carefully scribing, and hopes that others will pick up the threads he has lost. Relieved, he hears Zach ask another helpful question.

"What kind of woman do you want to be, Raquel? Have there been women in your life that you'd aspire to follow?"

Gradually, Raquel responds to the question, clearly enjoying the opportunity to speak in detail of many women who had inspired her, finding different qualities in each of them. She speaks of her high school chemistry teacher, of Jane Goodall, even laughs about being Katherine Hepburn afloat on the African Queen. Thoughtful again, she links her fantasies of her idealized self, represented by Joan of Arc and Florence Nightingale, and then comes back to Sophie, her step-sister, and is able to admit, "I'm jealous of the way Sophie loves being a woman. She's uncomplicated that way. Not afraid of being sexy, or cute. She can be gorgeously elegant one moment and a crazy bitch the next. It surprises me how envious I am of her."

Maria has had her eyes closed for some time, her creative spirit captured by the essence of the birthing process. Maria has been imagining that she is floating in amniotic fluid, immersed in the flow of invigorating life that Raquel is bringing to her as a listener. It wasn't long before she also feels her own internal story kicking and stirring wildly in her gut, and becomes aware of the necessity to keep grounded in the human circle. She opens her eyes and mentally holds the umbilical cord of the real physical presence of each person in the room. If she lets go, she is certain she could be swept away by her own turmoil and cease to hold Raquel at the center.

Over her years on the stage, Maria had been learning the complex art of remaining mindful in her character while also remaining conscious of the outside players, seen and unseen. She could hold the other actors gently in the space around her, not overpowering them with her strong physical presence. She knew something of the marvel of the dance of intimacy that unfolds when defined bodies yield to communal movement; each one dancing in harmony with the spirit of the music. Thus she is mystified by her internal response to Raquel.

Why do I want to sing a lullaby to her? I can't get this idea out of my mind. I hear the music and feel my arms invisibly rock her, soothing her. I long to soften the toughness of words with musical fluidity ... water and wind ... refrains from ancient songs sung to babies in mothers' arms through the centuries. Surely this is not the time to sing, but I hear the notes so clearly. Maybe, maybe ... no ... this is my quiet role today, to be a creative midwife ... to honor Raquel's passage with soothing, gentle music. Not rushed, nor frantic—she has all the time in the world. This is comfortable music, ripe and overflowing with rest.

Ahh... My body is responding to Raquel—how can I put this into words—as an offering? I don't want this to be all about me, or demand any particular response. Maybe it doesn't matter whether I speak at all. Maybe I just need to stay singing this inner song, this lullaby.

Silently, Maria keeps rocking Raquel. They were

nearing the end of the session when she finally speaks simply.

"What was it like to lie down in the grass by the side of the road today, Raquel?"

Her question prompts more insight and more supportive energy that assists the creative passage of soul birth—for all of them in the circle, and especially for Raquel. The time is soon over. The long minutes have flown by unnoticed in that soulful space that knows no marked boundaries of time and place. Each person has explored below the surface of the visible world, entering into that inscrutable zone of memory, imagination, and psychic glue that ignites the empty spaces with fire. It has clearly been a very courageous journey to take together.

The group ends with a few minutes of mirroring, speaking back to Raquel some of her exact words they have written down, ones that seem important to note once more. Then each person offers a few sentences of affirmation to her: a personal blessing and a thank you for this bold work of faith that has touched them all, in so many diverse ways.

In turn, she thanks them, struggling to express the gift of their caring presence. She is once again beyond words, but this time she can hardly speak because of the awe that has lulled her into peace.

Quietly, the group files out of the room, each one lost in their own reverie. It is good to have time to be alone before dinner.

CHAPTER TWENTY
REVERIE

Deep in thought, after her Clearness Circle, Mei opens the back door of the meditation room and steps into the chilly, late afternoon air. The rainstorm, now all washed out except for steady dripping off the trees, has left a hazy shroud that is enveloping the garden. The pockets of warmth still trapped in the ground rise like ghosts and hang eerily in the cool air. Shivering, she slips on the thick coat of wet leaves plastering the slate walk, but manages just in time to catch herself from falling.

The sudden seasonal change, combined with the downhill grade of the walkway, makes it difficult to navigate back to her cottage. She spontaneously takes off her shoes and walks on the grass beside the path. As the tingling raindrops on spiky grass tickle her feet, she laughs and jumps with sudden freedom. She kicks at a pile of wet leaves and giggles as they stick to her legs.

This is a snapshot of my life—right now, in this moment. Nature so often speaks in synchronicity with my soul. This image, my dancing journey off the slippery path, this is a picture of my complex world of family, business, and spirituality. This is what I have been talking about for the past two hours. Up until now, it hasn't really come clear.

She had left the room feeling jumbled, after spilling out pieces of this and bits of that—an old grandmother's grab bag of stories unraveling like yarn. From deep within, she had dug out antique buttons, unhooked clasps, and tested the elastic connections of her human relationships. She's been surprised at how much inner material she had stuffed away, the silent accumulation of a bountiful lifetime. After the session, she'd felt askew, off-balance, still tripping on the cut-off fabric remnants of huge swaths of her life yet to be untangled.

How can I find clarity? How do I reassemble my life-pieces in some fresh, creative way? I feel all spilled out before these kind strangers. Do they realize they saw colors inside me never witnessed before? Emotions that had never escaped until now? I feel like the storm blew right through me, washing my inner world clean along with the outer one.

After losing my husband, my seasons have abruptly changed—like today's weather. Who could predict how profoundly I would be affected? I'm only sixty. But stepping onto this path of older life seems like going downhill, like this path. Not a steep decline, but it could herald the slippery slope down ... toward death. I want to be entirely present for the rest of my days, but to do that, I have to get off the old path.

Inspired, Mei looks over at the old slate pathway and feels the grass under her feet. *Yes! Unknown green expanses are spread out before me, right at my feet ... things I have not fully appreciated before. I am single, childless, and have a lot of money. I am fluent in three languages, my body is extraordinarily healthy, and I have a lifetime of real connections around the world. There is a lot to dance for—a lot of ground to cover in the years ahead!*

She gives the leaves another exuberant kick. *These wet, sodden leaves are beautiful, so colorful still, yet such a hazard to walk on. Even scattering them won't make them go away. What an uncanny picture of my family inheritance ...it holds such tension for me.*

Mei gazes at the aged oak tree before her. Its colossal presence looms over a back corner of the property, but the tree is evidently in the process of decay. Several freshly splintered limbs lie on the ground, knocked down by the wind that afternoon. *Over the years, my family wealth has flourished like this tree. For generations, my family inheritance has been carefully tended. I have lived in bounty and opulence all my life, but somehow change is coming. What shall I do with this aging wealth now? One part of me wants to joyfully and foolishly kick it all away, give it all away. Strangely, it represents a living trap, stuck to me. But wealth is not who I am. I am much more than that. Nevertheless, nothing will ever separate me from the reality of my birthright.*

What does this mean? How do I learn from this oak? Can I let all this business stuff "fall down" like the branches, like the leaves? Is there some seasonal, natural process evolving? Do I have to keep on killing my private self, attempting to secure the glory of all the leaves? She continues to meander thoughtfully, back and forth in circles around the tree, her chilled body barely aware of the need to get indoors.

And how does my spirituality find life in all this dying, this eternal cycle that I have been steeped in from birth? What does it mean to be a Chinese Christian woman? I am changing. How is this new season calling me? What is being composted, like leaves into new birth? Oh dear,

209

I still have too many unanswered questions, too many threads jumbled up in Grandmother God's knitting bag.

At her cottage now, she quickly pulls off her damp clothes and finds her favorite old flannel pajamas that at the last minute she had stuffed in her bag. Wrapping herself up in the wooly rug in the armchair, she peruses the stack of handwritten notes from the people in her group. *Over twenty pages of handwriting to decipher and digest all over again. Could it be that I said all of this?*

Hungry to revisit what her soul had spoken in the safety of the group, Mei completely forgets about dinner.

*   *   *

If Charles the cook had known that Mei had lost track of time, he would have promptly summoned her to his prepared feast. If Charles the priest had seen Mei at this moment, he would have doubly blessed her with prayers for spiritual sustenance.

In fact, Charles the human being is happily enjoying a second bottle of wine with his new friend George. They had done a lot of talking over the past hours, and Charles had managed to cajole a much-recovered George into helping him cook.

Charles is creating seafood fettuccine, one of his most popular dishes. It reminds him of his all-time favorite meal of the year—the traditional Feast of the Seven Fishes dinner on Christmas Eve. His grandmother would concoct an extravagant banquet beyond all imagination. No wonder he turned back to the kitchen for solace.

Charles hustles around the kitchen at full speed. Well prepared, the counter brims with bowls heaped with carefully chopped ingredients. He stirs and pokes under lids of huge pots, dropping in spices and seafood, while George carries to the dining room the artfully arranged fresh tomato and basil salads they had prepared together. Charles had splashed his finest olive oil and balsamic vinegar over the crumbly goat cheese and chives topping—yet another of his signature dishes. *I'm sad it might be the last of the heirloom tomatoes, but I want this special group to savor every last morsel of my garden bounty.*

As Charles dumps the fettuccine into a large pot of boiling water, steam clouds his glasses. He hops backwards, jostling George who is leaning over to take a quick swig of wine. The resulting mayhem would have been a disaster in any other kitchen, but Charles's delightful Buddha nature turns the calamity into merriment. Both men, now a little tipsy, not only from the wine but from the powerful movement of their souls that afternoon, laugh uproariously, eventually throwing at each other bits of basil and tomato. They stop, a hair's breadth from an all-out food fight.

Soon, as Charles had desired and planned, Saturday dinner becomes a joyous celebration, as if the balance of energy within the retreat center has swung, from the solemn and often painful journey of the soul into a wild and crazy dance of childlike play.

As each person passes through the door, one by one they throw off their hats and coats of heaviness, eager to be drawn inside to revel in the sensory feast set before them.

In a few minutes the place erupts with oohs and aahs of delight, crackles with bursts of laughter, and hums with the pleasant energy of deep and happy conversation.

CHAPTER TWENTY-ONE
CONVERSATIONS

Leona and Michaela sit down together, admiring each other's jewelry while digging into dinner with relish. Evan joins them rather tentatively; he isn't up for a lot of chit-chat after his afternoon marathon session, but he likes these two women and feels drawn to get to know them. He struggles awkwardly when Thena sits down across from him, momentarily feeling obliged to make serious conversation with the leader. But the meal proves to be so delectable, that for a while, the four of them can only chat about food.

Michaela reminisces, "Giant crab dinners were our family treat. I had a Baltimore uncle who owned a crab shack by the shore. As a kid, I loved being able to whack unabashedly at the crab legs with my wooden mallet, even though I didn't even like eating the crab. But the picture that sticks most in my mind is seeing ribbons of butter drizzle down my grandmom's usually pristine face. It felt like such a cheeky triumph to see the mess she was in."

Laughing, Leona recounts the story of a family reunion dinner in a Georgia park. "The men on one side of a picnic table stood up together to race for second helpings of barbecue, completely oblivious that they'd sent an entire row of generous-sized aunties, who were seated on the other side, toppling over backwards."

"This sounds like my dad's church potlucks," Evan said. "My father is Pastor Emeritus in the largest Baptist church in town and is forever wheedling me back to church. The main reason I accept the invitation is to savor the huge pot of seafood gumbo that dear Adele Brown always prepares for special events. I can't remember a time when she wasn't there. As a teenager, she always recruited me to help carry in the prize covered-dish."

Thena joins in, "This conversation gives me flashbacks to my dad's favorite stories from his East Coast relatives, who worked on the lobster boats—how as a little city boy he was shocked by the sight of his first lobster, glaring at him from his plate." Tenderly, she concludes, "Then I remember how he would make a crazy googly face, snapping his hands like claws, and turn dinnertime into a game to catch and tickle me."

Leona sighs. "You saying that, Thena, makes me realize how much I miss not having the kids around anymore. It seems that much of our family culture disappeared when they left for college. We don't sit around the table together as much.

"Do you think this is a built-in part of our black family tradition? Maybe my husband's European one, too. But somehow, us black folks really know how to enjoy our food and one another, all mixed together. I get the sense sometimes that white families don't understand it the same way we do—how food and family really belong together."

Michaela responds quickly in agreement, telling

more of her unique family stories that hinge around the kitchen table. It hasn't occurred to Thena until then that out of all the other group members, the four of them shared their common ancestry. For whatever reasons, they have found each other this evening. The conversation turns a corner into deeper, more complicated differences around the issue of race and culture.

Leona is especially vocal. "It's only recently I realized how incredibly important my African-American heritage is for me." She confides how she had needed to "forget" a lot of that in her suburban upbringing.

"I realize now that it made it even worse when I married cross-culturally, because as the woman, I naturally felt like I was the one who needed to adjust and become more of the chameleon in the family. I still don't think that Gerritt gets it. Rarely, I have been able to show myself as a woman with real color. I guess I'm just starting to freely talk about it, so I can't only blame him."

Evan drops out, quite unable to engage this weighty topic. Instead he reaches for dessert: a luscious slice of fruit flan and a bowl of a white frothy substance. Assuming it is whipped cream, he ladles two large dollops on his cake.

Charles, standing at the edge of the room stares dumbfounded for a second, and then with the agility of a dancer, weaves around the seated guests and whisks away Evan's dessert just as his fork is descending for the first mouthful. Evan opens his mouth to remonstrate, but Charles with a flourish produces another clean piece of flan and whispers in his ear, "I didn't think you really wanted tartar sauce on your fruit flan!"

As Charles, saunters back into the kitchen, Evan attempts to explain what just happened. "I guess I'm still reeling from the emotional pressure of the last two hours. Sorry, Leona, what was it you were saying?"

Thena wipes her mouth with her napkin. "Leona, I really appreciate what you said, I know this is a really important topic—for me, too. But I need to go and get organized for this evening. I'm so sorry, please excuse me."

*   *   *

A burst of laughter erupts from a table of four in the opposite corner. Vanessa and Maria hold their sides, doubled up. George laughs too, although more reservedly. Sam is grinning from ear to ear.

Their hilarity comes from a conversation about women and their relationships, also triggered by their enjoyment of Charles's dinner. Maria had gushed to Vanessa, "To have someone in the house who could cook like this would be heavenly." Chatting, they discovered they both were good cooks, and in their households, each of them managed the kitchen.

"I told my husband that in my next life, I am going to marry a chef," says Vanessa. "Being cared for like this daily would be marvelous; but in reality, it's very relaxing to come home after a long day at work and slow down by cooking a great meal. We probably would end up fighting over what to make and who gets to cook."

"I'm the same way, Vanessa," says Maria. "When I'm home, I take over the kitchen, there's no room for my partner to even consider learning how to cook. She's simply useless in the kitchen."

"So we both foster our partners' helplessness by looking after them so much?"

Maria shrugs. "I guess that's one way of saying it. Sounds a little harsh, because I enjoy nurturing and caring for people. Providing food seems a great way to

216

do that. When I'm home, that's part of the way I feel good."

"So how do we find balance in our care-giving?" Vanessa looks at the two men sitting with them, "So, what do you guys think?"

George is happily spacing out, though keeping one ear on their conversation, hoping to glean some useful information about how women think. But Sam lights up with a previously unseen, daredevil enthusiasm. "I think it's inbred in women. The more they work, the more we men enjoy sitting around as couch potatoes, benefiting from it. A marvelous cycle! It reminds me of my college work in a laboratory one summer. Did you know that research institutes breed special fat rats for insulin experiments? I worked one summer weighing and measuring these gargantuan creatures that could hardly move, they were so genetically inbred. They were almost as wide as they were long."

The women snicker incredulously at his outlandish response—Sam is definitely an enigma to them—but then he tops it off by saying, "Actually, I wish I were a fat rat. I'm the domestic one in my home, too."

*   *   *

Thena has left the room without dessert, but is ruminating on what has just transpired.

I wish I could have stayed with that conversation Leona started, because to lead a retreat is to be present in communal dialogue with diverse people while inspiring each person to communicate more authentically from within themselves. This is a workable balance but it constantly shifts, weaving a series of conversations from the inside-out to the outside in. So now, I have to ask myself, as Leona did, "How truly unique is my African-American heritage and, in my case, my Jewish

217

background?" This is a significant question about important things that often aren't talked about. We politely ignore these topics, like racial or class issues in most social settings. How do I facilitate this deep dialogue? I know something new is percolating inside me...

She wanders into the little sitting room. *I need some quiet, to settle and think about how to follow the Clearness Circle gatherings. Dinner has been unusual, such a free spirit in the air, but now it's important to circle back. I've found in my experience that good conversation allows people to learn about each other while also relate more deeply to their own experiences. Everyone needs an opportunity, if desired, to put into words what they experienced this afternoon.*

The walls around her have been witness to centuries of conversations: silent inner conversation of the monastic seeker, multitudes of profound and boring oratories, secret confessions, and legions of public prayers of the faithful. As she muses, her eyes fall on a wall hanging. It is a faded copy of an elaborate ancient parchment. The typed note below describes it as a portion of the Rule of St. Benedict.

The illuminated text highlights the three vows of the Order: *Stability, obedience,* and the compelling term '*Conversatio morum.*' The words stand out, embellished with decorative spirals of Celtic knots and colorful floral motifs. Curiously, Thena finds herself drawn to it.

During these retreats, as in her everyday work, she is learning to trust a sixth sense. She knows that myriad conversations have already begun—many silent and invisibly waiting for engagement through creative human endeavor. The discourse is often not in words, so in some ethereal way it becomes important to slow down time, to pay attention through the far reaches of her senses: soft eyes, inner ears, and a finely tuned imagination guide these conversations, offering a new kind of energy to those present.

Thena thinks of it as *highlighting the unseen, discovering an invisible magic marker for soul talk.* How often has she heard someone say, "I was just thinking that," or "I was going to say that exact same thing"? *Energy blows where it wants to go, and yet I, as the leader, often provide a container, a shape to hold the flow of conversation.*

She mulls over these ideas, studying the parchment. *How can I embellish what has already transpired today? It's been such an intense day; surely I don't want to coerce anyone into more activity. Maybe it might be best to take the evening off—for light-hearted fun and private space. Ha! I wonder what the monks would say to that?*

Thena stares at the Latin words: *Conversatio morum.* What is this vow all about? *Conversatio—sounds like a conversation. Morum—sounds like dead. Hmm ... is there any link here? Maybe I should go and ask Charles, he was just talking about his vows earlier today.*

She laughs at her compulsory need for help ... and again from Charles, *as if all of life's answers can be found in the kitchen, or by dusting off the wisdom of ancient religion. As if I don't have all that I need, inside of me, right now in this moment.*

CHAPTER TWENTY-TWO
GROUP CONVERSATION

Thena knits her brows. *Luring the group from the seduction of the dining room will be no easy task this evening. Mei is the only one here. Evidently she has not been at dinner. But, better not to remark on this. I feel rather tender toward her after being in her Clearness Circle. That relationship feels quite private, almost the way two new lovers look at each other in the shy light of morning.*

Dylan ambles into the room with the air of a contented goose.

On the spur of the moment, Thena suggests, "Dylan, you have your djembe here, right? We need to gather the group. Can you play us into this next session? Drumbeats are so universally appealing. After the afternoon sessions, I get the sense we are looking for a rhythm of 'call and answer.' Don't you think the drum captures that conversational flow? It's an important mood shift for the group. Do you get what I am trying to say?"

"Of course, it's a great idea, Thena. You know how

music is my language. All day I have been experiencing the changes in the group as rhythm and flow, so it will be fun to discover the beat for right now. I felt like I wanted to dance in the dining room earlier on; there is something about Charles, the way he spontaneously brings joy to the other side of solemnity."

He grabs his drum and starts to beat out what his heart has been feeling. The rhythm comes naturally, so much more easily than words, as if his body had already silently recorded this hidden pulse of music and was bursting to be heard. He closes his eyes, allowing his hands and heart instinctively to carry him through this musical transition.

This is exactly what I had envisioned, thinks Thena, watching as the drum calls emphatically, and the group responds with their unqualified attention. Mesmerized, drawn into the circle of chairs, bodies undulate until they eventually sit down. Gradually the pulse intensifies to a more complex but less frenetic vibration; the polyphonic native rhythm soothes their heartbeats, softens breathing, and pulls each group member inside. Despite the throb of the drum, the air grows peaceful. Five minutes later every chair is filled, the circle complete. The last beat fades and the circle is left sitting in profound silence.

Thena waits for a long time before she speaks. *What more can I say? Words are almost unnecessary. What a reminder that spirit conversations are always in process, but much of the time are hidden, too deep to be heard. This afternoon's conversations have been retrieved and amplified by the drum.*

"Before we close this evening, after this long day, it's important to have a time of feedback about our Clearness Circles. I'm aware that there's no easy way to describe your varying experiences this afternoon, but I encourage you as you settle into the stillness here to remember how your inner teacher has spoken. I was just thinking about what I learned today in the conversation I was honored to be a part of. Clearness Circles are powerful experiences for everybody. We are transformed by the power of deep listening. Each time, I am consistently changed by these small circles of truth.

"Would the focus people like to talk about their experience first? Feel free to speak whatever you sense is appropriate and helpful to say here. As always, this is by invitation only. After that, the rest of us can share our personal reflections. And a reminder again, we really must honor the promise of complete confidentiality. It's important not to talk about any experience other than your own perspective. Let's first give the focus people a chance to speak."

*   *   *

Raquel is ready to dance into the circle. Not literally, although anybody looking closely a few minutes earlier would have seen the electricity as she came charging into the room following the throbbing drum. She could not have been more thrilled. Still overflowing with the energy from her recent meeting and now entranced by the heartbeat of Africa, she speaks.

"Dylan, thank you for your playing. It's an incredible gift, straight from the heart of Africa, just for me." She smiles warmly at him, then goes on.

"The time in our circle was like nothing I have ever experienced. Initially, I found myself frightfully scared, but the warmth of my group made all the difference. I could never have entered so profoundly into my inner world without their gracious receptivity. I felt tightly held—not that I couldn't get away, but they supported me, gave me strength to keep on and not run from myself as I have been doing for so many years.

"I was surprised by the breadth of what I processed, sorting through difficult feelings from years back, as well as getting clarity from a dream I had last night. It made me realize how much of my life goes unsaid. I'm a doer, someone who keeps moving and gets the job done, often to my own detriment. This is probably the first time I have sat down long enough to pay close attention to parts of myself that had gone unnoticed for years. It felt a little like gentle soul-plumbing—unstopping the plug. And the plug has been building for years.

"I have a lot more figuring out to do before I get the answers I need, but I have confidence in going forward without so much fear. Today brought me assurance that I can continue this search, with joy. It doesn't have to be like pulling molars. The drum music is an inspiration. It takes me back to my African village where I would love to go to sleep at night listening to the drums on the other side of the river. I'll carry that sound inside as I go back to sort out my future. Thank you all for helping me today."

Mei speaks next. "I came from my circle feeling like my grandmother's sewing bag. Spilling out fragments of my life in such a helter-skelter way is not my usual style," she points out with a wry grin. "I usually attempt to know what I am going to say before I say it. I like to have everything planned and organized, but this was an exercise in trusting myself not to get lost in the world of mess and disorder. I realize that, like my grandmother's bag, everything that spills out has a purpose and can be used again. Recycled. My life will come back together again—especially after the death of my husband last year—" She hesitates, surprised by the amount of feeling welling up.

"It was only after we ended that some things came

clear. I even forgot about dinner tonight because I got lost reading the notes I received from my group. Thank you for your quiet and wise attention. I never thought it possible to engage in a private soul search and be accompanied by others in such a safe manner. I am forever grateful for this process and for you, my circle of gentle people. Your questions were insightful, too. You have helped me believe that my soul will lead me through the decisions necessary this season. I had forgotten how communal support can be so meaningful."

Unlike Mei, Evan was not normally one who missed the opportunity to speak in public. Caught off-guard by the intensity of his time in the Clearness Circle, he is still reorienting himself and finds it difficult to open his mouth.

"I don't know what to say right now—and yes, as the son of a preacher, I know you will be surprised that I could be so tongue-tied. I'm still overwhelmed, in a complicated, good sort of way. My wife, who has a French heritage, taught me the word *bouleversé*—completely turned upside-down. I didn't realize how much I had lost my bearings until at dinner I absent-mindedly put tartar sauce on my fruit flan. I thought it was whipping cream."

The group hoots with laughter as he continues. "So I'm still sorting everything out and probably will be for a long time. I get the sense this has been a life-changing experience, but I have no idea what that means just yet. Check in with me a few months from now and I'll hopefully be able to say more."

The group keeps chuckling over this dinnertime incident, enjoying the lighthearted awareness that comes from such a compelling image of their muddled humanity. For everybody the colorful picture is a snippet of his or her own jumbled emotion.

Then, from out of nowhere, George clears his throat conspicuously, and as he speaks, every eye rivets on him. Thena, sitting beside him, feels their relief and curiosity. *I'm sure each of them has been wondering silently, like me, what is going on for him. How good no one interfered, but has given him the necessary time and space to find his way. Now, evidently something has happened. With each sentence he's growing more confident.*

"I …I …was not an official focus person, but oddly enough I…I…had an unplanned Clearance Circle this afternoon." George recounts his story, telling them a shorthand version of what had transpired before his arrival in the kitchen with Charles. "Everything exploded out of me—hook, line, and sinker. I have never been so upset, and was literally planning to leave the retreat. I'm not a Catholic, but I think I learned the value of a confessional, even though Charles isn't like any priest I've ever met. He stayed with me, listening attentively, pouring us wine while I talked and he prepared dinner. It felt like being in my local bar, but this caring bartender kept asking me questions, helping me unpack some of the most difficult issues in my life. What a mess I am …" George almost stops, but bravely pushes on.

"One of my biggest problems that I've not told anybody, until today, is that my business is in serious trouble. I probably should declare bankruptcy. I've been in complete denial of this: even my wife has no idea how desperately off we are. I keep careening ahead, blindly hoping something will change. Well, today it changed for me, just being able to face this reality."

*   *   *

Watching George makes Dylan uneasy. He glances

226

at Thena, wondering how she might intervene. In slow motion, George's speech staggers to a full stop. He appears for a moment to buckle and collapse, teetering forward, almost falling out of his chair under an invisible weight on his overburdened back. Dylan tenses, about to spring over to catch him, but in this moment, the power of the group seems to kindle as the group soul amalgamates as one.

Together, they forge a hidden elasticity. With this communal resilience, they catch the fearful, exhausted energy from George, and convert it back to him in a gift of grace. It feels like the uncovering of alchemical strength, reminding Dylan of a lacrosse game—one of those enervating moments when a line of athletes race forward, passing the ball back and forth, energy multiplying exponentially as they spring forward down the field, together.

The group sits, conveying through their quiet inspiration a confidence that holds George upright. It restores his strength to press on toward his goal—whatever that is to be. In the silence, George no longer feels alone.

Dylan speaks aloud for everyone in the room. "Thank you for sharing, George. We honor the courage it takes for you to speak today. We'll continue to hold you in our hearts these next hours as you prepare to go forward into whatever the future holds for you."

Then, turning his attention back to the group, Dylan asks, "How about the rest of you? How was it for you this afternoon?"

Leona promptly blurts out, "It takes a lot of guts for someone to be a focus person. I get the idea now how momentous it would be to make that decision. I realize that I envy those who found the courage to do so."

"Humbling ... awesome ... unnerving ... holy ...

227

energizing ... exhausting ..." One by one different members of the group share their experience.

Gerritt, who had sat with Mei, says how surprised he is with how simple this process was. "I went in rather anxiously, anticipating having to come up with good questions, but after a while, my anxiety filtered away. I could just be there, fully present and listening, not having to help or do anything. I didn't need to be a scientist, a healer, or anything else. I could just be me. I hope I can learn to relax and not work so hard; believing that eventually out of all my confusion, clarity will come."

Sam follows him, agreeing. "The more I trusted the Inner Teacher to be present and available in another, I could relax. I realized that if I couldn't physically hear everything that was said, then so what? I can let go of the need to have to control the world through what I hear or don't hear. I learned to begin to listen to a new inner voice inside myself, one that is not dependent on my ears to be heard. I sensed another dimension of inner hearing that I want to continue to ferret out. I found I could trust that the other group members would find questions to ask—it was not all up to me. I am realizing how much I have felt that everything 'all depended on me.' I had no idea how much stress this was causing."

"The same with me: being in the small group today helped me learn to trust," Michaela says. "I have also been somebody who thought that I was left to figure out the world by myself. How awesome to see the capacity of a soul to bare herself without shame or fear. What a remarkable gift we humans have deep within us, able to give unconditional love to one another. I witnessed the power of a small community to encourage someone back to the wisdom of their innermost self. I saw no shaming, or blaming, or fixing.

"I shouldn't be surprised by this, but I am. In teaching, I spend tons of time building a classroom environment that is safe and trustworthy. I try hard not to teach toward standardized tests because if a classroom of children lean into one another and become a fully functioning, caring group, then, everyone benefits—even test scores eventually. The problem is we are culturally taught to go it alone, to find a club or a gang that will protect us from each other. Each individual builds a wall of fear. Today I became aware that I must seek out this kind of safe group experience for my own soul growth. I offer this to my kids constantly, but I have ignored or repressed my own need for community. I need to find more safe spaces in my life."

Zach ends the group tonight. "I'm exhausted—I can't remember a day when I have felt so emotionally and physically wiped out. If this is what happens around all you guys, then I am going to grow old really fast!" Exhibiting his instinctive gift, he brings everyone to laughter.

Thena closes the circle, aware that Zach has spoken the truth, his joke partially true—definitely too much sitting still for one day. "We each need time to decompress, to relax as you choose. Charles has left a tray of extra desserts. I'm taking one to my room and will relish eating it in bed. That's one of the treats I give myself on these weekends—eating dessert in bed, by myself, at the end of a long day. If anyone wishes for popcorn, there's lots here, too. Feel free to build up the fire with more firewood if you wish to hang around.

"Have a good night everyone. See you all in the morning."

CHAPTER TWENTY-THREE
NIGHT CONVERSATION

Maria lies in the dark, tossing on the single bed. Finally she picks up her phone and presses 1 on the speed dial.

"Hi there, me again. I just had to talk with you. I can't sleep; the beds must have been built for midget monks from the past century. But most of all, I have too much going on in my head. You always calm me down."

"Hi sweetheart, I'm glad to speak to you, I can't sleep, either. How's the rest of your day been?"

"I wish you could have been with me this afternoon so you could know the power of Clearness Circles. Such an old-fashioned name for something so extraordinarily progressive. God, we need more of this kind of thing in our world."

"What are they like?"

"How can I possibly describe what happened? I think for now, all I can say is that it made me aware of many things that I need to get clear about— for me. So much to sort out. But first, how about you? I haven't even asked how you are? ... ... Grace, are you there?

231

How are you?"

"Not good."

"Oh, no … really? I am so sorry … what did the doctor say?"

"Let's talk about it tomorrow."

"No, please tell me now. I won't wait until then, I can't bear not to know."

"It's bad news, but we both probably already knew that."

"Like, how bad?"

"Like, probably I have less than a year."

"Oh, Grace, this is the worst news ever. I guess we did both know, but to hear it so clearly from the doctor … it's really awful that I'm not there with you right now. Everything's all messed up and backwards. You're not supposed to get that news when I'm not with you."

"Really Maria, believe me. I am okay. There is absolutely nothing more we can do tonight, or tomorrow. You'll be back soon and we can find our way from here. We still have each other … Maria … are *you* there?"

"Yes, I'm here … too choked up … can't talk, sorry. This is devastating … for you … for me. Thankfully, I'll be home tomorrow, I'll leave first thing in the morning. You are more important than anything else."

"No, I think it's important that you stay until the retreat ends. Promise me you'll do that for me if for nobody else. Besides, I still really want to hear what you learned about you."

"No, I can't say more. Your news is the most important thing for us to share right now. Nothing else counts. Oh, Grace, this is way too hard…"

"We'll be fine, now get some sleep and I'll see you tomorrow. Goodnight my love."

"Grace, don't go just yet. I just thought of something that might help us both. This afternoon at the end of the small group, all I could think of was a lullaby—a beautiful Brahms piece that I adore. It felt like my heart song for this woman in my group. My body wanted to rock her, to soothe her. I wanted to offer her my arms to rest in, to hold her tight and tell her that everything is going to be all right. You know, like that lovely quote from Julian of Norwich that we have hanging in the hall? 'All shall be well, yes all shall be well, all manner of things will be well.'"

"Yes, I love that quote, I was looking at it today." Grace sniffs.

Maria chokes back the tears, "I'm about to cry myself to sleep but I'll think of you doing the same thing, and we can be together. So tonight, maybe that's what our souls need, to be rocked and soothed as we sleep. Rest in my arms and in the tender arms of all goodness and love. Bye…"

"I love you. Good night, Maria."

*   *   *

On the other side of the wall, Gerritt lies in the dark hearing the muffled voice and then the sounds of a woman sobbing. Tonight it is his turn to be wide awake. He's wondering where Leona had disappeared to at the close of the session. She'd strode out of the room with a purposeful air about her. He hadn't talked to her since early afternoon, when they went their separate ways after lunch.

Seems each of us needed solitude. But then, she deliberately chose not to sit with me at dinner. Today, I wish I had come alone to this retreat. It's too confusing attempting to heal both a long-term marriage relationship and long-term anorexia of the soul, I think our marriage has been dying of starvation: famished for more of the powerful moments this day has brought to each of us as individuals.

I really was hoping to be with Leona tonight. Just to be able to talk. It's dawning on me how dependent I am on her for much of my emotional nourishment. I really feel her absence tonight. I long for her here beside me. I hope ... oh ... why am I so afraid I can't make it without her?

*　　*　　*

Leona had found her way back to the sitting room where she had sat that afternoon with Evan. Unconscious of what propels her back to this space; it makes sense for her body to return to the same wingback chair. She stares silently into the night shadows of the garden.

What a relief to find refuge. This intense day has left me quite unbalanced, over-stimulated, but I don't want to move a muscle. Even yoga wouldn't help right now. Just wait ... be quiet. She observes her inner energy patterns; imagines them doing cartwheels, ricocheting around her, exploding through the glass and falling in jumbled heaps onto the earth, which quickly absorbs them.

Sitting with the lotus flower, lying on the floor with my Möbius strip, the discomfiting walk and talk with Gerritt, those intense hours with Evan and all his stuff, the dinner conversation that brought up so much about family. ... In time, the images slow their pace, her body still pulsating with uneven waves, like the force of many streams colliding.

Maybe I can put what I am feeling into words—but action and sports are my thing. Gerritt is the academic in the family; I'm clumsy with words. Or, maybe I'll run through my yoga routine again. It was so helpful this morning Yoga is my language of communication beyond words. But I have to unscramble. Can I let my

234

life speak in a new way?

She finds a pen on the shelf and urgently fills up pages from one of the lined notepads left over from the Clearness Circle. She scribbles and scratches at the paper, ripping off page after page, tearing some up in frustration, while others she balls into a wad and throws at the window. A litter pile grows at her feet until eventually, her energy less frenzied, she begins to read aloud, needing to hear herself think.

> *People fail miserably. They mess up horribly.*
> *They leave inevitably.*
> *People are disappointing, unpredictable,*
> *and frustrating.*
> *I wish it were not so. I am that way too.*
>
> *I continue to hope that things will be different*
> *That today I will know the answer and tomorrow*
> *we will find love and yesterday's hopes will not be*
> *dashed again.*
> *It hurts to have faith, to believe, to wish for basic*
> *miracles. It is easier to doubt, to be a cynic.*
>
> *Is there no dream for tomorrow, no promise for*
> *the future?*
> *I give up. I lose. I opt out of this game of chance.*
> *I don't want to play with him on my team anymore*
> *because he is so unpredictable.*
> *I am tempted to entirely give up, roll over and*
> *admit defeat.*
> *The hell with my positive thinking that things*
> *might change.*
>
> *One more time my heart grows sick.*
> *Like a transient tenant of life that pays for my rent*

of joy one day at a time,
I stick my rental quarter in the slot and hear the
wheels of fortune turn.
Will the arrow land on joy instead of anger and
helplessness?
I don't want to roll those dice again.
There must be a better way to live.

She stares at the paper in front of her, shocked, hardly believing the sound of her own voice. *What a contrast to my recent positive and upbeat attitude. Is this what's lying below the surface of my mind? Where has this come from? Why did I come back to this room to write this crap?*

Was I feeling like this when I was listening to Evan? All this frustration stuffed down inside me while listening to him sort out his life? Did I need to re-enter this room to recover my lost feelings of this afternoon?

It came clearer then, that for the most part she had been able to listen with care and pay close attention to Evan. For most of the time, she had stayed open, holding him as gently as she could, thinking of the image of the bird they had talked about … *even though he didn't seem in the slightest bit like a helpless little bird. I found it hard not to judge this vigorous, forceful guy. Some of the things he said, especially about his wife, made me mad. Actually, I remember thinking of him as a great big jerk, tempted to wring this big bird's neck, and then feeling completely guilty about it. Burying those thoughts and going back to being the more gracious, loving Leona. Crap, I completely forgot about that entire transition, that whole sequence of thoughts and feelings. I was awfully angry and cruel for a while.*

Leona sits quietly, remembering the reminder from Dylan—the touchstone that spoke about "being curious

236

when negative feelings come up when we are with other members of the group."

Is this really about Evan? Did some of what Evan said somehow scratch away at my raw heart and expose some deep meanness and outrage—maybe toward Gerritt?

She mulls it over, rereading her words several times. *Interesting how the power has gone out of them, kind of like hot air released from a balloon. They are only words, and now that they are out in the open, on paper, they don't have as much power over me. I don't feel half as uptight as before. Almost airy, like things have settled down inside of me. Maybe I've come back to stand on solid earth—like in my yoga routine this morning*

It is now that Leona realizes her exhaustion, and after cleaning up the mess around her, she tiptoes down the hall. Grateful to hear snores, she opens the door to her room.

*   *   *

Similar to the night before, Zach was the last person left in the meeting room. He messed around with the art supplies; a large box of colorful pens inspiring him to play with some of the images of the day. His mind reeled with lotus and Möbius Strips, and then with impressions from the circle with Raquel: foreign images of birth, babies, and vibrant fantasies about African life. He wanted to fill the papers before him with these intense representations of the day, but it was mostly Raquel's African stories that shadowed him.

As a teenager, he had been intrigued with stories from those who had traveled abroad on church mission trips. He had almost gone to South Africa as a senior in high school, but a crisis with his grandmother necessitated his staying home, caring instead for his own family that summer. His mom and dad had left his siblings and the household pretty much to him to look after, so his dreams of going to Africa quickly faded— up until today.

At this point in his life, he has lost the missionary zeal of being the one who arrives with all the answers; in fact, he now feels much more painfully aware of having so little to offer. Still, today Raquel has stirred a fresh longing in him to serve the world. He recognizes how he has grown insular, without even knowing it. As much as he loves working with adolescents, he yearns to move out of the boundaries of his American culture, to explore outside the box of his experience and take in the wealth of the globe.

If I am going to continue my education, to teach or serve in any way, I have to explore and find more diversity in my life. Maybe that's the primary thing this retreat has taught me—to welcome diversity, complexity, into every pore of my being. I wonder what this might look like? What possibilities are there for me?

I've never thought of myself as a rigid person, but this weekend is helping me see beyond the straight-jacket of my family and culture. Maybe I can find a job in Africa somewhere? What could I do there?

For more than an hour, he has sat at the table and swirled colors without trying to make any sense of what he is doing. It feels good to let out his energy onto the paper, creating a plethora of colors and shapes, without having to figure it all out in advance

Then it comes back to him—Raquel's dream. He loves the idea about a part of her that is still being born. This makes so much sense; it is as if he had been the dreamer.

I wonder how that works. Can someone else's dream be for me too? Is there such a thing as a group dream

238

that can energize different members?

Crazy ideas—but as a male I've never before been able to personalize the powerful image of birth. That's always been the domain of women. But, this is exactly what I feel—birth pangs. I felt them last night here in this room, a kind of conception or even labor; some part of me being re-born. Could I also say that I am pregnant? What a wild metaphor.

His drawing begins to take new shape: the contours of a female body, a womb, and a well of bright color spill onto the paper.

Zach is glowing with pleasure as he lights the candle, turns off the lamps, and lies down on the floor.

*   *   *

Thena zips up her robe, turns the handle of her door, and quietly pads toward the meeting room. She is focused on one thing—checking for fire.

Sometimes this happens. Even at home, she would be lying in bed trying to sleep, and the compulsion arises, so she just has to get up and inspect the place: check for candles burning, fireplaces unattended, stove left on. She knows it doesn't make sense, everything is undoubtedly fine, but she has to do it or else she cannot fall asleep. Thena is also aware that it's all because of the fire many years ago; as a young girl, their communal farmhouse had burned down. Some crazed hippie had set it on fire. After that, Thena's mom became completely unhinged by numerous compulsive rituals. Inevitably, Thena caught her anxiety.

I know this fear is clearly a sign of stress—probably the flashing signal after an especially complex work day, the result of my hyper-active brain that can't shut down. Neither does it help that earlier in the day I was looking at some gruesome pictures of the fire-torn ruins of the old school next door... anyway, it's always slightly embarrassing, but I know it doesn't help to ignore it. Besides, I'm nothing like my mother. She really did have her problems ...

She slips into the meeting room, gratefully noticing the lights are out and the fireplace is not burning any more, and then with a shock notices that a candle *is* burning: The centerpiece candle has been left on. Swiftly, she pushes aside a chair and almost falls on top of Zach, who lies sprawled out on the floor, the candle burning on the small table above his head.

"Good God, Zach! You terrified me!"

Zach springs up onto his bare feet. His shirt is unbuttoned, and as he hitches up his pants to keep them from falling down, he stares out from under his unruly mat of hair, muttering at her. "Well, needless to say I thought you were some demented ghost of the monastery. Believe me; I'm more frightened than you."

They share a forced laugh, then Thena apologizes, "Sorry to have disturbed you, but were you actually intending on sleeping here in the meeting room? Isn't your bed more comfortable?"

"Yeah, I'll go there now, but I needed down-time here first before going to sleep."

Zach picks up his papers and blows out the candle, leaving them both to grope their way through the darkness, stumbling down the dimly lit hall, and finally back to the familiar comfort of their rooms.

SUNDAY

CHAPTER TWENTY-FIVE
EARLY MORNING

We watch as everyone at the Terra Center sleeps in on Sunday morning—even the weekend breakfast cook completely forgot her shift. Maybe it is the weather change; maybe it is some lurking spirit of sloth; or maybe everyone simply needs rest.

Even Vanessa sleeps. She rolls over at six o'clock, but is luxuriating in such a lovely dream that she curls up again under the covers, to recover it in the pleasant warmth. Her anxiety, which had faithfully woken her at the crack of dawn for the past five years, somehow knows better than to disturb these moments of repose.

Surprising too, Leona had migrated in bed during the night, unconsciously searching for warmth from the man she'd married thirty years ago. Gerritt wakes up reveling in this unaccustomed closeness. Thinking she must be awake he murmurs something amorous in her ear, but she remains heedless to the visible world. He slips back into a contented sleep, praying this might be a sign of her return.

After her outpouring of grief, Maria was left hugging her pillow, wrung out and empty of everything but the need to let go. She hadn't moved a muscle during the night, so when she does wake up, she thinks her body might remain stuck in fetal position—not a familiar place for Maria, but one that today she finds remarkably comforting. We note she has not an iota of desire to get out of bed this morning.

Not surprisingly, Mei spent the night in China, transported there by the ancestors; an army of them conspiring to channel her back to her aboriginal beginnings. Her dreams brimmed with sights, smells, and sounds of ancient dynasties; rich dreams, filled with memories of her people. She heard her grandmother's voice offering her soup made of boiled lotus tubers, and as she drank, Mei felt the nourishment of the fleshy roots infiltrate every crevice and pore; the sustenance of family percolating within her soul. As she wakes, she is still speaking Mandarin, but also, from the far side of her brain, able to distinguish the fading whispers of the hill country dialect. *How remarkable. I haven't heard that spoken since early childhood.*

Mei knows then, in the rawness of the morning, that she is melded with China—entwined like an ancient wisteria vine grown for a century on a rusted iron trellis. Nothing could ever separate her from her people. She apprehends this with acute clarity. "I am them. They are me," she whispers.

In response, the frogs in the pond croak emphatically. A flock of mourning doves whir to and fro across the property cooing and calling. Elm beetles in the dusty corner under Mei's bed roll over on their backs and shake their legs in hysteria. The curtains on the windows in her cottage gently billow back and forth. Mei's ancestors are celebrating their victory, their phantom hands clap exuberantly. For a few moments, everything rejoices.

George is the last one out of bed. He doesn't move until he hears the breakfast gong at 8:15. Breakfast had been planned to start at 7:30.

Thena had leaped out of bed at 7:45, aware that something was not quite right. When she saw the time, she threw on clothes and rushed to the kitchen, finding it cold and empty. *No sign of coffee, nothing. I hate to do this, but there's nobody else.* Digging out her cell phone, she dials a number on the wall.

Charles had been singing Handel's Messiah in the cathedral choir. Quite an adventure for him, considering that, as many had noted, he consistently sang off-key. He compensated by reveling in all genres of music, but respected it enough to rarely subject anyone to the sound of his voice. This morning, his excursion into Dreamland abruptly terminates with the annoying beep of his cell phone. In a few minutes he shambles sleepily over to the kitchen to cobble together a quick breakfast for the guests: yogurt, fruit, cereal, and bagels from yesterday. *As usual, I am doomed to never be able to sleep in. It must be a lingering curse for leaving the priesthood*, he muses grumpily.

We note that for the next half hour the energy emanating from the building swirls off-kilter, on the edge of apprehension rather than genuine disorder. After this organizational snafu, Thena exhales. *Coffee made, morning meditation shortened, and breakfast almost inhaled.* What she doesn't know is that an intriguing synchronicity had evolved earlier that morning.

By coincidence—or as we conjectured later, a posthumous good deed from the monks performing penance—two people did wake up early. Two individuals did rise as intended, both with plans to go for a run and be back in time for a quick breakfast. We watched with interest as they each quietly find their way out through different doors and startle each other at the convergence of the paths that led into the conservation area, both jumping off the path in surprise.

"Well! Good morning—fancy meeting you so early!"

Raquel bursts out laughing. "Good morning yourself, Dylan!"

At the gate of the property it seems natural to casually stretch together, both of them comfortable as their bodies move with the usual jogger's rhythm of preparation. They begin to run, chatting back and forth with easy familiarity, striding along the broad path, relishing the exhilaration of an early morning jog in the cooler air. Initially nothing momentous is said, but after fifteen minutes it makes sense to slow down and gain the capacity to pay more attention to one another, to listen to the stories that have begun to leak out. Then abruptly they stop and face each other.

"I had no idea you lived in Uganda!"

"Yes, I sure did … one of the most significant periods of my childhood," Dylan replies. "When I was eight my dad got this great job with USAID. We lived in Mbarara, in the south, for eight years, and for four years I went to boarding school in Kenya. So I grew up in Africa. I've always felt like I left part of my heart there. That's why drumming is so viscerally and emotionally important for me—it's like I can get back into that other world. Sometimes it feels like a lifetime away, that I'll never get back there again. My drum seems like my only link. Do you miss being in Africa?"

"Terribly. But another part of me is grateful not to be there now. I need to be back here in the States for a while. Yesterday reminded me how burned out I am. That's one

246

of the reasons I started to jog over this summer; it felt like a way I could let out all the energy within me, and at the same time benefit from great physical exercise. I used to be on the track team in college, but in medical school I quit, there wasn't any time to run. In Africa, I tried very occasionally to get out by myself for a jog, but inevitably the Africans would think I was crazy. I know I made a lot of them laugh—but it got too confusing to explain. Of course from an African perspective, we are nuts ... running like mad, going nowhere, but looking as if we are being chased. We can't be serious!"

Dylan laughs. "I think much of what we do doesn't make sense to the African mind, and vice versa. Our ways so often come from such fundamentally opposite modes of thinking and experiencing life. At times I'm still incredibly confused. ... How to be? Who to be? African or Western? I think I am both."

"Oh Dylan, you may feel confused, but if it is anything like yesterday, when you played your drum, you made perfect sense to me. All those rhythms somehow played out the inner music of what I had just experienced in my Clearness Circle. It was a highlight of the day for me, tangibly expressed in such a beautiful manner in the outer world. I desperately wanted to get up and dance—like an African woman. I was taught how, by some women friends; they used to grab me into their dancing circles at any opportunity for celebration. Yesterday that might have caused quite a scene!"

"I wish you would have Raquel—I'd love to see you do that ..."

We note that his voice trails off when he recognizes his not-so-subtle invitation. Disconcerted, he quickly switches topics by looking at his watch. "We'd better turn around. We've missed the meditation time and we're going to miss breakfast unless we get going."

Like clock-work, on the far side of the forest, a church bell peals, breaking the awkwardness, yet also highlighting the special moments that have just transpired between them. We hope they sense the bell as a Sunday morning benediction from the unseen, because for most of the way back, they run silently, each lost in their private world, yet fully aware of the other.

They appear to us like two disoriented actors coming on stage simultaneously from separate wings. Tentative strangers, who know that somehow they have been charged with parts in the same play, each unsure of the next lines and anxiously searching for the appropriate script. Each desiring interaction, yet suddenly fearful that their personal language of intimacy would not be adequate or even understood by the other. Neither speaks again, but both find relief that their bodies know how to run well and fast.

We enjoy their race home. They arrive back at the Center sweating profusely, but exhilarated. Like two kids who suddenly decide to prove their worth, they have found a common goal—competition. When the road ahead gets murky with the unknown, it seems humans resort quickly to the rat race of rivalry.

CHAPTER TWENTY-FIVE
THE SEEKERS PATH

Thena is reordering chairs in the meeting room when Dylan appears showered and glowing. He is hungrily devouring a banana slathered in peanut butter.

"Well … aren't you the picture of good health for a Sunday morning! How come you're so radiant and alive?"

Dylan stammers something about being out for a run, and Thena, oblivious to his sudden discomfort, keeps right on talking.

"It's been crazy around here. I could have used your help sorting out our schedule earlier on. The cook didn't show up for breakfast … somehow we all slept in. I've never had that happen before. It was one of those things that could have messed us up, affected our entire day's schedule, but it's all worked out now, thank goodness. So you're ready to lead us this morning? Shall we quickly go over the details?"

In a few minutes, Dylan is introducing the morning session to the group. He begins with playing a cheery, yet reflective song from Carrie Newcomer, "A Circle of Friends."

As the music plays, he looks around the room, conscious once more of how these circles quickly weave an extraordinary web of connection. *This song perfectly fits the mood of the day. It isn't as if everyone becomes lifetime bosom-buddies, but it does seem that when each person more intimately understands themselves, they are able to draw closer to each other; this intimacy feels unparalleled to most other large group settings that I have experienced.*

With such little time left in the retreat, Dylan had struggled for weeks with choosing the most appropriate program for this morning. He had looked for pieces of art, or poetry, or some window into the multi-faceted gifts of nature; all different "third things" which mine the depths of human complexity. Aware that significant works of art have a mysterious trajectory through the world, in preparation for a retreat such as this, he attempted to stay attentive; he's often been surprised at the way certain poems call his attention, how some poems "find" him. But consequently he also is discovering the confusion between the communal and his individual soul, how they readily scramble together. As a facilitator, it's quite critical to attempt to discern the difference—personal and/or communal. It is a nuance he keeps working to grasp.

He can remember with chagrin a difficult moment with his drumming group when he had insisted that a certain song must be played in a certain way. Finally, the woman in his group stood up and angrily questioned, "What might it take for you to pay attention to the whole group and not just to your own perspective?" That had been a shocking moment of self-revelation.

Eventually, he and Thena had chosen to begin with

a short quote from Tom Jay called "The Seeker's Path."

"This seems a good way to help us focus on our inner seeker: the mysteries, the questions that brought us here, and how we will take away fresh truth, finding new ways to act on the wisdom gleaned from the weekend."

The 'Seeker's Path' is about arriving at a place, a bottom, a foundation, where will and ego aren't big enough to serve the thing that you are after, which is the truth.

So you have to give up trying to control things.

You attend to them.

The difference is major.

The path is about a larger, more mysterious context, which makes things scarier and more confusing, but it also makes beauty possible.

Truth, like beauty, is not ultimately in your power, it is larger.

The curious thing about the path of the seeker is that if you stay on it, you come to understanding that you are part of a tradition.

"What images or words come to your mind when you think of a path?" Dylan asks the group. As a popcorn of words fly around the room, he thinks about meeting Raquel on "the path" this morning and risks looking in her direction. But instead, it is Maria that commands his attention.

Pallid and drawn, he hardly recognizes her face; it is so washed in grief. She sits with her tall body hunched over in a question mark, yet is attempting to appear engaged in the spirited group conversation. *She looks perfectly awful. She reminds me of an African mourner: a lovely face covered in the white ashes of death. I'd better check in with her as soon as I have a chance. I wonder, what happened? She's trying so hard to act normally.*

After giving several more questions to the group, he proposes a final opportunity for silent reflection. "After that personal time, we will meet in triads for forty-five minutes. Let's be sure to follow our process like we did yesterday. Each person has fifteen minutes to use however they wish, just remember to only ask open and honest questions of one another if you do respond.

"It might be helpful to beware that we, as a group, are turning a corner in our process—turning back toward home, back to the situations and people of our everyday lives. The purpose of this time is to gather the threads of your learning from the past days. Trust you will be guided to remember what is important.

"Maybe you still have questions. Write them down, speak them out, live into them—maybe you'll find more clarity as you talk in your triads. Take this last opportunity in the safety of your small groups to be bold. Communicate from your uncomfortable place of uncertainty. Stay long enough to be found by a truth larger than any you might discover on your own. Or, maybe you'll leave with even more uncertainty, taking home more questions than you arrived with; sometimes that happens, too. Everybody's path is different. Remember, it is the beauty of truth that we seek ... and our soul knows the way home."

*   *   *

Mei looks at the questions, and begins to journal. She is glad to have this reflective space to think before she needs to talk to others.

What has your seeker's path looked like these past two days? Is there a phrase from the "Seeker's Path" that stands out for you today?

As you go back into your daily world, where is beauty calling to you? Where or how does your soul yearn for beauty?

What are your fears? Might it be helpful to write or speak about where your confusion lies?

I came to this retreat as a seeker. My path feels like an earthquake overturned everything months ago. But during this weekend, I have seen some ways through the confusion. I think of the old stone paths in the garden here, patchwork patterns of rough fieldstones laid over a century ago. Yes, this is the raw material of my life, barely visible when grass and weeds cover it. But if I keep walking I can find the outline for the next step; another stone comes into view.

I think I'm struggling in three specific areas – my work, my relationships, and inside my soul. Does this make sense? Is it too simple to define myself this way?

All three areas have seen recent cataclysmic change, but my work might be the easiest, the most concrete, to figure out. Shall I put my company up for sale? Do I lose control by selling options, going public? Or, do I maintain the family business, continuing the legacy of my husband, the way he liked to run it? It's a business decision that has merit either way...

"Small" is beautiful. "Big" is profitable and alluring. But increased profits in the bank could be used even more creatively, also "very beautiful" from a business perspective. That would provide a great deal of freedom for many when used in appropriate ways.

Her pen stops moving, aware that like the poem, "*her ego and will*" are attempting once more to figure this out—for the hundredth time.

What does it mean to have "a bottom, to lose control, to let go of ego and will"?

Where does beauty call me to today? How does my soul yearn for beauty?

These questions hang around Mei, enshrouding her in solitary detachment despite the room full of people. She sits motionless, then practically jumps out of her skin when Dylan quietly announces that it is time to start the triads. Groaning inwardly, she wishes for more personal time, but realizes that *every opportunity for communal conversation this weekend has surprisingly led to something richer, more dimensional. What a circuitous path to clarity!*

Michaela comes toward her, smiling in a captivating way. "Mei, I'd love to join with you to talk again." Then suddenly aware of Maria, says, "You too Maria … will you join us? I think we'll be a wonderful triad of strong women."

Mei lets herself be guided again, but is clear that she wants to return to her favorite place in the sanctuary of the meditation room. They gladly follow. Maria, still evidently struggling to keep her composure, hides from any added burden of attention, silently looks to the others to lead.

Once more, Mei crosses the difficult threshold from private to public. She speaks out loud, starting up where she had left off in her mind a few minutes earlier. "I am trying to figure out where beauty is calling me in my life. Will you listen with me? I feel like I'm on the cusp of something new."

The silence for a minute is intense—so profound that even the miniature waterfall stops flowing for a heartbeat. The attending spirits of the ancestors suck in their breath expectantly. For an instant, there is no space, not even for water to flow.

"... Ah … China … my beautiful heritage … I think that is what calls me right now. Last night I had extraordinarily vivid dreams. I was transported into the wonder of my ancient tradition. I have no idea what it might mean, but I have decided to make a pilgrimage back as a seeker of the old ways. I have faith that over the course of this next decade—you know I have just turned sixty—I hope to discover how to creatively live out of my entire American, Christian heritage and still be fully Chinese. Does this make sense to you?"

Michaela and Maria listen, suspended, as if watching a chrysalis twirl before them, watching an amorphous beauty writhing in the agony of questioning. They wait, willing her to speak more, for confirmation in their spirits as much as for Mei.

"I think you know how my husband's death rattled me to the core. Last night, I started to feel joy and hope again, but I have little clue what to do. Can I trust that this desire for beauty that is calling me back to my culture will not fail me? Can I be sure other decisions will fall into place, in the right timing? I have such a sense of relief it is not all up to me, yet paradoxically, I do know what is best for me. The business decisions will follow—of that I am sure ..." Mei keeps on talking expansively, bringing wholeness to the moment as her past circles around to greet the future.

After a while, it is Michaela's turn to join the conversation. "I keep thinking about an old hymn my grandmother adored—a Mahalia Jackson song, "*It's always darkest just before dawn.*" I woke this morning with an ache in my heart, but knew it wasn't related to the day itself. Today seemed so full of promise. I've always tried to deny this sorrow because I knew it didn't fit the present. I felt it on the train, coming here to this retreat—messy, disjointed grief. I watched myself try to get rid of it then. Who wants a depressed person around? But what on earth am I supposed to do with it now?

"I came into the circle this morning, preferring to be positive, to focus instead on exciting challenges ahead, like my studies. Maybe I don't want to stay in education. Maybe I can teach in another career path. There are so many kinds of master's degrees I could apply for..."

Michaela stops and starts to laugh, "See what I mean—I could get off on telling you all about that right now and move far away from my darker, inner world."

She begins again more softly, "Mei, when you spoke about your grief and ensuing struggles, being alone after the death of your husband, I realized something. My lover died suddenly too—seventeen years ago. I have lived repressing how awful that time was for me. I don't want a magic wand of reversal, but now that I get the opportunity to make new choices for myself, all the old pain re-occurs, as if it were today.

"Someone told me recently that emotions know no sense of time. Now, I think I see what is happening more clearly. Letting go of my Emma as she goes to college, and me, heading out on my own, back to school, evokes all my aloneness again. Mei, your courage in resolutely going forward alone, while still in mourning, has helped me know I can do the same thing. I learned to become strong before. Now this painful memory, with all my sadness and fears, can only make me stronger. Thank you, Mei.

"Still, it sucks to be single. This weekend helps me realize I can find community in different ways, like in these trusting circles … and, if I'm honest, can I authentically answer the question, 'What is my greatest fear?'"

Michaela pauses, rubbing her tattooed arm, "I … I think I'm afraid of being single forever—that I'll never find another man to love in my lifetime. That really hurts to imagine, but it feels okay to say it too." Michaela finishes, silently hoping the two women might have questions for her.

"Where is beauty calling you, in this 'single' season of your life, Michaela?" Mei asks.

"Wow, that's one of the most intense questions I've been asked. I don't know. I need time to think about it. Maybe I'll do that as I head back on the train. It sounds a lot more pleasant than my thoughts were on my journey here. Say it again, so I can write it down and remember."

After Mei repeats the question, they are all quiet, realizing that Maria has not made one sound, although she has been engaged in the conversation. Eventually Mei speaks very gently.

"Maria, you are obviously struggling with something. You don't have to tell us, or even speak at all, but we'll spend this time just being quiet with you. Whatever you'd like—it's your turn to have us sit with you. I know I really want to do that for you."

After minutes of attempting to gain control over her emotions, Maria utters, "My partner Grace told me that yesterday the doctor gave her a year to live. She has leukemia and has endured years of every treatment under the sun. Now it's time to let her go. Less than a year … a year…" Her tears flow. All three women silently weep together, sharing the holy sorrow of human suffering, when there is nothing more to say, and nothing else to do.

Mei's mind races with images. *My own recent dark days full of loss. … Jesus weeping alone in the garden while his friends slept. … Peasant women sitting around an outdoor fire. … The comforting murmuring of hill country dialect whispering in my ears …* Mei realizes with awe the gift being offered in their small circle. *Maria will have to go through her trials by herself, but I want to stay awake and alert sitting with her in this ancient circle of healing. She must not suffer alone. It is too much to bear.*

*   *   *

The room charges with spirit. We cannot squeeze in one more ray of loving energy to hold them as they release their pain. A cloud of witnesses sharing her grief, hang around Maria, giving her momentary shelter from

258

the inevitable storm. The women's communal silence supports her into the waiting abyss. We know that as they cry for her, they cry for themselves secure in the awareness that these are healing tears, not just for now in this circle, but for tomorrow and for all those touched by death.

They hear the bell chime to end the session. Eventually they find the strength to move back to the larger circle. As they embrace one another, both Mei and Michaela whispered in Maria's ear, "I'll be praying with you."

Mei, the last one out of the room, stops, briefly wondering, *how did all that water find its way out of the fountain? There is so much spilled out all over the floor.* She closes the door behind her, too weary to attempt to clean it up.

We are grateful. We have been gathering all those precious tears. Now, not one will be lost. Replenished, the primordial healing circle continues, its path sustained by seekers throughout the history of this land.

CHAPTER TWENTY-SIX
LETTERS TO SELF

Now that he has been forced out of bed, Charles realizes he has no other honorable choice but to make the best of it. Not surprisingly, he decides to bake—luscious butter tarts, filled with rich sugary syrup and piles of organic raisins. While the triads earnestly talk, Charles putters around the kitchen in a solipsistic haze, reviving his soul with Gregorian chant and a strong cafe-con-leché. Scooping the perfect tarts from the muffin pans brings him such an immense rush of satisfaction that he resolves to employ his precious espresso maker to produce a large batch of this restorative potion for his guests. Mentally he figures that after such a paltry breakfast, a treat of magnanimous proportions is in order.

From our vantage point, we note that as usual, Charles is flowing in the spirit of the retreat. As we experience his soulful cooking from our world view, we become aware of the remarkable sensorial attunement he has with us and with humans. It is a shame that he is often unaware of how much of a gift he is to those around him. Unfortunately, his first instinct is to undervalue his work in the world, and to seek to be more holy. As if his very being is not holy enough.

After the triads, a break is essential, and correctly, he perceives the size and dimension of the many gifts that had been received that morning. Like a soul potlatch, his baking echoes the theme of abundance. He waltzes into the meeting room carrying the inviting tray, overflowing not only with the delectable pastries, but decorated with edible orange and red nasturtium flowers. He jokingly welcomes any adventurous eaters to test out the flowers for their love potion of the day. Dylan hoots with delight after Charles's pronouncement, briefly toying with the idea of offering one to Raquel.

Standing in a loose circle, Sam, George, and Gerritt gorge themselves companionably, each quietly content with reflections from their recent conversation together. How the three men self-selected their triad was not clear, but it has been a fruitful time. They joined in a serious dialogue around their personal issues of failure: George in his business, Gerritt in his marriage, and Sam now fully aware of his failing to trust his creativity. Each found quiet encouragement from their shared dread of the public appearance of failure. Each had valued the public path of success over the hidden, more elusive path of their souls. The reality is that each one in his own way has been unable to live up to infernal standards of perfection that drives him inexorably further from his deeper inner truths.

George dreads facing the reality of the demise of his business. Gerritt knows he has succumbed to delusions of grandeur from his success at work, and had thus sacrificed his marriage on the altar of mid-life idiocy. Sam is rather aghast to have his eyes opened to his internal striving for success in the academic world, how this has kept him rigidly plodding on in work that is no longer satisfying. When the bell rang, bringing the groups to an end, each man left with a sense that he had a lot of thought-provoking homework to do. Butter tarts were a welcome release from the need to push on.

As they enjoy their snack, it strikes Sam as comical to see Gerritt studiously picking out every raisin from his tart, piling them in a folded napkin. With the plethora of raisins, there was not much substance left to enjoy, just a sugary sticky mess, a ghost of former glory.

"Hey, man—that's a pretty obsessional behavior," he says jovially. "Have you ever had that analyzed? As a psychologist I can't resist saying something."

They both laugh as Gerritt says matter-of-factly, "Actually, I just don't like raisins—that's all. But I do love butter tarts, so this is the best I can do."

"Speaking of being analyzed," wonders Sam, "I have been thinking about the kind of inner work we are doing here. It isn't really psychological, yet it is—that and more. What do you think?"

By now Jean had overheard the conversation and joins in, remarking, "This work is quite different from most group therapy approaches. I have never been in a group where we have quickly felt safe enough to be genuinely authentic. I'm amazed and humbled by my own internal conversations that I've never had the chance to air in public. I surprised myself just now talking in my triad about how I have subtly fallen in love with one of my own clients. But just talking about it openly makes me realize I can move beyond this, understand what is happening, and neither feel guilty nor get caught in any unethical action, messing up my whole world."

"Me too," says Sam. "I'm aware of all that happens

inside my head. I use my professional writing and research to work out a lot of the rational detail, but my creative world has gone underground for years, unprocessed and unresolved. I laugh at you, Gerritt, picking out raisins, but my mind has been picking out and throwing away the best parts of the beauty of the educational process. I realize I'm hungry for creative adventure, for bright spots of color and texture in my life.

"I was just talking to Zach at breakfast, and realized to my chagrin that I was jealous of him. I wish I were younger and had fewer responsibilities. I think I would quit my job and travel around the world like he wants to do. Can't you see the creativity oozing out of him? What hope do I have if I stay in the academic world?" Sam takes a big breath as if he had just heard himself say something new, and then keeps talking.

"Did you guys feel the power of our group conversation? When was the last time you had a similar talk with a group of men, or a group of academics— anybody, for that matter? I'm a Quaker, so we don't have the ritual of communion, but talking together in our group today felt like communion. A celebration around all the broken bits of our lives. This power of communal sharing reminds me of my humanity. I can't tell you how often I felt like I was the only one in academia who feared going crazy inside my mind. My brain energy is way too dynamic for the rest of me … like ... speaking of dynamic, can you imagine eating snacks this size every day?"

*　　*　　*

As she stands beside the table, Michaela opens her mouth and then closes it again. Instead, she takes a drink of coffee. Evan cocks his head at her, raising his eyebrows. "You were about to say something?"

"No, it's not important."

"Go on, out with it," he teases her. Michaela looks embarrassed, so he continues, "Well then, I have a question for you. Tell me about your tattoo, it's very striking, I'm sure you have a story about that."

"Yes, I sure do. It has lots of meanings; over the years it has become quite the companion. I got it on the year anniversary of my husband's death, I knew he would approve as he loved his tats." She smiles with affection.

"The snake represents the divine feminine in Japanese tradition. It was my way of calling out for wisdom and at the same declaring myself powerful and free to live my life as a single woman. A lot of women spook at snakes, but for me it's healing, a symbolic way of mastering my fears."

"Well, I'm glad I asked; it makes it even more striking on you. I bet your kids at school are mesmerized by a lovely teacher with a snake tattoo!"

Nonplussed, Michaela wonders if Evan is hitting on her but it helps her forget her reluctance. "So I have been wondering something, too—about you. What's your last name? Is it Pierce? Were you the star Eagles player who had that awful accident and could never play pro football again?"

"Yup—that's me..." Then Evan adds softly, "You remember? It was a long time ago."

"Eighteen years this month."

"You really do remember!" Evan exclaims.

"Actually your accident happened the week after my husband was killed. He was one of your biggest fans. I became one too, but for a different reason. For months, I followed your progress, leaning into your courage to keep on going forward, for myself and my new baby girl. I guess I get to finally thank you for that. You were the closest thing I had to a saint."

"Oh, Michaela, you're too funny, I'm sure no saint, but your words make me want to cry. Thank you for telling me, I needed to hear this today. How curious that we just found this out now. Yesterday I was talking about my accident in some detail in my Clearness Circle, so it feels very fresh in my heart. ... Wow, we could have missed this if you hadn't found the courage to ask. Maybe after this weekend, we can get together and talk some more. Some of my favorite kids that I coach come from your school district; they probably live right around you."

Michaela's heart leaps, and then falls with his next words. "You'd really like my wife, Alycia. I'll definitely have to get you two together."

She smiles back at him, *Shit, why does it always have to end like this*? And after taking a long look at the snake on her arm, she declares, "I'd like that Evan—I'll wait for you to call me. I'm so glad we talked."

A few minutes later, they are called back into the circle, aware of the clock ticking. It is 11:00 and the retreat ends at 12:30, at lunch. Many are wondering how things will conclude.

Jean whispers to Gerritt, "How on earth are they going to wrap this up? Don't you feel like we're only just beginning?"

It is time for Thena to introduce the last activity. She points out a stack of plain paper and envelopes, and invites the group to write a letter to themselves. "This 'Letter to Self' is your personal way of summing up what's on your heart, what you'd like to remember from this retreat. It's a way of finding inspiration for the future. Here are paper and envelopes, write whatever you wish, then seal it up and address it to yourself. One day in the next months, I'll mail it back to you. These letters hopefully will arrive at a time when you need them most, as a message for you from your own soul.

"Let your inner teacher speak to you as you write. Trust your words. If you don't wish to do this, feel free to use the next twenty minutes for your own personal conclusion to the retreat, in whatever way is most important for you. Let's not speak, though. Remain quiet until we ring the bell and we come back for our final circle."

Silently, most of the group pick up a couple of sheets of paper and an envelope, and find a comfortable place to write. George, with a big sigh, gets up and walks reluctantly to the door as if he were feeling torn: one part wishing he could more easily comply and the other part needing to find another way. Finding his jacket in the hall, George wanders outside for a last stroll around the garden.

I need the peace of not having to do one more thing. Too much looms ahead of me, much that will demand careful attention. Now is my time to find quiet and hope— from somewhere. His body keeps moving methodically along the path.

Mei is writing as if in a trance—this time writing in English.

Vanessa scribbles furiously, three pages of looping script. All the while her copious tears keep dropping, leaving damp smudges and circular pock-marks on the pages below.

Sam writes only one short paragraph:

Dear Sam,
... Look for creative beauty everywhere—in
yourself, in your work, and in your family. Find

beauty at all costs. What is it that you long for?
What is it that you desire? Search after beauty.
She is everywhere. Don't forget.

Gerritt can't stop looking at Leona. She has moved over to the more comfortable sofa in the window seat and is writing with her long legs curled up—like a cat bathing in sunlight. Every now and then she stretches her neck, closes her eyes, and faces directly into the sun. She looks very much like the teenager he had first met—gorgeous and quite unaware of her seductive allure. But today, like a cat, she also looks distinctly unapproachable and fiercely independent. Her intensity screams, "Leave me alone."

No wonder no one else is sharing the sofa with her.

He continues to glance at her, hoping to see her relax, to smile; wishing for some sign of peace between them. *It's impossible to know what to write when all I can think of, is Leona. Maybe I should try drawing something again.* He moves tentatively over to the art table, clutching his paper and envelope.

Despite the aura of peace that has settled into the room, Thena can't sit still. She finds herself curiously agitated again; her shoulders feel tight, and as she stretches, she winces at the tenderness of her muscles. *I can't wait for this to be over. This is not like me. I usually hate to come to the end of a retreat weekend.*

She silently slips out of the room.

Dylan is surprised to see her disappear. He lets her leave; he needs the time to write about some of his new revelations this weekend.

Zach hugs his knees close to his chest. He's on the floor in a corner, looking as if he is trying to get out of the room, as far away as possible from the group, yet still remain a part of the action. He has been writing on and off all day since early morning, choosing earlier not to meet in a triad. Bizarre dreams had unsettled the peace of his late-night meditation. He had attempted all day to capture some of the relief of those images. Words have been pouring out of him erratically.

It feels to him like turning on an old faucet, and finding nothing but convulsions of stale air, then waiting, and more retching begins. Like gas and water trapped in pipes forcefully rising, his strangled thoughts erupt. He wants to spew uncontrollably. He senses it might be a long time before really fresh water will flow again.

BEING FORCED

The bile rises in my throat and I force it back down

I tenderly touch lifelong feelings

Of being made to perform, to produce,

Being the good boy was all I ever could be

Now I drop my anger like constipated bombs of wrath

On the unsuspecting world

God let me be bad for once

To vomit out all my pukey niceness

That has protected me from me

The little boy who was never free to let his crap fly freely

Don't you know the queen never farts? Really?

Hold yourself in, pull back your shoulders

Can't you see my anger monstrously growing to boulders?

Stones of depression and fear and anxiety

Built up caverns of rage protected by walls of propriety

I feel forced from within, forced from without

I've swallowed this shit long enough to doubt

If I ever will be free to stand on my own

And say no with a smile and yes with a frown

To curse when I want to and laugh with the angels

And revel in bed like the devil's archangel

To gently listen and softly speak

To roar loudly and lustily weep

To blast a woman right off the planet

And love her to death in the next moment.

I cannot be still, my guts are so shaken

My musings have me quite overtaken.

Dear God! May my life as a man, go passionately ahead

With confidence and joy that I am really not dead.

Well, if this is my letter to myself—so be it. Seems kind of rabid, to say the least. Maybe if I leave it here, it might stay here. All these feelings not haunt me. When it comes in the mail, maybe it'll be a good reminder for how much I've changed. I hope so... Zach picks up his pen again and writes quickly.

> *Use this as a reminder how much you have changed. Remember—keep enjoying your life! Travel! Have fun! With love from your soul ... Zach*

*   *   *

Dazed, Thena finds her way back again to Charles. He is sitting morosely, holding his head in his hands, the Sunday paper spread out before him. Quietly, she turns around, trying to exit the kitchen.

"Is that you, Thena?"

"Yes, I'm sorry. I don't want to bug you."

"No, come in for a minute; it's probably good you came."

"I've only got a few minutes anyway, before I have to be back in the group. This has been the most complex weekend I've had for a long time. I keep trying to figure out what is going on—I seem so erratic."

"Funny, you should say that—that's the word I was thinking too. Erratic—like a clock that keeps changing time. My emotions are powerfully on edge these days."

He pushes the newspaper around to face her.

"Look at this—a story about three people who have lost work in this recession. This man here? I knew him as a boy. He was in my parish, such a great young man. He's built his own business over the years, had a family, and look—now he is at the end of a financial rope, barely able to stay alive. He's lost his home and is now living in a homeless shelter. Inconceivable to imagine ... poor guy.

"The other two stories are the same, everyday folks

271

who have been run out of the system with nowhere to go. Poverty is so frightening and so soul-destroying. What chance do these people have? Who is really there for them? Reading this left me with a tidal wave of guilt, feeling badly that I'm not there as a priest anymore, second-guessing my decision to leave. Have I lost my drive to be a radical change agent? Here I am today, wrapped up in the sweet satisfaction of baking goodies for all of you. Crazy. For the moment, I'm totally lost in how to be and do all of this at the same time."

Thena gazes at him, her heart full. "Thank you for being so honest, my friend—I need to hear you speak like this. I love your compassion. It has no limits, even though you know you're still learning that you can't do everything. I feel like I am there too, so many longings to help … I can't articulate it. Today, I can't even help myself.

"I don't know why I came in here right now, other than to cry on your shoulder. It seems this weekend has been helpful for almost everyone else but me; it has left me more unglued than I started. I'm worried about this last session. I don't know if I can trust my emotions not to betray me."

"Yeah, I know how tricky that can be. Trying to lead wisely from a place of brokenness is enough to scare all of us out of leadership. I remember the last homily I gave, just before my complete meltdown. It was remarkable; despite my own confusion, people to this day tell me it was the most meaningful talk I ever gave. It's the one they all remember. It's confusing to realize that a part of us is genuinely more powerful in weakness than in strength. Soul energy emerges out of the humility of imperfection."

He gives her a quick hug and almost pushes her out

272

the kitchen door. "You can do it, Thena. This is what your soul knows how to do best. I'll see you at lunch in less than an hour."

Then, just as she heads down the hall, Charles calls after her, "Hey my friend, can you hang around for a bit after everyone leaves? Join me for tea—or maybe a cheery glass of wine will be called for."

CHAPTER TWENTY-SEVEN
LAST WORDS

By now it is automatic. As each person sits down, they find the company of silence. Many look around, drinking in this experience of community, savoring it for one last time. Others ponder the quote they found on their chair. A couple of them check their watches, hoping that the session will end on time so they'd be able to catch the earlier flight home.

Thena is the last to sit down in the circle. Dylan had rung the bell and was ready to start without her, even though it was her turn to lead. Feeling much like a sheep bleating in the wilderness, she begins to read.

"Our deepest fear is not that we are inadequate.
Our deepest fear is that we are powerful beyond
measure. It is our light, not our darkness,
that most frightens us. We ask ourselves, who
am I to be brilliant, gorgeous, talented, and

fabulous? Actually, who are you not to be? You are a child of God. Your playing small doesn't serve the world. There's nothing enlightened about shrinking so that other people won't feel insecure around you. We were born to make manifest the glory of God that is within us. It's not just in some of us; it's in everyone. And as we let our own light shine we unconsciously give other people permission to do the same. As we are liberated from our own fear, our presence automatically liberates others."

~ *Marianne Williamson*

Her voice seems about to break, Dylan thinks. *What's happening? How should I help?* He grows anxious on her behalf, but Thena speaks again, this time with an authentic quality that resounds through the room.

"I don't know about you, but as I come into this last circle together, I feel very inadequate in finding an easy way to close our time together. I'd like to feel strong and unequivocal, able to pass that courage on to you— out of my strength. Actually, this weekend has brought me closer to the reality of my own powerlessness, my human frailty that I continue to learn from. Needless to say, as a leader this is not easy to experience, or to admit."

She smiles at them, at ease now, back in the track of accepting all that is human. "It's interesting that I picked this quote several weeks ago, not having any idea how important it would be for me today. I need to think about it more as I head home. I need to reconsider the question. What *are* the fears that haunt me?

"After many years of attempting to live consciously and authentically, how do I persist in 'shrinking back' from 'living out my greatness'? These are huge questions:

ones I keep revisiting, ones I never fully comprehend, but which always end up offering me a different kind of security—the assurance that from these dark moments I always find deeper truth. Today, I offer you my honesty; revelations that come out of darkness, but not despair."

The silence reverberates until Thena speaks again. "How about you? How did you arrive in this room on Friday, and how do you leave today? What has your inner Light taught you this weekend? We have forty-five minutes to share with one another in whatever ways you desire."

I can't ignore Thena's invitation. After her example, I must trust my private self to communicate authentically. Mei opens her mouth and speaks first, in a clear, forthright voice.

"I came here quite afraid of being known. I am someone who has been forced to live a very public life but is actually a very private person." She smiles slyly, looking at Thena. "I actually registered using my maiden name so I would be anonymous this weekend.

"So I want to thank you all for giving me space to grow, to learn the wisdom of community again. I just decided to make a trip back to my roots. I will take you home with me to China. I am so excited.

"Also, I need to share something I wrote this morning. Here's my letter from my soul—it's about you as a circle, too. This is my gift to you. Thank you …"

I am here meeting myself all over again for
the first time through you
Beginner's mind meet ancient crone.
Embryonic longings and fearful demons
Welcome to you All.

Dark, introduce yourself to Light; you are One

277

*Let us hold the emergent energy of this encounter
as we have woven this circle of unity together.
Discovering hidden order strung like galaxies of
stars within the ever-circling web of our lives.
You have colored my outer fringes with your stories,
revealing new form that speaks in the tongues
of ancestors.*

*Let me rest in your silence, those rich unspoken
spaces where you live in your abundant otherness.
Tell me your story, listen to my dreams.
Ask me your questions, and I will find courage to
go deeper into those crevices where the crabs
live and the river flows.
Can you see the reflection of our deepest selves in
the turbulent rapids of our well-used lives?*

*I have often waited for you to come, my teacher,
the Other one, searching in countless sanctuaries
of truth. But you have been here all along.
Answering to my name and calling with my voice
Living out of the deep ground of my being.*

*This container for my life is a mystery.
How I become clearer as the droplets of your
truth touch the surface of my being, liberating
fresh energy to dance and play in the music of
our world. To return full circle and become
yet more still and quiet.
Resting, in quiet anticipation of
the Great Work that communes in us.*

*together
in our community of souls.*

Mouths hang open in silence for a time, but eventually the others begin to share.

"Thank you Mei," Michaela says. "That is a precious gift you just gave us. I realize that as each of you has told your story, you have helped me know my own story better."

Evan confesses: "I wished I had arrived on Friday night. I couldn't imagine this group being as helpful as it has been. My wife, Alycia, pushed me to come in the first place, but after such a terrible day on Friday, I almost didn't come at all. I was afraid this would be either really boring or too touchy-feely. In fact, it was exactly what I needed. Something new has begun in me. I am grateful I didn't stay away. Thank you."

Gerritt and Sam echo a similar theme; each in his own way saying that his work-life feels out of control, but spending time in the circle this weekend has brought them more in touch with things they rarely take time to think about.

Zach, still troubled with the rage of his recent writing, unexpectedly remembers a quote that brings him relief. "Unlike you guys, I am still looking for work, still absorbed in my personal career and spiritual journey. All my life I have been worried about finding my call. The fear of missing God's will haunts me. This weekend it's been hard to tolerate the intensity. In fact, hearing your life stories has increased my confusion and added to my frustration. I appreciate what you said, Thena. It's a breath of fresh air to have leaders who can be fragile and human. You helped me remember a quote from Frederick Buechner that I've always liked: 'The place God calls you to, is the place where your deep gladness and the world's deep hunger meet.'

"I guess it's okay to be full of passion for a while, giving myself time to sort out what direction to go in.

There is too much hunger out there, and in here." He points to his belly. "I want to hit the road and travel, live each day as it comes. I'll send you postcards."

After the chuckling stops, George clears his throat to speak, and then finds he cannot say anything. Struggling, he looks up, his eyes briefly scanning each face in the circle. "Thank you, that's all I can say. Thank you."

With a lump in her throat, Leona talks about her arrival, "…feeling so heavy and burdened, but I leave more aware that I do not have to do life alone, figuring out the way by myself. I haven't said much, but I've felt curiously supported by each of you, by the power of the group. It's like when I do yoga, I feel the energy of the earth sustaining me, and I can rest in all the love around me. I felt that same strength in you this weekend. Thank you."

Vanessa recounts how she was called to come to this retreat. "I thought it came from my friend, who told me I should consider coming, but I realize it was my own voice that called me here. As a woman, I am starting to trust this gut-quivering feeling, this deep urgency within me that says, '*Do it! I need this for me. The hell with the cost, the time, and other people's advice. I am doing this for me.*

"I didn't realize, when I grabbed the phone and committed myself to this weekend journey, how big a leap I was taking, but I'm glad I listened. I want to listen more, to hear the call of my own soul. I haven't been paying much attention to her. I have no idea what this is going to mean, but I get excited thinking about it. I wish we could meet and continue here again next month. Are you going to have other retreats like this, Thena?"

Thena smiles broadly. "I don't know yet. I have thought about it. I guess we'll see. I'll certainly let you know."

Dylan, as a leader, relishes this complex conversation, ripe with hanging questions and answers, delighting in each honest heart revelation. But, he too is concentrating inside, attempting to verbalize his story from the weekend. Much stirs within him, he knows he has something to communicate, yet so far he has no clear sense of how to be authentic. So he waits.

Maria too, remains quiet; still overwhelmed with emotion, yet strangely at ease in her silence. *The time together with Mei and Michaela has been encouraging. I just hope I can find the strength to go forward into the dark future.*

Then Raquel speaks up. "This weekend reminds me of so many African stories that talk about how, when people join together in community, enormous strength and ancient wisdom emerges. It seems that our North American culture so often honors independence at the cost of losing community and generations of cultural values. African village wisdom knows that when we stand united together as individuals, within families in community, we will not be broken. Life will go on, no matter how hard things get. My broken pieces have been knitted together this weekend through your incredible gifts of undivided and compassionate attention. Thank you."

Again, there is a pregnant silence. Thena is about ready to end as it seems everyone has spoken who wanted to. "We'll hold the circle open for a few more minutes in case anybody else wishes to speak."

Now Dylan knows. Raquel's words have inspired him. He reaches behind his chair and picks up his drum, then sits down again. Unlike the night before, this time the beat emerges from silence. He plays very, very softly, like the gentle rhythm of an unborn baby's heartbeat.

Gun-Gun, Gun-Gun, Gun-Gun,

GoDo Gun Gun Gun-Gun, Gun-Gun Gun-Gun,

GoDo Gun Gun

Each beat draws energy up from the earth, through his feet and out his body. Waves spiral into the space between each note, returning to silcncc. The symbiotic circle of sound and feeling, a multitude of unsaid words, reverberate within the bodies around the circle. Each person leans in, urging Dylan on with a secret desire to hear the drum speak—to speak of their lives, their past, and the unknown future. They witness the heralding of new birth, inside and out, in the creation of this music.

The drum plays itself. Dylan knows. *Let go, trust this process, my body speaks today.* After a few minutes, the rhythm becomes more complex, as if he is waiting for something, for someone else to emerge, for another soul to show up and dance in the circle with him. It becomes a steady beat of invitation. This is how Dylan has been feeling all weekend. *Invited to join the dance.*

Maria like everyone has been swaying with the beat. Her eyes close and almost unawares, she viscerally begins to respond—moaning, a quiet keening wail of response that only she knows how to vocalize. She groans and hums in harmony, putting music to her pain and sorrow, and all her hope. For the first time in her life, she plays to no audience, with no prop but herself. She releases her voice from the boundaries of page and script, and not being able to sit any longer, she stands up, singing in her full and authentic voice—a voice that no one in the room has heard before, not even herself. Maria's soul knows this language like no other. She responds in an expert vocalization of life without words, her voice responding time and again back to the call of the drum.

Entranced, each person senses the magic of witnessing this free-floating duet, this mini-symphony of vocal sounds and drumbeats. It is the hidden soul-music of the retreat—for all of them. Each person hears their own song, their own verse played, from the inside-out.

Thena, feeling the electricity charge through her body, feels compelled to get up and dance. The invitation of the drum and the freedom that Maria represents is emotionally alluring, but Thena also experiences caution. It is a sacred time of reverence—for the two of these musicians, for all of them. She just as easily could have fallen on her face on the floor in awe. Instead, she remains seated, caught in the tragic gap of leader and participant, thinker and feeler, be-er and doer. She continues sitting, powerfully attuned to the mystery of remaining there, solid and vibrating with energy while dancing inside.

There couldn't have been a more fitting end to their time together. Even Charles had by now been drawn down the hall and was peeking around the corner surreptitiously to enter more fully into the history being made in his home. When the silence descends again, he tiptoes away, his hands high in the air.

Thena gently closes the circle, looking around into each pair of eyes. "Thank you. Thank you—each one of you! You have each heard your souls speak today." She guides them to the printed poem lying under their seats.

"In closing I'd like to read this last poem as a parting gift, a grace-note for you to take home."

Kindness

Before you know what kindness really is you
must lose things, feel the future dissolve in a
moment like salt in a weakened broth.
What you held in your hand, what you counted
and carefully saved, all this must go so you
know how desolate the landscape can be
between the regions of kindness.
How you ride and ride thinking the bus will
never stop, the passengers eating maize and
chicken will stare out the window forever.

Before you learn the tender gravity of kindness,
you must travel where the Indian in a white
poncho lies dead by the side of the road.
You must see how this could be you, how he too
was someone who journeyed through the night
with plans and the simple breath that
kept him alive.

Before you know kindness as the deepest thing
inside, you must know sorrow as the other
deepest thing.
You must wake up with sorrow.
You must speak to it till your voice
catches the thread of all sorrows and you see
the size of the cloth.

Then it is only kindness that makes sense
anymore, only kindness that ties your shoes
and sends you out into the day to mail letters
and purchase bread, only kindness that raises
its head from the crowd of the world to say

**it is I you have been looking for, and then goes
with you everywhere like a shadow or a friend.**
~ Naomi Shihab Nye

Nothing more could be said. It was kindness to end.
After a few announcements, the group scatters to eat a
quick lunch, and to say their final good-byes.

CHAPTER TWENTY-EIGHT
ENDINGS

Still hungry for more of Charles's food, George leaves without lunch. Profoundly touched by the freedom of the last hour, he knows without a shadow of doubt that he must return home and reorient his life. He had already spoken with Charles, thanking him for his caring presence the day before, and knows eventually he will write to the leaders of the retreat, to be in touch again, *but frankly, I cannot stand any more emotion. Somehow, I always manage to avoid goodbyes.*

This troubling thought launches him out the door without looking back, straight into his car. *Thankfully I put my suitcase in the trunk before the last session. Oh well, I'll have time for some lunch at the airport.* George is the first to exit the driveway.

People are milling around the meeting room, hugging each other, generally looking as if they are unable to leave. Zach hates this part of endings: it reminds him of summer camp where kids would weep and wail, hanging on each others' necks, promising a lifetime of love and communication, and then never see nor talk to one another again—and then on top of it all, feel guilty about it. *What's done is done. It's over now.*

He tries to slip out the door as George has done, but Vanessa grabs him, smothering him in a flurry of warm motherly affection. He remembers then that he does want to say goodbye to Dylan, and finds him still sitting in the circle, packing away his papers thoughtfully, almost looking as if he were considering playing again. He appears comatose, moving on autopilot.

Zach rouses him from his stupor with a hand on his shoulder. "Dylan. Can we stay in touch? I have no idea where I'll be over the next months or years, but could we continue our conversation? This weekend you consistently helped me to think more clearly; I am so grateful. Thanks so much."

Dylan good-naturedly replies, "Sure, absolutely, send me those postcards—okay?" As Zach turns to go, Dylan glimpses Raquel out of the corner of his eye, and a flood of longing rises in him. *I don't want to say goodbye to her ... I am not ready to do that. What shall I do? Ask for her phone number, when she knows that I already have it? How do I let her know that I am interested? Should I wait until after ... just call her?*

Dylan moves through a gauntlet of farewells into the dining room, feeling like a frazzled bundle of nerves by the time he sits down. He picks at his meal, talking distractedly with Gerritt, who seems intent on digging up more meaning out of the last poem.

Sam wants to leave promptly because he has a three-hour drive ahead of him, so he interrupts their conversation to ask for Gerritt's business card, while handing him one of his own. This exchange seemed important to both of them, and Gerritt responds by spontaneously getting up and hugging Sam, and then shaking his hand.

"I really would like to get together sometime. I think we have a lot in common. I'd very much like to stay in touch."

Listening to this, Dylan realizes the gods have just spoken, so it doesn't unnerve him when Raquel sits down beside him. Both finish eating but once Gerritt has left, he finds the courage to open his mouth. Feeling like an African parrot woodenly repeating words, he sputters, "Raquel, I would like to get together sometime. I think we have a lot in common. I'd very much like to stay in touch."

Raquel blushes, taken aback by his candor. *This guy is gorgeous—how could I be so caught up in my navelgazing that I just start to see him now?* Stammering a bit, but looking in his eyes, she responds. "I'd … I'd love that, Dylan. Yes, please give me a call. You've already got my number…"

Flustered, she rises to her feet. The African in her is once again prodding her to bow, but she manages to exit the room with grace, neither turning her back on him nor falling over her feet, which had suddenly become a problem.

Dylan mechanically finds his way to the counter and grabs an extra dessert, which he devours for a few minutes until others come over to say their goodbyes. Before leaving the room he checks in with Thena.

"Should we have our evaluation, review everything together before we leave? It would help me to have that kind of follow-up. Sooner rather than later, I think."

"Oh, Dylan, I've had it—I am done. 'Completely knackered,' my British aunt would say. Let's talk on the phone in a couple of days. I don't think I could put two sensible thoughts together right now. Is that okay with you?"

Gratefully Dylan takes his exit, aware now that all he wants is some quiet before getting back to work on Monday.

*   *   *

One by one, the group members leave on their own, except Gerritt and Leona, who find each other back in their room. Both attempt to pack. Gerritt, normally a fastidious packer, had unceremoniously thrown his clothes and papers into his suitcase and is sighing loudly, frustrated that everything doesn't fit. Leona is in the bathroom, determinedly stuffing her cosmetics into her overnight bag. She hadn't tightened the toothpaste tube before it squirts out. The white goo, now thoroughly enmeshed in the zipper, is oozing everywhere.

"Damn it ... Gerritt ..." She stops suddenly, moving cautiously around the corner, eyeing him and laughing. "Look at us! You'd never know we've just experienced three of the most powerful days in our recent lives. I'm completely fried emotionally. You probably are too. I'm not at all ready to go home and face the world. All I want to do is either fight or make crazy love with you. By the way, when *did* we stop doing that? That seems like so much more fun than fighting. Didn't that used to work for us? Please let's not argue right now ..."

Leona and Gerritt fall into bed, together, for the first

time that weekend.

*   *   *

Maria is most anxious to get home now, having stayed a few minutes longer especially to speak with Mei who had hugged her warmly and thanked her profusely, "Maria your voice today was the crowning touch of my retreat experience. Somehow you found a way to put into music all the things I tried to say. Your gift in song is truly exceptional, I know you'll find your way over these next difficult months, but please, please know we can talk if it's helpful for you. Even though I'm in China, I'll try to be available anytime."

Now Maria waves at Sam as they exit the driveway in their separate cars. Just then a mammoth black limousine rolls up the driveway, surprising them and forcing them both to veer out of the way. *Who the hell is that for?* Flabbergasted, Maria almost drives off the road, watching in her rearview mirror.

To her surprise, Mei miraculously appears from nowhere and climbs into the back seat. A uniformed man with a cap stashes her suitcase in the trunk. *Is that Mei's driver? She really must be loaded.*

Michaela's eyes widen, as she teeters sideways, tripping on her suitcase. *I wonder who Mei really is? No, she couldn't be—not Mrs. Mei Tang! Her husband died this year, the papers were full of the story. They are major philanthropists in the area. Fascinating—no wonder Mei needed her privacy. I understand that now. If I had known who she was, I might have been tempted to ask for funding for our new school library project*

As the limo pulls out of sight around the bend in the

291

driveway, Michaela and Vanessa wait with Jean for the shuttle-bus.

"Where did you say you were from in Canada?" Vanessa asks, making pleasant conversation as they wait.

"I'm from Edmonton," Jean says.

"Oh!" says Vanessa knowingly, evidently not having a clue where that was in Canada. Jean chuckles to herself, she had given up her hostility about Americans years ago, yet now finds Vanessa's ignorance rather funny. In the interval, Michaela realizes what has just happened. *It's always been a mystery to me what happens north of the border, but I'm too embarrassed to admit it. I too have no idea where Edmonton is.* Deciding the retreat is not over yet, she speaks up.

"Vanessa, I bet you don't know where Edmonton is—I have no idea. We Americans are completely dumb about Canada much of the time. It must be totally frustrating when no one cares to really know you as different. I find that all the time as a black woman. White people are often too freaked out to say that they don't have a clue about me or my culture. They're afraid to ask questions and be interested in me. It's no shame not to know, but it is a shame to pretend we are wise when we know we are ignorant.

"I know that sounded awfully strong Vanessa, but it really is not directed at you, believe me. I guess it's a leftover from the freedom I've felt in being honest and open this weekend."

The three of them chat, gleaning more social details about each other's lives on the drive in the shuttle bus than in all the hours of the weekend.

As they part, Vanessa remarks to them all, "Isn't it interesting how little we've talked about the day-to-day normal things of our lives, like ... How many kids do you have? Where do you live? Where were you were born? All those polite social things you hear at a cocktail party and forget right away. This *was* a different weekend. It's going to be difficult trying to explain it. How will I ever tell Arthur about it, if I am still trying to figure it out myself?"

*   *   *

Thena comes outside for a final goodbye with Dylan, walking to his car with him, trying to make up for feeling small that she had not been able to tolerate any more meetings. She waves goodbye, her relief palpable. Dragging, she walks back to the kitchen to say good-bye to Charles and plunks down in his comfortable chair.

He studies her carefully. "You really do look wasted, my dear. Can I get you something to drink?"

She feels it well up inside her again.

I am simply not ready, not ready to let it out: not today, not here, not now. I can't and I won't say anything at all. I must keep myself together—until I get to the privacy of my own home.

Charles remains quiet, waiting. Then he offers a tentative answer to what her soul might be crying for. "Thena, why don't you stay here for a day or two—or as long as you can? Have a private retreat all for yourself. There is no group coming in until next weekend. I'll feed you and leave you alone. Do you really have to go home right now? Call in sick—you look that way to me."

Thena collapses, nodding her head as tears of gratitude run down her face. "Thanks, Charles, I didn't even think of that … but it is exactly what I need … and what I will do. Can I put my drink on hold for tomorrow sometime? More than anything else right now, I need sleep." For the second time that day, he helps propel her out the door of his kitchen.

Leona and Gerritt lie in bed, quiet now; their frenzy abated, they have settled into an unusual calmness. They snuggle together under the comforter, both attempting not to fall asleep before summoning the energy to pack one more time. They hear steps, then a woman's audible sigh—a distinct exhalation of tension. Across the hall a door snaps shut. They rocket out of bed and hastily reach for their clothes. Neither is able to speak directly to each other.

*   *   *

Today, George is more than grateful for his frequent traveler pass. He jumps the lineup and boards the plane early, settling into his aisle seat at the emergency exit, wishing he were home already. Flying in the crush of a Sunday afternoon airport jam is never pleasant. He closes his eyes, almost nodding off, but countless bodies bustle past him, jostling him, and then he is forced to get up for a couple to laboriously move into the seats beside him. He rebuckles his seatbelt, ready for take-off, able to relax once more. Then, out of the blue, he sees a familiar figure careening down the aisle, excitedly waving and calling his name.

"George! Hello George! Yoohoo …"

"Uh-oh…" he grunts in alarm. Hastily unbuckling his seatbelt, he stands up quickly and with a swift motion, firmly grasps her suitcase.

"Hi, Vanessa—here, let me help you with your bag."

AFTER THE RETREAT

Thena wakes up ravenously hungry. She has been dreaming of an exotic Indian banquet, awash with tropical color, spice, and every fragrance possible. Delighted, she had piled her plate high with chicken tikka masala, shrimp curry, and beef tandoori kebabs on a bed of fragrant basmati, and was attempting to bite delicately into a crisp poppadom, laden with mango chutney, when it broke apart with a snap. She is left holding only the luscious memory and sharp hunger pangs.

The clock says 9:00, but the room is completely dark. Groggily she swings her arm out to turn on the light, but instead collides with a wall. Completely disoriented, she lies still until, with relief she remembers that it is Sunday evening. *The retreat has ended, but I am definitely not at home in my bed. I've been zoned out since mid-afternoon: no wonder I'm starved.*

As she stumbles to the bathroom, she steps on a

piece of paper, recently slid under the door. Scrawled on it, the words:

"When you wake up and are hungry, help yourself to anything you can dig out of the fridge. Look after yourself. See you tomorrow. C."

We watch her flounder around the kitchen in a crumpled sweatsuit, opening and closing doors, until she finally settles on leftover seafood fettuccine and a cup of Twinings hot chai—which made us all smile. We note how relatively easy it has been to solve the problem of her physical hunger, but the look on her face tells us that she feels her commitment to resolve another deeper kind of soul-hunger. As she pads morosely down the empty hallway it is clear she is wondering if it had been a mistake to stay at the Terra Center. She looks so bereft.

I could pack up my stuff and leave; I'm wide awake now and could be home before midnight, back in the comfort of my own space.

Many others would have taken that option, but not Thena. She evidently has no desire to read, to fill her mind with new thoughts. For lack of anything better to do at that time of night, she climbs back under the covers and eventually sleeps again. We wonder about maybe influencing her dreams, possibly resurrecting those choice images of well-being, but we think better of it. This woman is physically exhausted, her senses overloaded like her body, and parts of her psyche definitely on the verge of snapping. She needs to sleep free from the need to respond to anything or anybody. Rest is the priority for the night.

It is cold outside, though not quite frosty, and as Thena sleeps, the season advances into a darker day of fall, when the light comes more slowly. That unfathomable enchantment calls everyone to pay greater attention. Somehow in fall, that loss of illumination becomes our gain. Nevertheless, as we commune that night in the counsel of darkness, we recognize a panoply of pressing forces.

We know Thena is here hoping not only for fresh wisdom, but also to gather up the fragments of her life, which dangle in disarray. Our burning thought, which she has yet to consider, is that she is now irrevocably linked to all those who had come to this retreat. We wonder what might become of this weekend alliance? We stagger at the potential for change unleashed in these humans; their many gifts into this world have barely been conceived.

What an engaging group they were. For us it was like watching a three-day movie, each life playing out their weekend drama inside and outside the group. No wonder Thena's center of gravity is jiggling off-center. She has little idea how much random unconscious energy she has attempted to contain. If only she might understand that the connection to those others is bound to eventually re-energize her, to bring her more closely into alignment within the matrix of her own life. That is how it always works.

Humans find it hard to hold the anxious tension of that living connection with each other; it seems almost impossible for them to glimpse the promise of renewal in those moments of dis-ease. Those of us who have been around for a while continue to offer our services as silent witnesses, understanding how painfully complex this network of life has become.

In the olden days it seemed easier somehow. It was

clearer to whom we belonged and who needed our support and connection. Physical space defined most of life then. Tonight, this group is already scattered across the face of the country.

As we watch Thena sleep throughout this night, we will offer our presence to her spirit as she gathers fresh vitality to face what is ahead. She has many decisions to make this coming season, and we are committed to being with her each step of the way. She is not alone.

ACKNOWLEDGEMENTS

From the first day to the last, Allene Riley-Kussin, my soul sister, has creatively walked with me in this project. Thank you, dear friend, for your art—for you.

This book would not have been written without the inspiration and life-long work of Parker J. Palmer and my friends and colleagues in the Courage Collaboration. Through you I have come home, full circle, back into my life story. Although this is my fiction, I trust that this tale creatively embodies our commitment to offer retreat experiences that represent our deepest values and principles—a place where we as individuals come home to ourselves within a loving and compassionate community. It has been a joy "to reconnect my soul with my role" in this writing.

I am grateful to the Center for Courage & Renewal, (CCR), for Terry Chadsey, and for Marcy and Rick Jackson for their trust in providing me a seed grant to support the research for this creative project. Big thanks especially to Sally Z. Hare and Bev Coleman, cheerleaders who brought me much courage along the way. To all the CCR facilitators who gave time by phone or in person for interviews and consultation, I am most thankful.

As a first-time novelist, I have been dependent on much help from my writerly friends: Betsy Morgan, Megan LeBoutillier, Debbie Black, and Howard Friend. Without the professional skills of Carol Gaskin, Caroline Evans, and Bob O'Brien at Prose Press, this book surely could not have emerged from under my mountain of words.

A word of recognition to honor retreat centers and their staff—those "thin places" on earth that offer hospitality to all of us modern-day pilgrims. Personally, I thank *Kirkridge* and *Pendle Hill* in Pennsylvania; *Dayspring* in Maryland: *Seasons* in Kalamazoo, Michigan; and *IslandWood* on Bainbridge Island, Washington State. You offered me sacred place where mystery is always whispering. My wish is that this novel brings many more seekers to your gates.

I thank God for my medical missionary heritage in Africa and for a lifetime of relationships that ground me in the native traditions of the earth. Thank you, Stephen Foster, M.D., for telling me your remarkable surgical experience of the "stone baby." As a psychotherapist, I am aware that my story also has become the story of my clients. Thank you for your courage to change—in the process, you have changed me. I am enormously grateful to Bev Keefer, who for many years helped me identify and weave the variegated "threads" of my life.

My life has consistently been connected in circles of love. I honor the midwives in my "women's circle": Mary, Gwen, Betsy, and Gwen, and in my "men's circle": Howard and Betsy, Tom and Barry. Our meetings and your precious persons have been ongoing sustenance for me to continue the journey of "The Retreat." I also honor my global friends in YWAM. You taught me about spiritual community—twenty-two years of abundant living.

And to my dearest family: Uli; Rachel and Skylar; Daniel and Christine, Jack, and Owen; and Jon-Marc. May each of you know the priceless blessing of many kinds of circles of trust to inspire and teach you for all your days. You are that for me.

For further information about Carol's work
at Stonehaven,
see www.stonehavencommons.com

For the work of Parker J. Palmer and the
Center for Courage & Renewal,
please visit www.couragerenewal.org.

PROSE PRESS

The origin of the word prose is Latin, prosa oratio, meaning straightforward discourse.

Prose Press is looking for stories with strong plots.
We offer an affordable, quality publishing option with guaranteed worldwide distribution.

Queries: E-mail only.
proseNcons@live.com

CPSIA information can be obtained at www.ICGtesting.com
Printed in the USA
BVOW081545241012

303811BV00002B/1/P

9 780985 188948